THE CATASTROPHE OF THE EMERALD QUEEN

by L.R. Manley

Strength in the next world!

Love, Manley

24/03/16

~COTEQ

~COTEQ

Copyright

~COTEQ

Quotations

"He who fights with monsters should be careful lest he thereby become a monster."
~Friedrich Nietzsche.

"In violence, we forget who we are."
~Mary McCarthy.

"To turn the other cheek once is noble. Twice is an invitation to brutality"
~The Emerald Queen of Alegria

~COTEQ

Dedications

For *Sophie Lancaster.*
I hope she found her own Alegria and that she reigns there still.

For **Robert Maltby.**
A man with dignity, courage, and a strength of character that I have always admired and dream of aspiring to.

For **David Rathband.**
No words can do justice to such a noble and brave man.

~COTEQ

Prologue

Tulips and roses mingled among the foxgloves that blanketed the garden. Giant poincianas towered over it, branches heaving with bright orange blossoms. Birds chirped gently above, drawing a stark contrast to the busy courtroom chatter coming from inside the castle. Sweet scents wafted through and past the tall hedges, following the path of lush grass to a set of stairs.

The queen strode down the staircase from her private balcony. Her bodyguard followed silently behind her. As they reached the bottom of the steps, the queen paused by the large, circular fountain.

"Should we take these rumours of Anghofio seriously?"

Her guardian paused for a moment, then answered. "My lady, I believe King James has long wanted your throne. His actions lately in the border towns have merely confirmed our suspicions."

The queen proceeded into the garden. The lush grass dampened her bare feet. She ran her hand absentmindedly along the hedge until they reached the locked gate. Again, the queen turned to her towering companion.

"I wish emissaries to be sent to King James. He knows better. Our power is greater than the other kingdoms put together."

Her bodyguard nodded. "It shall be done."

A small bird flew from the bushes, its belly a bright orange. The queen smiled and stretched out her arm. The bird alighted upon the jewelled fabric of her sleeve. She gently stroked its head with her fingers before it chirruped and flew away.

"We should return to court, my friend," the queen said. "Your counsel is always welcome."

"Yes, my lady," the hulking figure said solemnly. He tilted in a slight bow.

She linked her arm through his and they began to make their way back.

Halfway down the path the queen froze. She grabbed her stomach and cried out in pain.

Her companion tugged on her arm. "My Lady?"

"I, I...something's..." she stammered. She fell, her tiara slipping and tumbling to the floor.

"GUARDS!" the bodyguard bellowed. To his horror, the queen's body shimmered, fading to and from invisibility.

Two soldiers burst out of the queen's chambers and pelted down the garden towards them.

"By the gods," her guardian gasped.

The queen's eyes opened wide and uncomprehending. She faded to nothingness and back. "Where am I?" she whispered. "Who are you?"

Heavy footsteps stomped behind them. The queen reached out a hand to her companion. "Help me..." she implored, her voice barely more than a whisper, then she faded away, her fallen crown the only sign of her presence.

The guards thundered to a halt. They stared, bewildered, at where the queen had lain.

After a moment's pause, the bodyguard snapped, "Summon the council. The queen is gone."

Chapter 1

Hospitals are so boring. Jared thought.

It didn't matter that his parents raved about his cousin Susan's new baby; he just didn't like the smell of hospitals. All disinfectant and soap.

Tomorrow Susan would go home with Peter Tristan, her new son. Jared's family seemed more excited about the event than Susan herself. It wasn't that Jared disliked Susan; far from it, he thought she was lovely. The baby wasn't cute yet, just a helpless blue bundle with hands no bigger than a kitten's paws and Jared was frankly sick of hearing about the little creature.

He'd stood patiently for an hour at the foot of the bed before he asked if he could go and get a can of pop from the vending machine. Timing was of the essence and he'd learned a long time ago that he had to be exceptionally crafty to get treats. When Jared was born his parents had struggled to make ends meet for a couple of years until his father got promoted.

However, for reasons that Jared couldn't understand, his mother still liked to perpetuate the myth they were "poor." Yeah, right. His father was a bank manager and his mother now worked as a supervisor in an accounts firm. The only time he'd tried to argue, his mother had tutted and subjected him to a half hour lecture, with tears in her eyes. She told Jared about how young and naïve he was and that her and his father still "struggled" to make ends meet.

With this in mind, getting a can of cherry pop was something he had to time very well. He'd waited until his mother had asked for what seemed like the fifteenth time how Susan was, and then

11

quietly asked if he could get a can--with his own pocket money of course.

His mother had paused, the smile fading slightly from the pure joy of being with Susan and the baby. She'd tutted, reminded him that he was supposed to be saving his money, and told him to be quick. Before he made it out the door, she had turned back to Susan, her conversation with Jared forgotten.

Now he stood in front of the machine. He put in his money and was rewarded by the reassuring clunk of the can dropping into the tray.

It was nice to be alone, even if just for a short while. He couldn't take too long or his mother would fret about him, even though the hospital had security guards.

He opened the can and sucked the froth from the rim, the bubbles tickling his upper lip. This hospital looked more like a hotel, with wooden walls and dark brown tiles covering the floor. There were some paintings on the wall too, most of boring, predictable stuff like yachts and peasants ploughing fields

A souvenir shop stood to the left of the pictures. *A stupid idea*, Jared thought. *Hospitals were places you came to get better. Why would anyone want to have a teddy bear or a pack of playing cards to remind them of an illness?*

A clock chimed; he'd been gone for about five minutes. He could probably be gone about fifteen before they'd notice, so he decided to walk back the long way, past the children's ward. Anything to forestall the boredom of being back with his family.

The kids' ward was up one floor. Jared took the staircase slowly. At the top of the stairs, he turned left and walked along the corridor. Children's pictures drawn by little nursery-age kids hung on the Sister's station. It was empty, and further along he could see the white ward doors with round windows; they reminded him of those on an old sea ship.

The sound of the television came from the ward. Jared turned left again, taking another gulp from his can and stifling the burp that rose in his throat. A smaller corridor appeared with rooms off to one side and posters and notices on the opposite wall. One proclaimed that visitors should use the dispenser pumps to wash their hands, alerting everyone to the perils of spreading germs through contact. Another tattered sign read *"Watch Out, There's A Thief About"* with a silhouette of a thief making off with the "o" from the "about."

It never failed to amaze Jared just how boring life could be. *The problem with what you see every day is that you eventually stop seeing it,* Jared thought.

He passed a room marked "Sophie Roberts." Jared had heard her name before. Eleven-year-old Sophie had been on the local news about four months ago after being in a car accident. Physically she hadn't been badly injured, but she'd fallen into a coma. At the time, Jared had wondered where she was being looked after. Now he knew.

He glanced in the square window as he passed and something caught his eye. A strange multi-coloured light was pulsating from the room. He paused, uncertain but reassuring himself that nothing was amiss. He'd heard that sometimes they played TVs or radios for people in comas hoping they'd hear them and wake up.

The light was pulsing brightly into the central corridor and casting patterns on the window glass. Jared was about to turn around and walk away when he heard a strange sound. Something like whispering was coming from the room. It sounded like someone was having a conversation in there and it certainly didn't sound like a television. He was worried and a little concerned now.

The pulsing light was still playing colours across the window of the ante-room, purple gold and blue, then red and green. All washing over the glass like when you mix petrol and water. Jared hesitated and looked left and right. There was no-one about and he was curious.

Moving nearer to the glass, his can almost forgotten, he peered through and tried to see into the girl's room. The light was more subdued now, as if the source had been dimmed but he could still hear the whispering. It sounded creepy, like the wind in the trees mixed with the sound of a bully quietly threatening you.

He still didn't think it was anything to be afraid of. After all, Jared thought, they were in a hospital and the children's ward at that so there must be grown ups about who would be able to help and knew what was going on. If someone had got into the room who shouldn't be there, then Jared could see them, alert the ward matron and then everyone would think he was a hero. Jared always believed that people in control knew exactly what they were doing.

He gently pushed open the door and peered in, stepping quietly through. He expected only to take one look inside and then beat a silent yet rapid retreat if he saw anything suspicious.

Looking in, his breath caught in his throat and he froze.

The girl was lying in bed on the far side of the room. Pipes in her arm and a tube going into her nose. The sheets were pulled up to her chest and the gentle "beep, beep" of her heart monitor kept a steady beat. She looked peaceful as if she was just asleep with no signs of injury from the car accident that had put her here. Either side her bed were two cabinets. One had flowers and cards on it and the other was adorned with more cards and a large but old looking brown teddy bear. The moonlight shone through the window behind her and a small wall lamp in the corner casting a reassuring glow across the room. The shutters were half closed and the scene was more or less exactly the way Jared had imagined it.

Except for one thing…

Hunched on a chair, next to Sophie's bed was the strangest man Jared had ever seen. He had on a scruffy, blue blazer that was too big for him and the fabric looked worn, rips showing in a couple of places near the collar. He was wearing dark blue suit trousers, faded and old looking. He was completely bald and his head was angular, almost coming to a point. He was sniffing every few seconds as if he had a cold. As he leaned over Sophie he whispered quietly but frantically.

"Took so long to find you. Thought we'd never find you but we did. Don't want to do this, I really don't but you see if I don't then they'll punish me. I like my fields and my house you see. I want to be nice to you, I like nice people but they told me I have to do this."

Jared watched mesmerized, realising something was seriously wrong but not knowing what to do.

The man moved slightly and Jared realised that the multi coloured lights he'd seen were from something he was holding in his right hand. The man held it up slightly and Jared saw it was a knife. His stomach knotted with fear. The blade was rainbow coloured and bright, casting vivid shades over the girl's bed, the lights playing over her face.

"Don't want to but I have to you see? This is not something I enjoy but each to his own life and all I wanted was to live mine and then they found me and said I have to do this." The man grunted irritably and sniffed loudly again, his shoes scuffing in a quick pattern on the floor beneath his chair and then going still.

He raised the knife over his head and spoke to the sleeping girl once more. "So, you see I am so sorry little girl but they told me this is a must and I have to do musts you see. I will try and make it quick for you."

Jared realised what was about to happen and dropped his can from numb fingers. It hit the floor with a wet thud, the remaining soda foaming crazily over the side of the rim and on to the floor, leaving a damp sticky puddle. Instantly the man stood up from his chair and turned quickly to where Jared stood, the knife held before him.

"WHO IS SPYING ON ME?" he shrieked loudly and then Jared saw his face clearly and the terror took almost complete control of him. The man wasn't a man, but some kind of monster. His forehead and chin sticking out a full few inches beyond the rest of his face. His nose was prominent and large, jutting forward, while his mouth was a slash of teeth, jagged and yellow. The skin on his face was smooth and taut, stretched tight as a drum and his ears were tiny against his head, more like little stumps. Most terrifyingly of all, he had no eyes, just smooth skin where they should have been.

He stood up and the chair scraped back on the floor. "Spying on me! Come here!!!" he snapped, beckoning with his free hand and sniffing the air loudly, moving his head from side to side. Jared shook his head and stammered incoherently. He tried to move backwards but the creature sensed his movement and raised the free hand in the direction of the door, waving it in a small circle. The door, which had already been closed, now glowed briefly a bright, brilliant blue around the edges. There was a sound like rustling paper, the light glowing in a rhythmic pulse and the window turned black, impossible to see through. Jared managed to stagger back and put one hand on the handle to get out. It was stuck and wouldn't open.

"No way out now nosey little boy," the creature said, sniffing loudly again and moving two steps towards him raising the rainbow coloured knife, which glowed in his hand. "Now come HERE!!"

Jared staggered again and tried to back away. He looked at the girl, still peacefully asleep in her bed, oblivious to this.

"Look I won't hurt you," the creature said smiling at him and then laughed. "Be easier for you if you don't make me wait." The snicker was like the giggle of some demonic clown and it broke the spell of fear Jared was under. He tried to slide along the wall of the room to the main window but the creature moved to block his path. "Naughty, nosey little boy," it said waving its finger at him. "Nosey boys shouldn't meddle."

It moved towards him once more and Jared watched as it raised the knife higher, the blade glowing. He felt his palms

17

sweaty on the wall, the tiles warm beneath his fingers. He glanced past the creature to Sophie, desperate to cry out for help but too afraid to try.

Then he noticed something near Sophie's bed. The shapes and shadows in the plastic curtain nearest to her head started to move. Jared stared as the shapes broke and then came together, swirling and spinning and what he was seeing was even harder to comprehend than the foul monster approaching him. The forms merged into what looked like the shadow of a head. Then in the heart rate monitor to the girl's left, the reflections in the glass over the readout display began to impossibly flow, bleeding into the shapes near the plastic curtains like food colouring dropped into water. Madly churning and flowing, drawn as if by some crazy form of gravity. Then the cards on the right bedside cabinet next to her head bled their colours upwards and at an angle to make a lopsided kaleidoscope.

He watched the scenes before him as if in slow motion, his heart racing. The creature still bore down on him, but the steps seemed slower now as if it was walking through water. It hadn't noticed what was happening behind it, its whole attention focused on Jared.

The colours stopped forming and Jared could vaguely see what looked like a shadow of a head and shoulders with a chest and arms below. The image was unclear and as he looked it made less sense, his perception slipping as he stared and the image faded under his frightened gaze.

The shadows under Sophie's bed and from the creases in her top blanket then detached like banana peel and moved suddenly upwards, like water drops when someone throws a large stone in a river. The explosion of shadows merging at their zenith to join the original shapes.

The creature's smile widened, the yellow teeth shining with wicked malevolence and its breath foul in the air as it raised the knife once more, reaching out with its other hand to grasp Jared's collar.

Finally the light and shadow play in the background finished. The shadow was fully formed and with a sudden burst of white and blue next to Sophie, a figure appeared, thrown from the light into the room. It landed on its feet and stood in front of the bed, erect and tall. The explosion spilled the cards from the cabinets, whipping round the room in a maelstrom. Sophie's hair blowing over her face in the sudden storm, the cards and teddy bear on the other side swept away and tumbling to the floor. A plastic beaker of water fell, cracking open and spilling its contents in a widening circle. The cups next to it clattered down, burst from their cellophane wrapping.

Jared glanced up as the lights dimmed and then the bulbs exploded, shards of glass scattering over the room. As he raised his arm over his face he saw the heart rate monitor screen fizzle out, flat line and then come back to normal.

The creature turned at the sudden noise while Jared sat on the floor and stared transfixed at what was in front of him.

The newcomer was tall. Taller than anyone Jared had ever seen. He was dressed in a black robe secured with a cord at the waist and a hood that completely covered his head, the face just a dark shadow. He had a huge sword strapped to his back in an old, red sheath and secured with a purple sash.

The creature shrieked in anger and fear at the newcomer and dropped its knife.

"MORDALAYN!!!" it hissed in disbelief and fury.

The newcomer made no reply but advanced in three strides and grabbed the bald monster with both hands by the lapels of its scruffy jacket.

"No! Not my fault, don't hurt me!" The creature pleaded pathetically, trying in vain to break free. Jared watched speechless as the wriggling creature was hauled into the air, squealing and kicking madly, trying to prise free of the grip. The newcomer pulled it forward to stare at its face.

"You would DARE?!!" he growled at the monster in a deep, gravelly voice and with a *"snikt!"* noise unsheathed claws from the fingertips on one hand which pierced the tips of his black glove. They were at least three inches long and looked sharp as razors. He slowly put his hand near the struggling creature's face.

"No, please have mercy, not my fault, they made me do it!!!" The creature wailed, kicking like a fish on a line.

As the newcomer seemed to be on the verge of deciding what to do, he glanced in Jared's direction. Jared shook his head and after a pause the figure grunted angrily and threw the pathetic form down to the floor. The creature whimpered and covered its head with its arms. "Don't kill me, I'm sorry." It gibbered frantically, trying to curl up into a ball.

The man scooped up the rainbow knife and held it for a moment. The colours faded out and the blade turned a dull brown. The metal changed to a lump of jagged rock which the figure placed in a pocket in his robe.

He glanced at Jared and then reached into another pocket. Jared staggered slightly and his legs collapsed and he fell back against the wall. The man turned to the fear stricken would-be assassin and picked it up by its collar again. It shrieked indignantly and continued pleading. "No, no!!! Let me go, I'll be good."

The huge figure opened his hand. In it was a green jewel, encased in silver. He blew on the jewel which rose up and hovered over the squirming creature. The bald figure's shrieks rose like a tocsin in the room and the jewel began to spin fast over its head. The newcomer then let go and stepped back and as the jewel span, a brilliant green light enveloped the thrashing creature in a diamond shape and held it.

Just before the light flashed brightly and closed in on itself, taking the creature with it, the bald monster turned and glared at Jared and flung its hand out; the gnarled, twisted fingers pointing at him. "Nosey little boy!" it shrieked and a bolt of black energy launched from its rotten fingertips. Jared was frozen for a moment, unable to scream as it entered his chest and pinned him immobile to the wall. The hooded figure glanced quickly at Jared and shouted in anger but then the monster was gone, the sudden wind from the explosion signaling its absence, once more scattering the cards that littered the floor.

The man leaned forward and neatly caught the now clear jewel as it fell, spinning from the air, putting it back into his pocket. Straightening up he turned to Sophie and walked over to her bedside. Dropping to one knee amongst the chaos littering the floor he bowed his head, placing his hand on her arm. He whispered quietly and taking another crystal, held it in front of him in both hands and broke it in two. A glowing orange liquid, just a few drops, fell to the girl's sleeping body. They ran backwards and forwards as if on a sheet of glass, forming lines and lines and then vanished. Sophie glowed for a second and then was normal. The man rose and turned, crouching down in front of Jared, his face hidden in the dark depths of his hood, a scarf covering his mouth and nose. He had eyes of emerald green, shining brightly amidst the shadows of his hidden face.

"Don't be afraid," he said softly but in a voice that was deeper than any Jared had ever heard before.

Jared shook his head, his ears still ringing and his vision full of dancing white dots.

"What's your name boy?"

"J, J, Jared" he stammered after a few seconds.

"Are you hurt?"

"No, he didn't touch me. You got here before he could."

The figure rose. He extended his hand and Jared took it and struggled to his feet.

Just then there was a frantic banging on the door. "It's locked," one man's voice said.

"Kick it in!" someone else shouted.

"I have to go Jared," the man said taking him firmly by the arm. "The spell he placed on you means his people, my enemies can track you." He pulled back Jared's right sleeve as the pounding on the door and the frantic shouts grew louder. Removing a bracelet from his own huge forearm he placed it on Jared's wrist, whispering something as the metal curled in and shrank on itself to fit his smaller arm. The round jewel in its centre briefly glowed before returning to a cloudy green. Jared tried to pull away but the man held him firmly.

"This is a warning sigil," he explained over the increasing din as the people outside hammered on the door. "It will alert you if my enemies are close. The jewel will glow and become warm if they are near to you. If it does so, hide wherever you can, don't let them get hold of you, do whatever you can to get away." Jared nodded mutely, still confused and frightened. "I promise you I will come to protect you" the man continued. "One final thing. Do NOT tell anyone about me."

Jared was about to answer when the door to the small corridor behind them finally broke in and the people from outside spilled into the small room. Almost too fast to see the man let Jared go and sprinted the three or four steps to the window behind Sophie and hurled himself at it, his arms out in front of him. The glass shattered loudly and Jared watched dumbfounded as he disappeared into the night, the rain of glass following him down.

Jared turned from the shattered window to the security guards and a nurse who were piling into the room. They looked around quickly and saw the chaos and disarray. The nurse moved quickly to Sophie and checked her vital signs and pulse, then turned to the others. "She's ok," she said, exhaling heavily, relieved. Then she glared at Jared and seethed. "Just what the HELL happened in here young man?!!"

~COTEQ

Chapter 2

As Jared got out of the taxi at Heathrow airport he felt dizzy. The holiday in Malta had been planned for about nine months and like Susan's baby, his mother had fussed and fretted the whole time. For the last seven days she'd gone into anxiety overdrive until even Jared's father had got sick of it as she worried about the house in a frenzy of laundry, suitcases and countless repacking of everybody's luggage.

The incident in the hospital a week earlier had been awful and when the man had leapt out the window Jared had been left alone with the comatose Sophie. Initially hostile to him, the nurse and security guards had softened when his visible fear and tears had made it quite clear that he'd simply interrupted someone who had come to the girl's room to cause mischief. The police had interviewed him a short time later with his distraught and tearful mother present alongside his ashen-faced father. Jared had decided to lie and had stated only that a horrible man in a nasty suit had been in the room when he'd walked past and had trapped him and then jumped out the window. For some reason he felt that he should respect the stranger's wishes and not mention him or the unbelievable things he'd seen. He'd managed to keep the bracelet hidden, which was difficult as he couldn't take it off no matter what he did.

His mother had initially been skeptical about his involvement and had asked him in front of the police if he'd not smashed the window himself and was "fibbing" in order to cover up. He was secretly pleased when the female detective interviewing him had abruptly told his mother to shut up, after she interrupted their conversation for the third time to ask if Jared was "sure" he wasn't hiding something.

The police had said they'd be in touch and had phoned a few days later to say Jared wasn't a suspect. They added that he was in their opinion a brave lad for trying to stop whoever was in the room. They then stated that in future he should call for help and not try to intervene himself.

His mother's stress levels had gone through the roof and he was glad that now finally they were about to go on holiday and hopefully she would relax.

His father paid the taxi driver and they got the suitcases out the boot. Jared's slipped and fell onto the tarmac.

"Watch what you're doing Jared!" his mother snapped angrily. "If you looked after other people's property as much as your stupid comic books then you wouldn't keep breaking things all the time" she seethed.

The taxi driver looked uncomfortable and Jared's father looked away.

Jared knew she was just being spiteful but kept quiet, knowing arguing would simply result in an embarrassing display outside Terminal 5.

They moved into the departure area. Only a few people were milling about as it was 6am.

"Quickly Jared, come on Paul," his mother said bossily. As they walked along Jared felt his wrist get warm. He pulled back his sleeve to see that the green jewel in his bracelet was glowing faintly. He shrugged and pulled his sleeve back, glancing quickly to check that his parents hadn't seen.

As they moved deeper into the huge room Jared squinted at the bright glare compared to the gloom in the shadowy area they had been in before. The roof and walls were glass and metal, towering above them in vast skeletal forms. Huge metal pillars with vast nuts and bolts linking it all together. His father spotted the departures screen nearest to them and moved towards it. Jared felt the warmth get hotter on his wrist and was starting to worry, he pulled his sleeve back as the glow from the jewel became brighter.

His father returned and smiled. "The flight checks in at desk 17, on the left."

As they moved towards the desks a hooded and robed figure stepped out of an elevator and looked around slowly, eyes finally resting on Jared. Moving forward holding a large tube in one hand, like for mailing a poster, it moving lithely and soundlessly between people, never bumping into anyone.

Above them through the glass structure were clouds of the early morning. Blue sky was spattered amongst them and Jared hoped the day would have good weather.

There was only one person ahead of them at the check-in desk. Jared's mother's insistence that they arrive a full 4 hours before the flight was due to leave to cover for "complications" meant that they wouldn't have to queue. The lady on the desk smiled brightly as they approached and asked for their passports. Jared glanced down at his wrist; the jewel was bright green now and hot enough to feel like sunlight on his skin. It wasn't painful but it was impossible to ignore. As he glanced at it, it began to pulsate in a steady rhythm and Jared remembered what the man in the hospital had said. He was frightened now and just as he looked to his father there was a deafening crash above them.

Everyone looked up as chunks of glass rained down, three or four thudding against the luggage conveyer belt and one splitting a suitcase open, the clothes bursting out. The cascade spattered around them and people shielded their eyes and turned away. A loud whooping could be heard and, almost too quick to see, a figure swooped down in a graceful arc from the ceiling. It swerved in mid air and stopped in front of Jared and his terrified parents. It was standing astride some kind of hover board and it grinned wickedly. Dressed in tattered black leather and wearing what looked like flying goggles and a black, tight fitting leather cap. The check-in woman screamed in terror and dived behind her desk. The hooded figure from the elevator began to run towards them from the other side of the hall, sprinting fast while prising the lid off the large tube he was carrying.

"We-e-e-lll," the creature on the hover board cackled malevolently. "What do we have here then? Time to come with me little boy." It grinned evilly and licked its lips, reaching out to Jared.

"No use to run, we catch you boy. We love the chase we do," the creature laughed loudly and glanced at Jared's father who was standing rigid, his mouth silently opening and closing.

His mother screamed and fainted, hitting the floor with a loud thud. The creature maneuvered the board to where Jared's father stood and gave Paul a hard shove, propelling him backwards towards his prostrate wife where he toppled over and sat down hard on the floor.

"Poor daddy," the creature snarled snatching its head round to glare at Jared. It spied the bracelet on his wrist and tutted theatrically. "Oooh, toys have we? Not going to do you much good now."

Jared was dumbstruck and scared beyond belief. The creature had slitted, orange eyes that glowed brightly and its smile was like a row of kitchen knives.

Everywhere people were frozen to the spot. The robed and hooded figure was pounding across the floor, tearing the top off the long tube and reaching inside.

The creature leaned over and cocked its head conspiratorially. "Come with us boy, we take you for a ride," it said in almost a whisper, winking as it did so.

The people around them were staring, unmoving. The check-in clerks were clearly petrified but the nearest one scrabbled with her hand for the panic button under her desk.

Jared backed away. Chunks of glass were still pattering down from the ceiling where the creature had burst through. It snorted loudly through its nostrils as Jared staggered back further, the jewel in his arm bracelet now glowing with a vivid and almost blinding green light, as clear as a freshly cut emerald. A piece of glass tocked against his shoulder and snapping out of his fear he turned and ran. He remembered what the man had said in the hospital *"don't let them get hold of you, do whatever you can to get away."*

"IT TICKLES!!!" The creature whooped with delight and kicked the side of the black, bobbing board with its heel. Weaving after Jared as he tore terror stricken down the concourse, people staring dumbfounded as he ran past. The creature threw its head back and laughed loudly, clearly enjoying the thrill of chase. Jared glanced over its shoulder and

saw the creature's brown and yellow, crooked teeth jutting from it mouth. *"God,"* he thought suddenly, *"don't any of these people have dentists?"* and then wondered why he'd thought that at this of all times.

He turned down a side corridor and saw that it branched off to left and right with closed shops either side, their grills down. The creature swerved the board round the corner with an impressive curve, the front end rising up and laughed again. "Run boy, tickle all you want. We will find you so we will!"

Jared turned and the creature smoothly powered the board towards him. He staggered backwards and tripped over his feet, landing hard on the floor and wincing.

The creature lowered itself and the board to just above ground level and then its voice took on a serious tone.

"You come we take you, you don't come we take you. Your choice boy."

Jared sat staring through frightened eyes at the triumphant creature. As he looked past the hovering monster he saw the hooded man charge round the corner and pound up the corridor towards them. The creature grinning at him was oblivious and simply stared at Jared and reached out its hand, the filthy, curved nails on its fingers clawing the air.

The hooded figure grasped something inside the tube and tugged hard. A sword in its sheath was pulled clear. He dropped the tube, grasped the sheath with one hand and yanked the weapon free. Jared saw to his amazement that it had three golden blades which shone brightly, a big, engraved central blade and a thinner one either side. As the man hurtled down the corridor he raised the sword and just as the hovering creature turned to see what was behind it the running man launched himself in a flying kick. A booted foot caught the creature in the chest and with a whoosh of air it flew back, smacking into the large window facing the runways and then collapsed on the ground. The man ran past Jared and as the creature furiously struggled to its feet it tugged a long, thin blade free from its belt. Jumping into a squatting position, it hissed madly as its attacker thundered towards it.

"Cursed meddling swine!!!" it hissed loudly, raising the blade. Before it could do anything else the figure swung the three bladed sword towards it and on impact the creature seemed to explode. One second there was an angry hissing monster, the next the air was full of what looked like black dust. It reminded Jared of watching a vacuum cleaner bag explode. The dust shone and glittered crazily and swirled around the man who drew the sword back into a defensive stance. With a disembodied scream the particles flooded into the man's chest, who stood impassive and unmoving. Then there was no sign that the giggling monster had ever existed except for its hover board, still bobbing slightly in the air. Then, that too turned to dust and after a second the particles sank to the floor.

The man sheathed the sword and slung it over his shoulder by the red strap.

He moved quickly towards Jared and without saying anything scooped him up under his arm and ran quickly down the left corridor.

"HEY! Let me go!" Jared screamed in shock and indignation, futilely struggling against the powerful grip. The stranger ignored him. Jared saw signs they were heading for the shuttle train platform that led to the other terminals and he kicked madly. The people around them were pointing and shouting, one or two taking photos on their mobile phones and cameras. The man holding him skidded around a corner and then ran down a flight of steps, bounding over them three at a time. He barged a woman out of the way on the escalator and in four quick strides was at the bottom and running to the train platform. The few early morning passengers turned at Jared's screams for help as the huge figure jumped down onto the track and bolted into the dark tunnel. Jared caught a glimpse of the digital clock on the platform wall. It said "next train in 2 minutes."

The man ran, the fact he was also carrying Jared seemed to make no difference to his speed as he sprang nimbly along the track. "Let me GO!" Jared cried out, thrashing madly.

The light of Terminal 3's train platform was getting ever brighter. Jared could see the train on the platform and to his horror saw it start to move towards them as they ploughed down the tunnel.

The train's lights were dazzling and as they ran Jared could see nothing and closed his eyes as the blinding glare shone in his face. The man ran up to the platform edge and just as the train reached them he leapt onto the platform. Jared's scream was drowned out by the roar of the locomotive and the wind blasting his face. Without pausing, his captor ran through the nearest exit and made for a service door. People stared gobsmacked. He charged up a darkened staircase and emerged at a security entrance. Jared winced as he saw the door looming towards him but the man twisted at the last moment and turned his shoulder to the frame. Pushing Jared behind him he barged into it and the magnetic security seal cracked loudly. They were on a similar area to the one they'd been on when all this started in terminal 5. He craned his neck to look up as the figure holding him scanned the area frantically. A police officer nearby was talking on his radio and staring at them in astonishment.

"Hey!" he yelled, releasing his grip on the radio and raising his machine gun. "Armed police! Stand still!"

The figure paid the officer no heed and suddenly sprinted off to the right. The officer lowered his gun and grabbed the radio again. "1142 to control, he's here and he's headed to the Departures area!"

The hooded figure leapt agilely around, then vaulted the security barrier and hurtled through the queue, shoving people aside. He charged towards the metal detectors while bewildered security personnel stared blankly at them both and scattered. The alarms screamed loudly as he ran through and hurtled on. Jared had ceased to struggle now. He was too frightened and confused. In the back of his mind he realised that keeping quiet meant he might have a chance of getting out of this without being hurt.

The man bolted along the linking tunnel to the Departures lounge, the few early morning passengers flinching to one side or the other as his heavy boots thudded down the carpeted corridor. Another armed cop came out ahead of them and dropped to one knee, raising his machine gun and yelling at them to stop.

Halfway down the corridor was a fire exit, the handle taped up with a big red sign saying "DO NOT OPEN EXCEPT IN EMERGENCY." The stranger skidded to a halt and ran at it, kicking the door hard. It shook in the frame but remained closed. Cursing loudly he booted it a second time and the door opened.

The restraining tape snapped and fluttered outside, caught by the sudden blast of cold air.

He leapt through the door frame and Jared had a terrifying glimpse of the tarmac, realised it was at least eight metres to the floor and before he could scream they were suddenly down. The man's knees bent and he grunted slightly but then straightened and ran, this time parallel to the building. A large aeroplane was pulling away from the building, the turbines in the jets whirring loudly. Suddenly the man skidded to a halt and dropped Jared on the tarmac who scrabbled into a sitting position and found himself next to a motor cart, loaded up with luggage. He looked up to see the hooded figure draw his sword as two more black-clad shapes on hover boards swooped down out of the sky, the same maniacal laughter heralding their presence. Jared glanced over to the cockpit of the large jet and saw the pilot and co-pilot's looks of confusion turn to fear. The jets whirred loudly and the plane halted its withdrawal from the terminal.

"Meddling oaf," one of the flying creatures cackled maliciously as it flitted past then up and away, taunting them.

"Oafish meddler," the other said as it flitted past and away.

The man turned to Jared and stared at him, his face still hidden behind the large hood he was wearing. "Stay there boy!!" he shouted in a muffled voice and whirled as the second creature flew down shrieking and then swooped away as the big sword was swung at it.

The driver of the luggage cart that Jared was next to looked out in fear from his cab and then jumped down and ran into the building via an open staff door. Jared wanted to run after him but was too petrified to move.

The two flying monsters flew back up into the air, about 20 metres from the ground and pointed at Jared while whispering to each other. One snickered and they flew away from each other in opposite directions. Then they rushed in at almost blinding speed towards where Jared sat with the man above him, standing guard like some immense statue.

As the two howling figures dived in the swordsman adjusted his stance and correctly guessed that the first one was simply to throw him off. He ducked as the board shot by where he had been a micro second before, fast enough to take his head off. Then, almost too fast to see he swung the three bladed weapon in a powerful arc at the second creature that was rushing in, teeth showing in a yellowy, terrifying grin with its arms outstretched to grab Jared. The blades cut through the front of the board and it veered away, wobbling dangerously with red smoke belting out from the gaping hole.

The creature screamed as the board bucked and weaved in the air, careening around and looping the loop, barely missing its colleague as it spun wildly. Then with a deafening screech the board and the rider flew straight into the left hand jet engine of the plane. There was a grinding crunch and flames billowed out. Jared saw the pilot grimace and shout into his radio. The same explosion of grey shimmering particles hung in the air for a moment, dancing above the orange flames and then the smoke from the fire smothered them and they were gone.

The second creature glared furiously at Jared and his savior. "Nasty little interfering PIGS we have don't well!" it hissed and launched its board straight at them. The figure stood impassive as the monster hurtled towards him and at the last moment shifted his grip on the sword to one hand and stepped to one side, grabbing the creature by its leather coat and pulling it clean off the board. The board zoomed forward and embedded itself in the wall with an ear splitting crunch of grinding metal.

The man flung the creature to the floor and pointed his sword at its throat. The creature showed no fear but instead glared up at its victor and spat. "To the Sea of Glass with you! No one can stop us. That child will DIE!!"

Without saying a word the man brought the sword up over his head and then swung it down hard. The creature exploded in a final screech of fury, a shower of sparkling grey particles which again swirled around before making a path to the chest of the swordsman, his body momentarily shining and then returning to normal. Jared glanced over and saw the board disintegrate like the previous one.

The man sheathed his huge sword and turned. Jared glared at him and snapped "I'll come ok, just forget the baby carrying."

The man paused for a second then shook his head and scooped him up.

"Oh, for God's sake!" Jared shouted but chose not to struggle as he'd realised this did nothing except tire him out. The jet engine was still on fire, black smoke and orange flames pouring out from the crippled motor.

As the man ran on with Jared tucked under his arm, the door ahead of them burst open and four armed police officers spilled out onto the tarmac. They saw the sprinting figure. One shouted the challenge as they raised their machine guns. He didn't slow in the slightest and bounded forward relentlessly. The guns wavered and suddenly the man jumped high, sailing over their heads and landing with barely a break in his speed. The confused cops turned round and one shouted. "HEY!!"

After another fifty or so metres, he came to a piece of wall that looked older than the rest and in the middle was an old service door. Jared could see that it looked ancient, rusted and red and had clearly not been opened in years. The man pushed Jared against the wall next to it and shouted. "Don't move!" Reaching into his robe he pulled out a bright red crystal. He gazed at it and spoke some strange words then hurled it at the door. Jared flinched but before it could impact the metal, the crystal exploded into rainbow coloured swirls. They spread slowly, the colours forming into a square that fit the doorway exactly, the frame glowing with a pulsating light. The man lunged forward and grasped the handle. Jared expected it to remain stuck with the rust but it opened easily and he looked away as pure white light dazzled him. As it quickly faded and the view cleared, instead of an old service corridor he was met by a mesmerizing sight of a red field and a sky lit by what looked like the most spectacular sunset he'd ever seen.

This incredible sight was suddenly interrupted as the police officers ran up behind them and a police car made its way from around the corner, siren blaring noisily as it skidded to a stop. The man glanced over his shoulder then leaned forward and grabbed Jared by his collar and belt. As Jared yelled in protest, he swung him back and then flung him through the open doorway.

The police ran to a halt ten metres from the figure who whirled and stood there facing them, his sword still sheathed. The car driver killed the siren and someone shouted. "Armed police, stand still! Do NOT move!" The man stared at them silent and unmoving, his face hidden in shadow, the door open behind him.

The driver of the police car had two gold pips on each shoulder and appeared to be in charge. He raised a megaphone and shouted through it. "Place your hands on your head and drop to your knees."

The silent figure made no attempt to comply and simply stared at them. The cops shuffled nervously, their headsets crackling with frantic chatter from their control room.

The officer shouted through the megaphone. "Just do as we say. Put your hands on your head and drop to your knees."

Without a word the man simply turned on his heel and walked through the door, slamming it behind him.

Jared staggered backwards, his view of the runways and skyline at Heathrow airport now gone as his kidnapper marched towards him. Impossibly, the door he was now facing appeared to be the back door of a shed on a farm He was all dusty where he'd landed and while before he'd been too caught up in what was going on to be really scared he was now very frightened.

The man walked forward and stood over him, the dying sunlight bathing his robe in red light. As if sensing Jared's unease he reached up and grasped the sides of his hood and pulled it back and yanked down the black scarf that covered his mouth and nose. Jared gasped as he saw the man wasn't a man but had the head of a large Caracal hunting cat. The ears were tall and black sticking up from its skull, its nose coloured with a black tip, the whiskers long. The fur was a light brown and it had long hair, like a human, extending from behind the ears, tied back with a purple cord.

The cat man looked at him and after a pause said slowly. "Do not be afraid. My name is Mordalayn and I will not harm you."

Chapter 3

Jared tried to stand up but his feet slipped and he fell over. Mordalayn reached down and gently took his arm. Around them was a field of what looked like tall red wheat stalks, waving lazily in the fading sunshine. The sky was a magnificent array of orange, red and purple, the clouds lit up by the dying shades of dusk. The house next to them was ramshackle. The bricks looked old and the chimney on the top was crooked. Smoke was puffing from it slowly and Jared could smell something like stew cooking.

The farm creature nearest to them broke from its grazing to see what had interrupted its task, then looked away disinterestedly and carried on. Its four small horns moving as it munched away contentedly.

The wooden door was closed and Jared somehow guessed that if he opened it he wouldn't find himself staring at Heathrow's runways.

"Where are we?" he said to Mordalayn while trying to brush the dirt from his sleeves.

"I will tell you later," the huge figure replied, his deep voice somehow reassuring despite the fear and confusion Jared was feeling. "Come inside, I will find you clean clothes and food and you can rest."

He put his hand on Jared's shoulder and gently steered him through the dusty field, Jared's shoes picking up the dirt as they made their way round the front of the house. In places the ground was split but in the cracks was a bright orange, thick substance like smooth marmalade. It bubbled slightly and a steam rose from it.

"Watch your step," Mordalayn said, steering him around the ooze.

A large black horse was standing in a pen, it raised its head and snuffled as they approached it. Mordalayn extended his hand and rubbed the creature's nose soothingly. He ducked down under the tiled awning above the doorway and grasped the round metal handle, shoving the door forwards with a grinding noise.

Checking that the room was secure he then beckoned Jared to enter. "Come," he said, "it will be colder soon." Jared gingerly stepped inside and saw that the room was a basic living space. There was a large wooden table in the centre with a few metal plates and mugs. There was what looked like a fruit bowl on it, but the main item in it looked like a cross between a pineapple and a cactus plant. Looking closer, what he thought at first glance was an apple appeared to be silver in colour. Further back were a couple of closed doors and to his left was a large window.

Mordalayn turned to Jared. "Your arm with the bracelet, show it to me."

He hesitated but then extended his arm. Mordalayn pulled the grubby sleeve back and saw the oval crystal was still cloudy. He unslung his sword and laid it on the table, then removed his robe.

Jared jumped as a male voice suddenly went. "Well, back again. Just in time for tea."

A short man wearing an apron emerged from one of the doorways. Jared could see a stove through the open door with a couple of large black pans on. He felt his stomach rumble in protest.

"Hello young man," the man said cheerfully, wiping his hands on a large cloth "and who might you be then?"

"He appears totally unfazed by the sight of a hulking, cat faced man who's just walked into his front room and lain a sword on his table," Jared thought.

"My..." he squeaked and then coughed to clear his throat and cover up for his nervousness. "My name's Jared. Jared Miller."

"Ah," the man said beaming.

Jared looked at him puzzled. "Now then," he said to Mordalayn who was wrapping his robe up into a ball. "You both must be hungry. I have some stew and sweetsomes for eating. You are both welcome of course."

Jared glanced around the room. The place had a high ceiling and wooden beams supporting it, criss crossing here and there. The windows were old looking and diamond shaped from the lead patterns on the outside. There were many ornaments on the various sills, large cabinets and chests of drawers. One was a small statue of a woman, wearing a long green dress and holding her arms out as if wanting to give a hug. Another was of a ship, the rigging and sails exquisitely rendered. The man caught Jared's wandering eye and chuckled. "You like my boat?"

"Yes, errr...it's very good."

"Thank you," he replied smiling and then, "My, my, where are my manners," he tutted to himself. Putting the rag he'd wiped his hands on into the pouch on his apron, he extended his hand. "Fellicone," he said beaming and shaking Jared's hand hard.

Mordalayn had finished wrapping up his items and he turned around. He was hugely tall and was dressed in green leather trousers and calf length brown leather boots, buckled severely. He wore a brown jerkin with several pockets adorning it, over a green shirt of some heavy looking fabric with the sleeves rolled up. He had what looked like a silver coat of arms pinned to the left breast. The buckle on his belt was large and had a carving of a hand, with a crown in the centre. Writing above and below said "MANUS HAEC INIMICA TYRANNIS." The cat face showed no emotion. He gestured for Jared to sit down. "Please, we owe you an explanation and I do not want you to be afraid."

Jared thought that being afraid was something he might have to get used to but took the proffered wooden chair and sat, looking from the smiling, friendly face of Fellicone to the unreadable one of Mordalayn.

Mordalayn sat opposite Jared and placed one arm on the table, his huge fingers still, the gold ring on his middle finger had the same hand and crown crest on it.

The cat figure leaned forward and spoke quietly his voice resonating in the room. "You were in mortal danger when I chanced upon you in the hospital. The creature who was in that room was an assassin, sent by evil men to kill our queen." Jared looked puzzled and Mordalayn paused.

"Do, do you mean Sophie?"

Fellicone and Mordalayn exchanged glances and Mordalayn leaned slightly further forward. "Her name to you is Sophie Roberts. Here she is our queen and ruler, bringer of light and joy to all in Alegria."

He paused for a moment and then continued with his explanation. "She was hurt, four months or more by your calendar, much longer by ours. She is greatly vulnerable now."

Jared stared at him confused and bewildered. He had no idea what was going on and far from reassuring him, this explanation was just tying his brain in more knots.

"Sophie was hurt in a car crash, at least I thought she was. How is she your ruler here? Is this like Africa or something? Is she a princess staying in England or something?"

Mordalayn again glanced at Fellicone whose face creased in concern.

"Jared, we are not in Africa. This is Alegria."

He paused and Jared looked at him even more confused. "Where's Alegria?" he asked.

Mordalyn paused. "I cannot tell you everything now, for your own safety. I dealt with the assassin and placed a protection spell on Our Lady so they cannot find her. But that spell he threw into you means our enemies can track you."

Jared looked around and was still uncomprehending. "But again. Where ARE we? I have to go home, my mum and dad will be worried about me."

Mordalayn sighed. "I promise you all this will be made clearer later. I need to get you to a safe place. We are safe here for a short time only but we are on the borders of Alegria. Those who would hurt the queen may find you here."

He stood. "The corvo he placed within you has to be removed."

Jared paled. "But, but I feel nothing. What is it?"

45

"The corvo is not malignant, it simply resides within you, but our enemies can track you with it. We need to remove it. Now.."

Jared was scared and stammered. *"But, but what will you do?"*

"I promise you this will not hurt or do you damage but you MUST do as I say ok?" Mordalayn's feline face looked deadly serious and Jared squirmed under his gaze. Fellicone stepped forward and smiled reassuringly at Jared.

"It's ok my boy. This is quick but we need to do it immediately. Please be assured we mean you no harm."

Jared looked from Fellicone to Mordalayn and back. "What do you want me to do?" he asked, his voice cracking.

"Just sit still. This will be over quickly," Mordalayn said and looked to Fellicone who moved forward.

"Please don't be scared, but be aware you may be shocked by what you see."

Mordalayn moved to the windows and drew the heavy curtains, blocking the final rays of sunlight. He lit a fat green candle in the middle of the table and another on a cabinet near the front door. Locking it he pocketed the key and turned to Jared.

"Stay in the chair and do not speak or move, no matter what happens. Do you understand?"

The flickering candles cast an orange glow across the room and the shadows were long and deep. He braced himself in the chair as Fellicone stood in front of him and smiled once more. Gently he took Jared's hands in his large, pudgy ones. He closed his eyes and began to say very softly:

"Eye of evil, we see you. We know you. None trust you and none want you. You are bereft and alone. Begone from this boy."

Jared looked around but nothing was happening. Mordalayn stood next to Fellicone, his face emotionless.

Fellicone repeated the phrase and this time he raised both arms with the palms facing down and moved to stand over Jared. After a pause he began a third time and Jared felt something prickling the skin on his chest, like pins and needles. He squirmed slightly but Mordalayn whispered urgently. "Keep still."

Fellicone loudly shouted. "Eyes of treachery, beacon of betrayal leave this boy and go. You are not welcome."

Jared could feel his skin getting hotter and it felt like something was moving in his chest. He fought to remain still but then he felt a bump against his ribs but from the inside and he yelled out and squirmed. Suddenly Mordalayn was behind him, pinning his arms to his sides and whispering. "Be still, you must be still."

Fellicone again chanted and then Jared saw a ghostly, shadowy shape appear through his t-shirt. He gasped as it pushed through and saw that it was the head of some sort of large bird. The beak was open as if it was trying to cry out. He couldn't feel the bird moving, only the prickling sensation but he struggled against Mordalayn's grip as the bird continued to emerge.

It was like a huge black crow, faded slightly as if in an old photograph. It looked like a projection from a movie camera. It's eyes were red and angry. Fellicone chanted, raising his arms higher. The bird thrashed its head from side to side and then pulled clear of Jared's chest, its huge wings beating slowly as if they had been trapped. The bird shook itself and raised its head in anger at Fellicone and silently screeched, its long curved beak open in fury. Then as it finally wrenched itself free of Jared it hovered in the air and finally made a sound. A horrible, piercing screech that made the very air echo, as Mordalayn held Jared fast against the chair. The monstrous bird raised its wings and lunged forward as if to attack but then suddenly faded, the screech dying out as it vanished.

Fellicone opened his eyes and slowly breathed out in relief. Jared blinked and looked around. The candle nearest the door had gone out and the room was dull in the sputtering flame from the other. Mordalayn released his grip and moved to stand in front of him.

"The corvo is gone," he said. "You will be fine."

Jared nodded slowly, sweat on his forehead and Mordalayn moved away from him. Fellicone moved to light oil lamps on the walls and another on the table.

Jared gulped, then found his voice. "What was that thing?"

Fellicone smiled kindly and said. "A tracker. Rancidrain placed it in you as a spell when you happened upon him in the presence of Our Lady. Have no fear, it is gone now." He paused but then added, "had he known what he was doing we could not have removed it so easily or without harm to you. Fortunately our enemies used someone they would never miss so luck was on our side."

Jared looked at Mordalayn who was checking out the windows of the house, moving the curtains aside to look at the view across the fields to the dense woods further back. Far in the distance was a high hill and at the top was an elegant white building. In the dying sunlight the last rays cast a beam across the huge cat figure. Mordalayn turned to Fellicone and asked. "You are shielded here?"

"Yes," the fat man replied. "The woods themselves offer protection as you know. You are as safe here as you can be."

Mordalayn turned to Jared. "You must be hungry" he said.

Jared realised his clothes were dirty. Fellicone saw him look down and chuckled. "Don't worry; I can take care of that. There are clean clothes in the bedroom that will fit you. They were my son's but he's outgrown them now."

Jared stood and moved towards the room. Fellicone called after him. "There is fresh water in a pail for you to wash with before you change too. The meal will be ready when you are."

Jared stepped into the bedroom and closed the door behind him. His jacket was spattered with dirt and his trainers were caked in it, along with his jeans. He pulled off the jacket and dropped it on the floor next to the empty metal bathing tub. He was glad there was very little grime on his jumper and none on his t-shirt as he had to pull them over his face. He washed quickly and turned to the pile of clothes laid out on the foot of the bed. There were brown trousers of a heavy fabric and a light, green shirt that had no buttons but went over the head. There were no shoes so he realised he'd just have to wear his muddy trainers. He used the remainder of the water to clean the worst of the filth off and then left them to dry. There was a small belt bag, like a bum bag, made of brown leather and he put in the few items out of his pockets. About five pounds in change, his mobile phone, MP3 player and a keyring with a pocket torch on it. He tied it around his waist. Emerging from the room he saw Mordalayn was already seated then jumped at the sight of a tiny creature standing on tip toe and dealing with the dirt on the chair he'd sat on. It was small in size and looked like a little man until you saw its head which was the shape of an elephant's, the tiny trunk slung over one shoulder. It muttered to itself as it worked, the dirt drying as it waved its hand over it and then brushed the flakes into a gold coloured dust pan.

As Jared moved forward it finished and Fellicone said. "Thank you Ribbledonk."

The creature grumbled, glanced up at Jared and tutted and then waddled off into the kitchen.

Mordalayn was eating from a large bowl, the stew in front of him was meaty and the smell was inviting. There was a plate of bread in the centre of the table and he broke a piece in half with his huge hands and dipped it in the liquid.

"Come young master" Fellicone said pulling the clean chair back for him. "You must be hungry."

Jared sat down and Fellicone put a generous helping of the stew into a clay bowl and handed him a spoon. Jared was about to dig in when he paused. He didn't know where he was and he had just been abducted by a cat faced giant while an elephant-headed creature cleaned furniture. He paused and Fellicone chuckled. "I think our young friend fears poison," he said not unkindly.

Mordalayn glanced over at Jared and without saying anything leaned over and dipped his spoon in Jared's bowl, taking a big helping with a chunk of meat and then putting it in his mouth. He looked directly at Jared as he chewed slowly and then swallowed. Jared didn't hesitate any more but wolfed down the stew as fast as he could.

Chapter 4

Mordalayn rode slowly on the large, black stallion with Jared behind him. After dinner the night before they had told him to try and get some sleep. That had been impossible and he'd lain awake wondering just what on Earth was happening. Mordalayn had stayed up all night, prowling around the small house and the outside grounds. As the sun came up the cat man had come to fetch him. After a brief breakfast of bread and what Jared thought might have been milk they had saddled the horse and ridden off.

The horse trotted at a leisurely pace through a dusty path that wound its way through lazily waving stalks of red grass. As they approached the line of trees Jared glanced behind and saw Fellicone in the distance, waving slowly. He raised his hand in reply and then they were inside the wood, the sudden change in light startling him.

"*Where did the doorway take me?*" Jared wondered. "*Somewhere unusual,*" he thought but he had no idea where. In the distance he could see the sun, huge over the horizon, over twice as big as the sun he was used to seeing. It was light green and orange, the clouds around it a glorious display of reds, purples and oranges that changed every minute as it rose higher in the sky.

Mordalayn sensed the fear in Jared. "It's all right boy. Don't be frightened. See the lake in the distance through the trees? That's where we're going."

As they rode along a whispering voice suddenly said. "Master why are you here on this path?"

Jared jumped. The voice was like the wind whistling in the grass. It was as if it wasn't actually spoken but more inside his own head. He looked around frantically as Mordalayn gently reigned the horse to a stop.

"Good friend we are on our way to Alegria. Two travellers, surely you can allow such innocents as us to pass?."

"Master Mordalayn?" the whispering voice said again with curiosity. Jared glanced around and to their left he saw that the leaves of a large tree were twisting in the breeze. As he stared at it the leaves rippled and formed, breaking into patterns to suggest there was a face in there. The large lips and eyes formed and then dissapeared, to reemerge in the next tree and then into a third. Finally the voice spoke while the leafy face looked at them both.

"Oh, master Mordalayn you are with a young friend. Pray, who is this young boy?"

"This is master Jared, a very important friend of the Emerald Queen" Mordalayn replied in a friendly yet totally formal tone. "We are on our way to the palace so he can help her in her time of trouble."

The face in the leaves rippled, broke and reformed and the green lips appeared to smile. "Gooooood" the voice whispered. "Master, you are always welcome in this wood. Please tread carefully. Take only what you need from it."

"You are very kind my friend, Our Lady will hear of your kindness to one who serves her. Have a good day."

The face seemed to smile once more and with a final flurry of the leaves and a whistle of wind the trees became still.

Mordalayn tugged the reins gently and they continued on the path. "What was that?" Jared asked bewilidered.

"Forest guardians of the border lands" Mordalayn said quietly. "They guard their own. They are friendly enough if they like you."

"And if they don't?" Jared asked.

"Then, well you've got a big problem." Mordalayn replied.

Jared glanced to the left and saw the lake Mordalayn had referred to in the distance. They rode in silence and then dismounted near a long wooden fence. Mordalayn took their packs from the horse and then slapped its rump. The horse bolted, headed back to the farm. Jared's feet got stuck in damp patch of mud but Mordalayn caught his arm. "Careful lad, this ground is treacherous" he said sternly.

Near them was the same orange ooze that he'd seen at the farm. Steam twisted from it. "What is that stuff?" he asked.

"Old magic." Mordalayn said and then added "since Our Lady is hurt it is building like sewage. Don't step in it."

Jared nodded, fearfully.

They moved towards the lake on a path cutting from the field down to an area with an enclosed paved section with a large wooden table and seats. The path veered right to a fence that appeared to be made of some sort of livid, wet looking brown plant.

They walked down further and before them was a large lake and a bridge of maybe fifty metres in length extended out to a square dock port. Moored there was a small yet elegantly carved boat with oars lashed to it. The bridge was rickety and old looking with nothing to keep someone from falling in, although wide enough for two people to walk comfortably side by side. The water was a vivid, rich blue and impossible to tell how deep.

"Look, I know you did something weird back there but this is crazy" Jared said, stopping and turning round to face his escort. Mordalayn stared at him impassively, towering over Jared. He remained silent for a moment then said:

"There are many things I need to tell you but we're not safe here. Unless we keep moving we can be found. I promise you I'll tell you everything you need to know once we are somewhere beyond danger."

Just then heard there was the sound of hooves in the distance. Mordalayn whirled, pulling Jared behind him. From behind the large copse of trees there appeared five riders on large horses. They were all hugely powerful beasts. The riders were all men, all dressed in long, red cloaks and carrying sheathed swords at their sides with what appeared to be a bundle of short spears behind the saddles of their mounts. The horses were shining with the exertion of the gallop.

Mordalayn whispered. "Don't move and don't say anything."

The horses slowed at a signal from the foremost rider and stopped a short distance away forming a line. Then the riders dismounted and stood looking towards them, hands on their swords.

The leader strode toward Mordalayn, smiling broadly, one of his front teeth glinting. He was white haired and clean shaven with broad shoulders and reminded Jared of a rugby player his dad knew. The mud on the shore caked his dark leather boots. Flipping his cloak over his shoulder he bowed theatrically, making a flourishing gesture with his gloved right hand as he dipped low.

"Well, well, my friend. Seems you have collected a stray."

Mordalayn said nothing. Jared peered out anxiously from behind him.

"Come come Takoba, this is no time to be belligerent or unfriendly." He gestured behind him to his men who glanced quickly at one another and their grips tightened on their sword hilts.

The man moved forward slightly, his smile broad. "My thanks, it is indeed an honour."

Mordalayn's icy stare never changed. "You have no honour Siavy" he hissed angrily. "You are a mercenary and a thief."

The man's smile never faded but he took one step closer. "Mordalayn you are a loyal servant to Alegria, however the boy comes with us." He signalled to two of his men to move forward and they did so, striding forward purposefully.

Mordalayn snarled and stepped clear of Jared, unsheathing the huge sword. The metal hissed free of the scabbard and two men stuttered to a halt on the muddy shore.

Siavy shook his head slowly. "I will offer you one final chance. Give us the boy and you can go. The alternative is that we kill you and take the boy anyway."

Mordalayn said nothing.

Siavy sighed. "Very well" he said with a resigned air. His smile faded and he turned to his men. "Take him" he said curtly.

Mordalayn whirled, turning quickly to Jared and shoving him hard. "Run to the boat" he shouted.

The soldiers charged at Mordalayn with their swords drawn.

"Yield!" one shouted. Mordalayn didn't pause but raised his sword above his head and as the man raised his own to parry the expected down swing, Mordalayn kicked out with his left leg, his wide foot landing square in the man's guts. With a whoosh of air the man flew back four feet and dropped his sword, grasping his winded stomach and heaving in pain.

Mordalayn then turned to the other and brought the sword down in a vicious arc towards the man's head. The man countered in terror as the three blades rammed down with furious force upon his own steel. Before the soldier could react Mordalayn brought the hilt of his sword into the man's head, knocking him out cold.

Jared stood mesmerised on the bridge watching this unfold. Mordalayn had put the first two soldiers down in the space of a few seconds. He turned and ran. *"I don't want to fall in,"* he thought but noting through his fear that the boards seemed dry despite how close they were to the water.

Mordalayn ducked a blade aimed for his head and, holding his sword in his right hand, grabbed the man's sword arm and kicked his legs out from underneath him. He put his right foot on the man's neck, the soldier gasping as his throat was constricted. The final of the four hesitated, unsure of whether to proceed or not. Siavy looked bored and as the soldier glanced at him he jerked his head angrily. "Take him down! Unless you want to face me later!"

The soldier lunged at Mordalayn who brought the flat sides of his huge tri-blade down across the man's head, simultaneously dodging the blow aimed at his own neck. The man fell to his knees and then pitched forward in the mud face down.

Mordalayn contemptuously flipped him over onto his back with his foot.

"Hmmm....impressive. I was thinking maybe you'd got rusty after so long babysitting" Siavy said, adjusting his cloak.

"Count yourself lucky I didn't kill them" Mordalayn growled.

"Whatever" Siavy said waving his hand dismissively and looking with disdain at the prone and groaning figures scattered like fallen dolls. Mordalayn turned on his heel and marched quickly to the boat, not sparing a backwards look to where he had wrought so much chaos. Jared stood transfixed, still unable to comprehend exactly what he was seeing. The cat man strode towards him, then took him firmly but gently by his shirt and turned him towards the boat. "Come" he said. "We need to go, mind your step as you get in."

The boat was green and red, the paint chipped and flaking in many places. It was big enough for about four people to sit comfortably, with two benches with purple cushions across the middle of the boat, one behind the other. The cushions were also faded. Mordalayn gestured for Jared to sit down and then stepped into the boat himself, the small capsule rocking slightly as his weight momentarily upset the balance. He turned and began unlashing the oars, the knots undoing easily under his strong fingers. He released them with a grunt and dropped them into the boat, turning his attention to the mooring rope. Jared glanced around. The had cleared the horizon. Jared saw it was a gorgeous red colour. As he stared colours and ripples danced across the surface, reflected in the blue water.

"Who were those men?" Jared asked glancing back across the bridge to where the leader could be seen attempting to stir one of his prone men by kicking him.

"Mercenaries" Mordalayn replied. "Their commander is Galfront Siavy."

He turned and extended his left foot, pushing against the dock hard so the boat moved away from the bridge and the water lapped against the sides. He picked up one oar and pushed against the wooden surface, the boat turning slightly with the pressure. He then slotted the oars in place and sat down, begining to haul on them, pulling clear of the dock. Then both he and Jared turned to the unexpected sound of running feet thudding hard on the wooden boards of the bridge.

Galfront was furious that Mordalayn had bested his men so easily. It was bad enough he'd been forced to cover so much land tracking this child. To add insult to injury Mordalayn, once a general, had for the last twelve years been the personal bodyguard to the Emerald Queen of Alegria. Yet it didn't appear to have dulled his fighting abilities. He had needed to be sure of the Caracalic's skill so ordering his men to attack had been informative to say the least. Still, he had to admit that he'd proved his mettle.

Angrily Galfront kicked the man nearest to him to wake him up. The soldier groaned and grabbed his sore head. "Get up you mangy dog!" he cursed at the man, who winced in fear and staggered to his feet. "Get after him and stop that boat."

The man saluted, knowing better than to argue, even on the rare occasions when Siavy was in a good mood. He turned to the boat in the distance and winced as Siavy barked. "I said stop them, don't dawdle man!."

The soldier bent down and picked up his mud spattered sword and then ran towards the boat. Galfront folded his arms and leaned on a tree to watch, as one of his other men slowly made it to his feet and shook his head groggily.

Mordalayn couldn't understand why the man was running at them. They were already clear of the dock and the distance was increasing with every passing second. The mercenary hurtled towards them. Mordalayn stared at him and shouted. "Stop man, you won't make it."

The soldier paid no heed and with a roar leapt the distance from the bridge to the small boat. He fell short by a foot and splashed into the water. His hands scrabbling for purchase on the side of the craft. Mordalayn stepped back putting one hand on Jared's shoulder. Puzzlement crossing his features as the man floundered, his sword slipping from wet fingers and clattering into the boat.

"You fool, don't you know how dangerous these waters are?!!" Mordalayn shouted angrily.

The man snarled and his back legs kicked frantically as he tried unsuccessfully to heave himself up. Jared watched mesmerised.

Mordalayn reached down to the man and grabbed his arm, kicking his sword out of reach.

"Stop struggling and I'll pull you in" Mordalayn told him firmly.

The soldier reached behind his soaking cloak, scrabbling for something.

Just then Jared heard a new sound. Whispering on the air, similar to the sound of leaves rustling in the trees mixed with chattering. Mordalayn glanced up at the noise and winced. "Quickly you fool, take my hand."

The whispers got louder and sounded closer. Jared looked around quickly but could see nothing. Two of the other soldiers ran up the bridge. The distant figure of Galfront stood motionless, watching what was happening.

As Mordalayn moved to take a firmer grip on the man's arm to pull him up the soldier brought out a dagger from his belt and swung wildly. Mordalayn contemptuously grabbed the knife arm with his other hand.

"Let the blade go" he hissed in the man's face.

The whispering got louder as the boat rocked wildly, water spilling into the vessel as the two figures struggled. Jared fought to keep his balance on the bench, moving back further from the entwined figures.

Jared glanced past the two struggling men to see they had made some distance from the dock and shapes were forming in the water. Something was underneath the surface.

"For the love of the sun man, LET THE BLADE GO!!!" Mordalayn shouted, finally losing his composure as he tried to prevent the man from sliding into the water yet fighting to keep the dagger away from his face.

The whispering now had a sinister edge to it, a noise like a child chuckling. Not sweet like a baby's giggle but dark and horrible. The soldiers on the dock were gesturing frantically at the boat, while the disturbances in the water became more numerous, the motions and ripples getting nearer to the vessel.

"Soooooo sweeeeeeet" a voice said on the breeze as Mordalayn finally succeeded in twisting the man's knife hand far enough to make him drop the blade into the water.

"Nauuughty!!!" the voices echoed, seeming to come from everywhere at the same time.

The man kicked and struggled and Mordalayn tried in vain to pull him into the boat.

"Sooooo looooovely" the voice snickered as the water rose and fell.

"For the love of life you imbecile, STOP STRUGGLING!!!" Mordalayn shouted in exasperation.

The whispering was intrusive. Jared could feel shivers running down his spine and clapped his hands over his ears to shut out the sound.

A hand suddenly appeared at the far end of the boat, reaching over the stern. White as bleached bone with long pearl coloured finger nails it drummed gently on the wood. Drops of water fell from the fingertips.

"Oooursss" the voices cooed, the sound of leaves blowing in the wind was now matched with what sounded like birds' wings beating madly and frantically.

Jared watched terrified as the hand moved slowly along the side of the boat towards Mordalayn and the soldier, steam rising in wisps from it. Further back you could see the two men on the dock pointing madly and shouting.

The hand was connected to a wrist which wore a bracelet made of pearls, the same colour as the nails on the hand. The middle finger was wearing a large pearl ring.

Mordalayn saw the hand approaching and with a look of regret let the man go, who slumped back and fought to retain his grip.

"It's too late. You're beyond help now," he said solemnly shaking his head. He stood near Jared as the thrashing soldier finally realised his danger and turned round as the hand reached his shoulder.

"Soooo taaaasty!!!" the voice whispered again and then giggled like a little girl. The fingers on the hand pinched the flesh of his upper arm through his leather tunic.

The man shrieked in fear and pleaded. "Please, don't leave me." Mordalayn shook his head as other arms came sliding from the water and took grips on the man's upper body. He kicked and screamed and with one final burst of energy managed to half heave himself into the boat. Jared then saw something that frightened him more than anything else that he'd seen. The arms were not attached to a body, they were just loose, the sleeve of a gown that appeared to be made of sequins covering each one. As Jared reacted in fear, one of the arms paused in its approach. The hand turned towards him, the palm raising itself upwards, rearing back and the fingers flexing like spider legs. Then it turned to the soldier who was screaming in a high wail that carried over the lake, his two colleagues frantic on the bridge but powerless to help him.

Suddenly the thrashing stopped. A yellow light emanated from the heavy pearl ring on the middle finger of every hand holding the man. Jared couldn't tell how many, maybe seven or eight, the last one slithering over the man's wet forehead from behind and grasping his face. The light grew until the different points merged and the soldier was coccooned in light. He went rigid but his eyes still moved between the fingers, darting wildly to Mordalayn and Jared.

"Strength in the next world" Mordalayn whispered as the light completely covered the man's body and suddenly, without any warning he tipped backwards, his grip on the boat gone and was pulled beneath the surface. There was not even a ripple in the wake. Only a yellow light that faded slowly until the waters were calm and blue.

Mordalayn stepped forward once the light had gone and picked up the man's sword. Without hesitating he threw it out across the lake, the blade spinning wildly as it arced through the air before splashing into the water.

Mordalayn turned to Jared. "Keep your hands and feet inside this boat, if you do that then the boat will not overturn, even in a storm. Do you understand?"

Jared was white, still terrified by what he'd seen.

Mordalayn could see his fear and said more gently. "The lake is guarded, as is the perimeter. None may swim or hunt here, although that in itself is not a death sentence."

"What happened to him?"

"He tried to harm me." Mordalayn replied. "For that he paid with his own life. The guardians of the border lakes do not tolerate aggression...unless of course they are the ones dispensing it."

Jared glanced at the shore. The remaining soldiers had returned to their master who was already on his horse and signalling them to join him.

Jared looked back at Mordalayn. "You tried to save him? He was trying to kill you," he asked, confused.

Mordalayn looked grim. "The man was a soldier. His master is cruel. I only kill if I have to." He unhooked his cloak and placed it around Jared's shoulders. "Here, it's a long journey and it may be cold. Take this."

With no further word, he turned and sat on the bench in front of Jared and took the oars. Heaving hard to take the strain of the current and the weight of the water, he began to row towards a destination that was for Jared unknown.

Chapter 5

The sun, though huge in the sky was only as warm as a spring day and Jared wrapped the cloak he'd been given around himself, more to feel safe than anything else. The dock was now empty and the soldiers had gone. Mordalayn rowed hard, the oars slipping into the water in perfect unison as he heaved. For a long time there was no conversation then he glanced back towards Jared.

"Are you tired boy? Sleep if you wish, there are cushions in the hatch at the back near your feet."

"How on earth does he think I can sleep NOW?" Jared thought angrily.

"No, I can't sleep, in fact I don't think I'll ever be able to again" he snapped, pulling the cloak around himself.

Mordalayn half turned. "Look, I know you must feel overwhelmed by this but....."

"You'll tell me later. I know."

Mordalayn paused for a few moments then pushed the oars into the locking position and stood. He sat to face Jared and the boat rocked slightly.

"Jared....please be patient. I am sorrier than I can tell you that you have become involved in this but...." he looked up as a flock of crimson birds squawked past them noisily, wheeling up into the sky.

"This world is in turmoil. We cannot sustain ourselves while the queen is in this state." He paused then said, "She is Our Lady, the guardian and keeper of this world. While she is hurt we are greatly vulnerable."

"That...man you stopped in her room. Who was he?"

"He comes from the dark, a weak individual with no honour. Our enemies gather and they have great reason to believe that this world should end in its current form."

The boat rocked slightly in the water. Jared glanced over the side and saw the water rippling gently in the wind.

"I have to get you to the Shores" Mordalayn said, taking the oars again. He sat down and began to row hard. "Around to your right you can see what we're heading for."

Jared stared sullenly at the floor of the boat for a few moments and then looked out to where Mordalayn had pointed. In the distance and still obscured by the mainland was some sort of large building, a vast entrance gawping at its front. As the boat slowly edged round the curve of the land Jared saw that it was huge. The construction was dark grey stone, gleaming wetly like it had recently been rained on. The opening was rounded but came to a point and a large tip of narrow stone pointed out from the apex of the doorway.

There was no door visible, only a dark maw. The building continued back from the vast entrance like a gigantic snake, the view of the mainland currently blocking the sight of the rest.

As Mordalayn rowed Jared glanced around him. To their left was dark green land mottled with red. The land itself was very high with tall, thin trees dotted about and slightly ahead and to the right a small hut, alone on the hillside. A path ran in a rickety fashion, crookedly zig zagging along the steep face until it terminated at the top. A few animals could be seen clinging to the cliff face, munching on the grass that grew in abundance on its surface. On the other side of the boat the water ran out into an expanse of blue, the mist about a mile beyond them hiding the land on that side. There were only grey shapes visible through the fog.

As Jared turned back he saw more of the huge building they were headed for. The impression he'd had of the opening resembling a mouth turned out to be accurate. With a start Jared sat up and realised that he was looking at an enormus, sculpted recreation of a face with the mouth wide open.

They gradually inched up on it in the boat under Mordalayn's constant hauling.

The huge face appeared to be helmeted. The artwork was unbelievably detailed and flawlessly sculpted. The nose guard extended down to form an overhang in the entrance and the eyes of the soldier were open wide. It looked as if anything entering the mouth of the face would be swallowed. The sun played in vivid spills over the metal, splashing over the surface. Jared stared awestruck.

As they came nearer and rounded the land on their left Jared could see people working. Some appeared to be tending to fields while a few men were riding on horses near them as if supervising the work. Mordalayn rowed closer, taking their small vessel to within about 100 metres of the dock. No-one paid them the slightest notice at all. Eventually they came to a docking area close to the gaping entrance. Mordalayn whistled to a group of scruffily clothed men standing near the dock. They looked up and moved to the silver, riveted mooring points.

Mordalayn threw them the ropes from the bow of the boat and two of them reeled them in, lashing the lines securely around the metal with a complicated series of knots. Then he leapt nimbly from the boat in one fluid skip. He turned, tossed the nearest of the men a coin then extended his hand to Jared who stood, unsteady on his feet and handed the cloak back before stepping up. He took a deep breath and lunged forward. His shoe scraped on the loose grains of stone as he gained purchase on the solid floor and then staggered forward. Mordalayn took him by the shoulder.

"Come boy, we need to hasten. I promised you an explanation and one you shall have." They moved towards the huge entrance before them. A small, bright purple creature with an unbelievably long nose passed them pushing a small hand cart loaded with odd looking vegetables of some kind, the smell rich and sharp in Jared's nostrils. The creature was mumbling irritably to itself as it pushed the cart on, the wheels trundling noisily against the stone, one of them squeaking intermittently. The creature grumbled on, seemingly loathing whatever it was doing.

There were people milling about in every direction. It reminded Jared of ants entering an ant hill. The huge entrance was now completely over them. Jared craned his neck to look around. The inside of the entrance was like a dome, dark red in colour and his eyes took a while to adjust to the change in light.

Most people ignored them or failed to notice their passing. One or two bowed their heads or spoke a greeting to Mordalayn A tall, spindly creature with long skinny legs and webbed feet even bowing as he passed.

The entrance hall reminded Jared of when his family had gone to Rome and visited the Vatican. The ceiling there had nearly caused him to fall over backwards trying to look at it all at once.

Ahead the hall narrowed to a large tunnel. At the entrance to it were several soldiers. As Mordalayn and Jared approached a tall man in silver armour stepped forward. He nodded acknowledgment to Mordalayn, saluted then looked Jared up and down quickly, appearing agitated.

"Greetings Takoba" the man. "May I ask who is the boy?"

"Greetings to you Captain. I need to take him to The Council chamber." He put his right hand on Jared's shoulder reassuringly.

"Who is he?" the Captain asked again, looking nervous.

"Wait here" Mordalayn said quietly to Jared then gestured to the Captain to step to one side. He spoke quickly and rapidly in the man's ear. The soldier looked at first surprised and twice glanced over in Jared's direction. He nodded at whatever Mordalayn was saying and then signalled to two of the other guards who had been watching them.

"Take the Takoba and the boy to the council chambers" the Captain said, staring intently at Jared.

The two soldiers the Captain had nominated as escorts moved silently in sync to step either side of them. They began walking to a large wooden and ornate door. The Captain said something to another officer who glanced with a shocked expression at Jared. Mordalayn put his hand on Jared's shoulder and gently nudged him forwards. As they approached it the door on the left hand side swung inwards with a groan and hit the wall with a loud bump. The guards moved, one taking up a position to the front of them and the other to the rear. They were expressionless.

The corridor on the other side of the door was dark and Jared's eyes took some time to adjust to the gloom. Some way ahead of them was a brighter area that looked like a larger room. The guard at the front marched quickly, Mordalayn keeping up easily, Jared stumbling along briefly as he tried to increase his step. The walls either side seemed to be made of jagged rock but it was very dark and Jared couldn't really see.

They came into a brightly lit area that took Jared's breath away. Hanging from the ceiling was a huge chandelier like a crystal tree hung upside down. The jewels in it glittered with a dazzling display of white light, cut with flashes of rainbow colours. The floor was paved with what appeard to be white marble and in the centre of the room in a circular pattern below the vast chandelier was a dark, ruby red pattern of tiles. There were various soldiers and people moving about, one or two wearing white and gold robes, like priests. Doorways in arched frames led away in several places, via little flights of steps.

"Stand here" Mordalayn said as they arrived at the centre of the room. The two soldiers took up position either side on one of the dark tiles while Mordalayn turned around and stood behind Jared. "Don't be scared and don't worry. This is a short journey" he said gently. Jared felt his stomach lurch slightly as the tile began to move. The circular pattern of other tiles, identical to the one they were standing on, then flowed around and one at a time lined up in front of theirs. With no sound at all the tiles formed a line and then theirs moved forward. The tile in front of it slid underneath and replaced it in the first position and every time they cleared a tile the one ahead slid back to take its place.

They moved towards a large gap between two small flights of stairs. Again the corridor was dark and at the end Jared could see bright light. As they entered the dark tunnel the tile they were standing on lit up slightly, illuminating the space around them. The walls here were smooth and black as ebony. Jared felt slightly scared but stood still as Mordalayn said. The tile continued on, its successor silently replacing the space it left as they carried on their journey. After a few minutes of travelling the tile reached the lit up area and Jared could see there was a vast wooden table in the middle. It seemed that wherever he was, the people here did not do things on a small scale. There were no doors and the room was dome shaped with only the table and the entrance they had come from. As the tile they were on stopped, the soldier at the front stepped clear. Jared glanced over his shoulder and saw that the corridor was pitch black. The tile itself had dimmed.

"Don't step backwards!" Mordalayn warned gruffly. The guard behind followed them off silently and as they walked forward Jared looked over his shoulder and realised with shock that the tile had gone and the corridor had no floor, the blackness below was simply bottomless.

They moved towards the table and the guards took up position either side of the entrance they had come through. Impassive, their spears held rigidly by their sides, they stared straight ahead.

"It's ok, we are expected here" Mordalayn said.

"Who's expecting us?"

"The council know we are coming."

Just then there was a crackling sound and Jared glanced across the large table to his right. As he watched, the air above and slightly behind it rippled. The ripples played in the air, making Jared's eyes feel funny. They slowly merged to a central point and, just before they closed in on each other completely, a bearded figure like the ones they had seen out in the main hall, appeared sitting in a large, leather backed chair. His body was see through at first but as the ripples finally closed in on themselves he gained solidity and stared around him quickly before letting his gaze rest on Jared and Mordalayn.

"Ah, there you are" he said irritably, adjusting his white and gold robe and reaching into a pocket, bringing out a pair of spectacles and then putting them on.

Mordalayn nodded at the seated figure and said respectfully, "as you wish Prime Guardian."

Jared looked around nervously, unsure as to whether they would be invited to sit or not.

"Rancidrain has been received Takoba. He is persistently stubborn and uncooperative, as you would expect. We will assume you didn't have him arrive five metres above the floor on purpose," the old man added staring at Mordalayn over his spectacles.

Mordalayn said nothing.

"Hmmph!" the old man said loudly, and just then the air resounded with the same crackling sound Jared had heard before and then a third time. The rippling effect occurred to the right of the old man and around the table. As he watched various figures began to appear from out of the the air. Some dressed as the old man was, others in robes of red and then two women, middle

73

aged in green dresses. One after the other they appeared in the seats.

When the appearances had stopped, the table was now full of people facing them with the old man at one end and a vacant space with a much more ornate chair at the other. In front of Jared along the vast length were roughly ten people of various types. One had the head of a rat, the eyes piercing black. It was wearing a black tunic with bright gold-coloured buttons on it and what appeared to be medals on the left chest pocket. Another was a woman but she had only one eye in the middle of her forehead. They all greeted one another with curt nods.

"Now then, let's not waste time" the old man said. "We all know why we are here. Takoba, your mission appears to have been a partial success. The would be assassin is in chains. However you have brought this child here. May I ask why?"

The assembled council turned to look at Mordalayn who replied. "This child is called Jared. He was in the room when I caught Rancidrain." Putting his hand back on Jared's shoulder he continued. "His intervention prevented a murder. However Rancidrain threw a tracker into him. I took him when Glavers attacked. Here our enemies cannot use Jared to find Our Lady. They are careless in their methods and risked exposure by such an open attack."

There was a murmur amongst the gathered people. The one eyed lady looked intently at Jared. A man on her right with closely cropped black hair and the biggest sideburns Jared had ever seen conferred with the rat creature, both staring intently at Jared who was now more uncomfortable than scared.

The old man gestured to Jared to step forward. "Come boy, don't be frightened. Tell us what you saw."

Jared started to reply but his mouth was dry. "Could I have a drink please?" he stammered after swallowing.

"But of course. Excuse our eagerness," the old man waved his hand and a jug of water and a tankard appeared. Jared gingerly reached forward and picked up the jug. It was cold against his fingers as he poured, splashing the liquid onto the floor due to his shaking hands. He raised the cup to his lips. It tasted of strawberries and was very cold. He gulped it down then replaced the mug.

"Now," the old man said gently. "Please can you tell us what you saw? Don't be frightened."

"The man...thing....Rancidrain, whatever you called him. I heard him in the room of the hospital, Sophie's room. I looked in to see what was happening and he attacked me. When I tried to leave he did something to block the door. Mordalayn saved me and there was a bright light and, and..."

The council members looked at each other and then back at Jared. The rat figure then spoke, his voice deep and gravelly. "Did he say anything to you?"

Jared thought and then added "he was just horrible to me and he was begging Mordalayn not to hurt him but...." Jared thought for a moment then added "before he knew I was there he said something about not wanting to do anything but 'they' had made him and he just wanted to be left in peace."

There was a murmur around the table. The man at the far end stood up. He was dressed in armour like the soldiers on the dock but the colours were purple not red. He glared at

Mordalayn and Jared then said to everyone. "I believe we all know who is responsible for this!"

The old man held up his hand. "Lighvoor while you are clearly angered over King James's attempts to usurp our authority our entire standing army is only two thousand men. The majority are trained only in ceremonial duties."

"But Council this boy has heard..."

"Precisely nothing that can aid us in any way." He turned to Jared. "Did Rancidrain mention any names that you heard?"

"No sir, just that 'they' had made him do it. He said that more than once."

The old man turned back to the assembled council. "I believe the best thing we can do is keep the boy with us. We can find out whether he's in danger and exactly what our enemies are planning to do. This attempt was deliberate and audacious. The fact that they sent someone as useless as Rancidrain makes it clear that they are unable to move en masse."

Mordalayn then interjected. "With respect Council, the creature had this on him."

He approached the table and placed a block of brown stone from his pocket on it.

The one eyed woman gasped and there were angry murmurs from the table. She leaned forward and picked up the rock. It morphed and changed in her fingers to the rainbow blade again, the lights bright and this time there were what looked like fireflies flashing above it, the colours lighting up her face and the wall behind her.

"So you think you have no proof" she hissed. "Who but an Anghofian assassin would wield a rainbow blade?"

There were murmurs of agreement from the table. The man in the purple robes banged his fist on the table. "Since Our Lady was taken from us this...usurper of power, this, this hateful, ungrateful wretch...! We MUST act now, we have all the proof we need. We shall have more when Rancidrain has been questioned."

The old man spoke again. "Lighvoor your passion for your given role is commendable but we need to know exactly what is happening. Any move or accusation against King James will only further convince his cautious allies that he is in the right. Further, Rancidrain is stubborn as he always was and may tell us nothing or a mixture of lies and half truths."

"He won't if you give him to me."

"Lighvoor, remember your place!" the Prime Guardian shouted, his calm finally cracking. "Our Lady granted this assembly temporary power in her absence, she did not give us the right to torture her subjects...regardless of the reason."

Lighvoor sat down, still fuming and the old man addressed the whole table.

"We have, unfortunately let our guard down. Our rulers are immensely powerful and for that we never envisaged a time when they would be anything else. Our predecessors never, ever believed a moment would come when the power so carefully guarded would be trapped and impotent. He turned to Lighvoor. "When were your men last in battle?"

Lighvoor said nothing. The old man continured. "Have they ever seen battle? The answer is no. They are loyal men but they are no match for Anghofio's soldiers. Again I tell you, their elite battalion alone numbers half our entire army. We have become

77

complacent. None of us, in a thousand years ever believed we would lose the power of our rulers. Anghofio will not move upon us if there is the slightest possibility that the Emerald Queen could return. However they will try anything they can to find our secrets and to end her life."

Lighvoor looked away, his anger deflated and his cheeks flushed red.

"There is a traitor in Alegria, someone who knows our innermost, most precious secrets and we need to be vigilant until such a time as Our Lady returns or..." and he paused at this time and looked around before saying slowly, "..or she dies and we need to re-elect."

There were murmurs around the table. Everyone seemed to be in agreement.

Lighvoor sat back in his seat, tight lipped and looked at Jared. "So what about him? Where is he supposed to go?"

The Council turned to them. "Takoba you are to take the boy and present him to the Brotherhood Orphanage in Arkale village. He will be safe there."

Jared spoke up. "I need to get home. My parents will be worried. That mess at the airport will have everyone looking for me."

The Prime Guardian shook his head sadly and added. "The magic to bring you here is ancient, precious and very, very rare. All the portals are closed now, bar Our Lady's pathway. You cannot go home."

Jared's mouth opened in shock and he looked around, almost in tears.

The old man said kindly "You will not be missed as much as you think. Takoba Mordalayn will explain all this to you. Now, I believe we have covered everything. This meeting is over."

Without any further discussion the old man closed his eyes and from around his chest it appeared as if someone had dropped a stone in water. It was similar to when he'd arrived but in reverse. The air rippled in circular rings around him and as the ripples expanded he started to fade. Within a few seconds he was gone. One by one the other members of the meeting followed until only the rat faced figure was left at the table. He stood and addressed Mordalayn directly, ignoring Jared.

"Takoba, be cautious. While this council appreciates what you have done and what you will do, you will be forever in danger now."

"Thank you Degrezen" Mordalayn said stiffly.

Degrezen looked at Jared. "Boy, what city are you from?"

"Warwick...sir" Jared stammered slightly, realising he was speaking to a rat faced man, who was speaking to a cat faced man.

Degrezen widened its eyes in surprise. "Hmmm...that gives some explanation to....well, never mind for now."

He nodded to them both and then vanished, the air rippling around him.

Jared turned to Mordalayn. "Where are you taking me now then?"

"I promised you a full explanation and one you shall have."

"What did he mean I won't be missed as much as I think?" Jared said impatiently, tired of all this waiting.

"Time here is slower than in your world" Mordalayn replied. "Three days for us is a day on your side."

"But I'll still be missed," Jared said in exasperation. "Just for a day, not for a week."

They walked back to the opening they had arrived by. The two guards still standing impassively and rigidly to attention. Jared jumped slightly as caramel coloured tiles on the floor of the room slid silently under his feet to line up at the entrance like last time. The soldiers took up position then Mordalayn and Jared stepped on. The other soldier took up the rear. Without any word the tile moved off down the dark corridor, its light illuminating the dark walls and emphasising the void they were over.

"Why did they call you Takoba?" Jared enquired as Mordalayn faced away from him.

"That is my rank," he answered without turning around.

"Were you in the army?" Jared asked.

"I was."

Jared could tell Mordalayn didn't want to speak any more so he fell silent.

As the tile arrived back in the main hall they all stepped clear and walked back to the entrance. The area was still teeming with people and the light from the huge chandelier was dimmer than when they came in. On Jared's left a team of short creatures were working on a statue. They looked like the irritable, long nosed one that had passed them outside, pushing a barrow. They were about 15 of them, using their noses to hold onto the cylindrical pillar at various heights while polishing the statue with cloths. Two nearer the top were chiselling away with tiny tools at the face of the statue. None of them looked happy to be there.

"Come on" Mordalayn said as they moved towards the officers manning the entrance. The captain who had spoken to them when they came in turned around as they approached.

"Takoba," he said, bowing slightly. "I trust your meeting was satisfactory."

"Yes, thank you." Mordalayn replied. "I need transport to Arkale. Do you have something to spare?"

"Of course," the captain said and signalled to another of his men.

Chapter 6

As Mordalayn and Jared got down from the cart the Caracalic was tight lipped and surly. A grocer's cart had lost a wheel and was blocking their path. The driver of their vehicle reigned in his horses and watched as the irate owner yelling at his driver.

"What's wrong?" Jared asked seeing the look on Mordalayn's face.

"We should not be here," he replied glancing around as if expecting trouble. "This village is too close to the border. The Council should have known that."

Around them people worked, unloading other carts or selling their wares in the street. A young man holding a tray of glazed fruits bowed respectfully at Mordalayn as the cat figure glanced towards him.

All around people were hushed and obviously a little intimidated by Mordalayn's presence. He took Jared by the arm, and then whispered urgently. "This area is safe if you do as I say. Do you understand?" Jared tried to smile, still feeling competely overwhelmed.

They moved down the side of the street. People moving aside, bowing their heads as they approached.

"Why are they so nervous?" Jared asked quizzically, uncertain of why everyone appeared so awestruck.

"Hush, wait till we are indoors," Mordalayn snapped and Jared fell silent. He was getting tired of being told to wait for answers but was equally nervous by the reaction their presence was having on everyone.

They stopped near a shop with pots and pans outside. The brassware shining brightly in the sunlight. Mordalayn checked the street and a rider on a horse saw that they wished to cross and gently tugged on his animal's reigns, bringing the beast to a halt. All around them people waited, nodding or even bowing to Mordalayn.

Just as they were about to move off, a figure ran round the corner looking over his shoulder shouting frantically. "Oh my! Oh my! OH MY!." He was dressed in baggy red trousers and a pair of worn, grubby shoes, his toes poking out of the front of one. His shirt was torn and over it was a too-big green waistcoat. His hat was floppy and peaked, falling back over his scalp and his hair was shoulder length and looked filthy. As he hurtled towards them Mordalayn whirled and grabbed Jared, shoving him forward into the open doorway of a tavern. He landed with a thud, the air rushing out of his lungs. As Mordalayn turned the man collided with him and they both went sprawling into the road. A fine cloud of dust flew into the air as they skidded to a stop, the dried earth layering them both. Mordalayn tried to extricate himself from the wriggling man. With a grunt he shoved him off and stood up to dust himself down.

The people watching them were silent for a few seconds then the man on the horse who had stopped to let them cross began to chuckle. "My, my" he said shaking his head. "Our Lady's bodyguard seems to be not such a strong warrior after all."

Someone else laughed and soon three or four others had joined in. Jared staggered to his feet and put one hand on the door frame of the tavern, gasping for breath. Someone else piped up. "Yes, maybe he's a spoon not a Takoba."

Others began to join in. Their former respect of Mordalayn giving way to something sinister and nasty.

Another added. "All the ballads they sing of the Queen's Sword. Maybe they should sing of how he was finally knocked down by a runaway urchin."

More were laughing now. Jared watched, uncertain of what would happen.

The man who had bowled Mordalayn over was clearly dizzy, holding his head and trying to sit up. His hat had fallen off and he felt around for it. "Dearie me, oh dear" he said trying to stand up but still too disoriented to use his feet. He sat back down with a bump.

Mordalayn glared at the man and reached down with one huge hand to grab his collar. The man squirmed and wriggled, squealing "I'm sorry sir, I didn't see you!"

"I know you didn't you clumsy oaf," Mordalayn hissed at him lifting the kicking man off the floor and holding him up, his feet making pedalling motions in the air. The crowd still laughed at the scene in front of them while Jared fought for breath.

Just then two uniformed and armoured men came round the corner. They saw Mordalayn and one nudged the other.

"Don't bother yourself Takoba. Give him to us," he said, standing back with his hands on his hips. The crowd were silent, their amusement at the scene had vanished.

"Be my guest," Mordalayn said with a sneer, still clearly angry and turned, dropping the wincing man in the road. The man landed hard and grunted as he hit the floor again.

"I'm sorry sirs, I didn't mean to offend" he stammered as the guards reached down to pick him up.

"Come on" Mordalayn said. He saw the look on Jared's face. "Don't worry about him, he's an escaped prisoner" and turned him around, walking back into the street.

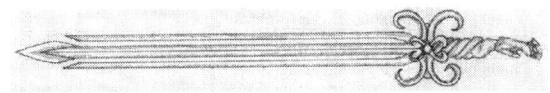

The guard who had spoken to Mordalayn was furious and very, very drunk. Scious was only a petty thief and he'd managed to get out of the prison cart when they'd stopped for a drink or two on their way back to jail. If they hadn't managed to find him they would have been in very serious trouble. Luckily the wretch had run into the once proud queen's bodyguard and some brat he was with. No mind, they would have him back in no time but first he needed to be taught a lesson.

He grabbed the man by the ear and hauled him up. Scious squeaked loudly and grabbed at the fingers that held him. "HOW DID YOU ESCAPE VERMIN?" the guard seethed.

"Please sir, I didn't do anything. The door was open at the back and I used it to slip out"

"Oh right, so that's why none of the others followed you?" He drew his dagger and held it up in front of Scious's face. The wriggling man blanched and kicked harder. "Maybe I should teach you a lesson you pig. What do you think about that?." He turned to the other guard who laughed. The crowd around them stood speechless. Some had ducked back indoors but others stared transfixed, horrified but too afraid to intervene.

The second guard grabbed Scious's arms. The one with the knife said loudly for the benefit of the crowd. "Those that steal and rob shall be punished." Just as the blade was about to touch the petrified little thief's ear, a huge hand grabbed his arm and twisted it hard.

Mordalayn was embarrassed, humiliated and angry. His reactions had saved Jared from a threat that didn't exist but he had been so wound up that he'd not reacted quickly enough and had been knocked down by a tiny little thief. He was also hungry and hadn't slept in days. He needed to keep Jared safe and being shamed in front of people who were clearly in awe of him did nothing to help that cause. He turned to the winded boy. "Are you ok?" Jared smiled and gave a thumbs up sign. "Good. I'm sorry you were hurt but I thought you were in danger. Come."

Jared glanced back to the scene in the street and couldn't believe what he was seeing. One of the soldiers was holding the man down by his arms, the one who'd knocked Mordalayn and laughing while the other was apparently going to cut his ear off. He tapped Mordalayn frantically on the arm and rasped in a croaky voice. "Look!" pointing. The warrior glanced round and his face transformed into a mask of utter fury.

As the hand grabbed his wrist the soldier winced in pain and then his anger took hold. "What in the name of...?!!!" he yelled and then twisted round to find himself staring into Mordalayn's green eyes.

"You miserable thug!" Mordalayn yelled and hurled him into the wall of the tavern. The man bounced back and fell face down. His knife skittered across the floor. Luckily for him his armour had taken the force of the impact. He leapt to his feet angrily.

"How dare you intefere with a lawful arrest!!" he shouted back

"The queen's absence is no excuse for barbarity," Mordalayn said angrily. Turning to the other soldier he snapped. "Let him go."

The soldier hesitated, his gaze flicking between his colleague and the powerful figure in front of him.

The man Mordalayn had thrown reached for his sword. The crowd around them watched in terrified silence. Mordalayn glared at him. "You are both clearly drunk. Does Provost Marshall Lighvoor know that his men drink on duty and torture prisoners?"

The guard paused and then lunged at Mordalayn who sidestepped contemptuously and tripped the man face first into the street. The soldier jumped up and Mordalayn moved as if to lunge but then brought his foot up at blinding speed and kicked the man hard in the knee. The man screamed, dropping his sword and collapsing. Mordalayn moved and stood over him, planting his foot on the man's chest and drew his own sword, the three blade tips quivering.

"Puh, please," the soldier stammered.

Mordalayn turned to the other soldier. "Let him go or I swear on Our Lady I will kill you both!"

The soldier released the still struggling man and moved to his injured colleague. "Get him out of here. I see either one of you again and you will regret the day you were born," Mordalayn snarled. The man stumbled and almost fell on his friend. He reached down and picked him up and together they limped off in the direction they had come from, the injured man whimpering loudly.

The crowd were still staring at Mordalayn and he glared back silently. Slowly they moved on, their amusement at his embarrasment now replaced by their original sense of awe.

Mordalayn turned to the little man who had knocked him down. "Are you alright?"

"Yes thank you sir, he didn't touch me, no no. Just scared me a little bit so he did sir, I thank you" the man replied, rubbing his ear as if to check it was still there. He scrabbled over to recover his grubby hat and pushed it back onto his head. Then he stood and bowed to Mordalayn and Jared. "Kind sirs you have been most kind to poor Scious, who is less fortunate these days than he was. My gratitude for your service. For that you may call on me any time to help you."

"Most noble of you" Mordalayn replied resheathing his sword and then looking Scious up and down. "What did you do?" he asked inclining his head back towards the corner the man had run from.

"Oohhh, vicious lies sir. They blamed me for stealing a ring from an elegant lady but it was lies sir, LIES so it was!"

"Be on your way little man" Mordalayn said quietly. "They will come back sooner or later and you had better be gone."

"Thank you both sir, most kind," Scious replied, glancing frantically around him to see if anyone was already following him. "Remember, I will come to help you if you need me" he glanced at Jared and smiled. "Either you or your young companion. Just say my name five times and Scious will be there."

The man bowed one final time before clasping his hat to his head and scurrying off across the road, darting down an alleyway between the pan shop and what appeared to be a butcher.

Mordalayn turned to Jared. "We need to move. Spies for our enemies may have seen this." He turned to the tavern owner who stood behind Jared in the open doorway. "My apologies for the mess my old friend but we need to go. I will return one day for a plate of your famous stew."

The innkeeper smiled. "I'll keep a bowl warm for you Takoba" he laughed and raised his hand in farewell before moving back inside.

Jared looked at Mordalayn. "Why did you hurt that soldier? You did everything you could to save the man on the lake."

Mordalayn was silent for a moment then replied. "The man on the lake was an unfortunate victim. That cur acted in defiance of Our Lady's rules."

"But you busted his leg!" Jared replied, still shocked by what he'd seen.

"Look boy!..." Mordalayn said angrily then looked away. "The Queen...you don't...there are RULES here." He looked down as he said it and Jared could see the anger but also sadness in the tall cat man's eyes.

"One of those people called you Our Lady's Sword. What did that mean?"

Mordalayn paused and Jared could tell he was thinking about telling him to wait but then...

"Our Lady is an elected monarch, a child chosen to rule us who is pure and good and kind. I am her protector. The rules she laid down are just and fair and were like no other ruler's for a long time. Those that flouted them paid dearly. Those that respected them flourished. She forbade all but necessary force. Even her enemies were treated fairly." Mordalayn then stopped and looked at Jared for a long moment before continuing.

"She laid down plans about how this world would be governed if she was absent for a long time or unable to get back. Her work is everywhere and there is the work of others before her."

"She loves her people more than any previous ruler has been known to. No one is treated unfairly and through all of this she kept peace and joy in this world. For many years she has been our ruler and then...."

He paused.

"Rancidrain's cowardly attack on Sophie was not something we expected. I got there in time and had you not been there he would have killed her. The magic the queen wields here cannot help her now but...we can use it to help her. Were she to return she would be able to end all this in an instant. But while the kingdom is weak, the forces of darkness gather."

Mordalayn turned up a side street heading out of the village and they walked slowly along it. There were less people by now and ahead Jared could see a building that looked very old. Either side of it was woodland, spreading out as far as he could see.

Another man walked past them pushing a wheelbarrow and touched his hand to his forehead respectfully. "Takoba," he said..

"You are going to be safe here" Mordalayn said as they walked up to the old building. "Keep what I have told you to yourself." A small black dog ran past them, span in a circle as if chasing its tail then bolted back down the road, yipping happily until it was out of sight.

Chapter 7

As they moved up the wide stone steps to the arched doorway Jared was nervous again. He still had very little idea of this world he had been thrown into and was constantly confused by the changes and situations he found himself in.

The door was of a dark wood in a tall arched frame. Two halves with a bright, brass plaque. Jared squinted to read it, the sun shining brightly off it's polished surface. "Bretheren of Alegria" it said simply and next to it was a large brass knocker. There was a face moulded into the metal, at the bottom.

The building was only one storey high and of a creamy coloured brick. It reminded Jared of the dentist he went to near Warwick, a very old but elegant building with smooth designs and vast angles on the walls.

"This is the orphan home of the Bretheren," Mordalayn said. You will be looked after here. It's only temporary."

Jared looked up at Mordalayn, who towered over him. "What are the bretheren?" he asked.

"This is an orphanage, for children whose parents have been lost or died protecting this world. For the children of those loyal to Our Lady."

Mordalayn reached up to grasp the brass knocker and the face on the handle suddenly moved, transforming from a static expression of ugliness to an uglier one of anger. As Mordalayn took hold of the ring surrounding it, it bit down hard on his finger.

"Aiaya! Be cursed!" Mordalayn said, fanning his fingers and quickly inspecting the bitten one for injury. There was none.

"What was that for you miserable little monster?" Jared looked on in shock.

The face glared at Mordalayn and then the eyes shifted to look at Jared. They examined him for a moment then appeared to get bored and looked back at the cat man. It then said in a high pitched voice. "How would you like it if I banged your head against a door?"

"What?!!" Mordalayn snapped in irritation, "that's your job."

"That's your job," the face mimicked angrily then closed it's eyes, stuck out its tongue and blew a long raspberry. When it had finished it replied. "Stuck here all day, people banging me into the door at any given moment and then just as I think I'm going to get some peace one of these little wretches comes and puts metal polish all over me. Do you think it's nice to get that stuff in your eyes, nose and mouth and not have hands to wipe it away?"

"My apologies doorkeeper, I meant no offence," Mordalayn replied solemnly.

The face continued to glare at him.

"If you could tell us how to communicate our presence to your masters, I would be grateful."

The sullen expression didn't change but after a pause, "use your fist on the door," it snapped and then the animation in its features melted away and it was back to being an ornament.

Mordalayn pounded the door with one huge fist and after a couple of minutes an elderly man opened it. His face was round like an apple with bright red cheeks. His head was almost completely bald apart from snow white tufts over his ears. His green shirt seemed huge and the buttons were straining to stay in place against his belly. He looked about 60 and as he opened the door he squinted at the two visitors, the sun shining off his large round nose..

"Can I help you?"

Mordalayn replied, "come Jorehlo, surely you haven't got so old to forget an old friend?"

The man paused for a moment and then as his eyes adjusted to the change in light, recognition flashed across his face and he beamed broadly. "By Our Lady! Mordalayn!!!" he exclaimed loudly and stepped forward extendng his arms. Mordalayn hugged him briefly and the old man clapped him on the back. "It's been such a long time. I hear you are now the Queen's Sword," he said stepping back and looking the tall, imposing figure up and down as if examining him.

"That I still am" he replied "but as you know things have changed."

"That they have Takoba, that they have." He glanced at Jared. "Who's the boy with you?" he enquired, smiling at Jared in a friendly fashion.

"His name is Jared Miller, Jorehlo, I need to speak to Susan Veer urgently."

"Of course, of course. Anything for you my old friend," the old man smiled again and stepped back to allow them in.

As they stepped inside the door knocker muttered. "Not a word of thanks and still I have to stay here all day."

Jorehlo opened the door wider, stuck his head round and snapped "shut up you or you'll find yourself adorning a pull chain in the latrines!"

He slammed the door as the knocker continued to mutter loudly.

"Now then my friends," he said stepping ahead of Jared and Mordalayn and rubbing his hands together briskly. "I suggest we make straight for Madame Veer's rooms immediately."

He walked ahead of them down a corridor, arched red doors either side. One had the sounds of singing coming from it but off key like the people inside were still learning. As they moved further up a boy dressed in scruffy brown shorts that came to just below his knees was standing outside a door. He was leaning against the wall with his arms folded and gazing up at the ceiling, whistling softly. His shorts had multiple repairs on them and there was a small hole above the right knee. He wore a green shirt, similar to the one that Jorehlo had on. The sleeves were rolled up and around his neck he had an orange stone on a piece of black cord. His brown hair was unkempt and messy and he looked about 12.

As they approached him Jorehlo tutted loudly and said to the boy. "Master Bue. Being punished AGAIN? Not suitable behaviour for the heir to the Valley Keys is it?"

The boy ignored him but grinned broadly when he saw Mordalayn and Jared. He had a large gap between his two upper front teeth. He straightend up. "Alright there. Haven't seen you in a while who's your friend?" he said looking at Mordalayn

"It's Takoba to you Bue," Jorehlo corrected him formally.

Bue ignored him again and looked at Jared. "If you're moving in here then come see me later, I'll show you around."

The door next to the boy opened and a woman's head appeared. "Master Bue you are not suppose to be talk....oh sorry." She blushed as she saw the three others.

"Not your fault Miss, our young friend was just telling us how sorry he was to have been sent out of class," Jorehlo replied.

"No I wasn't," Bue replied indignantly, then turned to Jared. "Seriously mate, look me up if you're sticking around yeah?"

He leaned on the wall as they moved on and the woman closed the door. After a few moments he began whistling softly and staring off into space.

The rounded a corner and on their right was a courtyard, the centre decorated with a neatly cut lawn and many flowers. A small fountain was in the centre, water gently cascading over a basin of grey stone. Across the other side was a corridor open to the air like the one they were now in, pillars every few yards forming arches along the way.

Jorehlo stopped outside a door that was blue instead of red and knocked three times gently. "She'll be so pleased to see you" he smiled at Mordalayn.

"Come in," a voice said loudly, muffled by the door.

Jorehlo opened the door and in the small office they could see a small boy standing in front of a desk. Behind it sat a woman dressed in dark green with her hair tied back in a tight bun. She looked serious and appeared about 50 years old. As they entered the room she turned to the child in front of her.

"Please may I? Is that clear? Please MAY I?"

The small boy looked at the floor with tears in his eyes.

"Is that CLEAR?" the woman snapped.

"Yes Ma'am," the tiny figure said, almost in a whisper.

Still retaining her serious expression the woman, picked up a piece of paper in front of her and held it up. "Now let this be the last time I have to speak to you about your manners."

97

"Yes Ma'am," the boy stammered and looked up at the visitors, clearly embarrassed and scared.

"Now, off you go," she said, writing a comment on the paper and handing it back to the boy who scurried out the room.

"Now then," the woman said, turning to the newcomers and smiling. "What brings you here Takoba? I must say I am pleased to see you again."

Mordalayn replied formally. "The pleasure is all mine Madame Veer. "I see you are still strict with your charges."

She stood up, extending her hand which Mordalayn shook. She turned to Jorehlo. "Thank you. You may go"

Jorehlo looked to Mordalayn. "Speak to you later Takoba."

"Indeed you will my old friend," Mordalayn said. He turned back to Madame Veer as the door closed. "This is a serious situation we find ourselves in. I am sure you have been made aware of the gravity of the current situation regarding the Emerald Queen?"

The woman adjusted her neat, long, green skirt and sat back down, gesturing to Mordalayn and Jared to do the same. They took up seats opposite her and she looked at Jared for a few moments before replying. "Is it safe to discuss this in front of this child?"

Mordalayn nodded. "This boy is the only link to what happened and he also needs our protection."

Jared glanced at both of them, unsure as to where this conversation was going.

"I am happy to take him in. Need I remind you that this is unusual to say the least?"

"I am aware of that Ma'am but this boy needs protection. While he is with you he is safer than if he is with me or the Council. Our enemies have spies everywhere."

The woman looked at Jared and smiled, her face transforming from a serious, scary look to a pleasant one. "Don't be scared boy, we are all friends here. How old are you?"

"Eleven" Jared replied. "Can I ask, why do I need to stay with you?"

"Here you will be safe, this place is protected by agreement. No-one may enter here without permission, my permission to be precise."

Mordalayn stood and turned to Jared. "I have to go now, there is work to be done. However I will return for you as soon as I can." He turned back to Madame Veer. "Thank you kindly. Your generosity is appreciated."

"You are always welcome here Takoba. May Our Lady protect you."

Mordalayn left the room, closing the door quiety behind him.

Jared felt scared and looked at Madame Veer. Her face was very serious but she appeared to realise his discomfort. "Don't be nervous, I promised we would help you and we will." She took a sheet of paper from a sheaf on her desk and took a feathered quill pen. She wrote a note and handed it to Jared. "Go back the way you came. The first door on your left. Challandra will see you and give you something to eat and allocate you a bed for the night."

Jared felt his stomach grumble at the mention of food and Madame Veer smiled. "All is safe for you here."

Jared walked down the corridor holding the piece of paper. At the first red door he came across he paused and glanced down the corridor. The boy from outside the classroom was gone and the singing had stopped. He raised his hand to knock when the door suddenly opened. Standing in front of him was a woman not much taller than him. She had shoulder length black hair with two lighter streaks of brown at the front. The hair was dangling in her face and she pushed it to one side as she opened the door. She was pleasant and friendly-looking, like the sort of person you could imagine taking care of little kids at a nursery school. She appeared to be young.

"Hello there," she said chirpily. "What can I do for you?"

"I...I'm not sure." Jared stammered, handing her the piece of paper.

"Let's have a look," she said, squinting at the page and then said excitedly. "AHA! So you're the special guest. OK we need to get you something to eat." Reaching down she took his hand and with her other closed the door behind her. "We'll get you to the dining room. I bet you're hungry."

"Just a bit," Jared said, his stomach rumbling.

She led him down the corridor, her shoes squeaking on the hard marble floor. "The boys will be so pleased to see you. We've had no one new for a while now. By the way my name's Challandra."

They came across two large red double door, arched like all the others. Jared could hear laughter and the clattering noises that a busy school dining room made at lunch. "Here we are" she said brightly, pushing the doors open with both hands.

As they entered the room every head turned in their direction and the conversations instantly ground to a halt. Jared was facing two long, wooden tables with about six boys on each. All were dressed in green shirts like he'd seen as he came in to the place. Their trousers and shorts were in varying states of repair and most boys were wearing leather slip on shoes with no laces. He looked at them blankly feeling embarrassed as the silence hung in the air. Behind the two tables was a hatch in the wall where a fierce looking woman with a face like a rhino stood holding a ladle and wearing a green apron. The ferocious expression was softened somewhat by the cap she was wearing on her head. At waist level were several large metal containers of food.

Challandra smiled and as the boys stared at Jared with mute curiosity she beamed at them brightly and clapped her hands together. "Hi there everyone, this is Jared. He's going to be staying with us. Can you please make him welcome."

There was another long pause and then suddenly a rush of excited voices began babbling.

"What's he got on his feet. Never seen shoes like that before."

"Where's he from? Don't recognise the clothes. You think he's from Coulen?"

"Strange haircut. How come we can't get ours like that?"

They continued to talk amongst themselves like Jared was a species of interesting monkey in a zoo. While he was standing there feeling like an ant under a magnifying glass he looked up and saw the boy that had been outside the classroom earlier stand up from halfway down the left hand table and walk towards him and Challandra. He smiled at her. "It's alright Miss, I'll look after him."

"Good lad Bue and thank you." She turned to Jared and put her hand on his arm. "Now Jared if you need anything please come to me or Madame Veer ok? You are safe here provided you stay within the confines."

"I'll be fine," Jared said smiling but still feeling incredibly nervous.

"Come on mate you can sit by me," Bue said smiling his crooked smile and taking Jared by the arm as Challandra left the room, the double doors banging a few times as she went through.

Bue moved back to his original seat while the excited buzz of conversation continued. All the boys were looking at Jared, the ones on the other table craning their necks to get a look at the newcomer in their midst. Jared noticed there was only one chair and paused but Bue slapped the boy to him on the back of the head. "Beevor, where's your manners? Get our guest a seat."

The other lad complied and scurried off to a stack of chairs against the wall of the large hall they were in. He pulled the top one free with a grunt and tottered back, setting it down between Bue's chair and indicating Jared should sit before squeezing back into his own seat. Bue looked at the boy opposite and jerked his head towards the hatch where the rhino faced creature stood looking bored.

"Makeo, get him some grub. You're hungry yeah?" he said to Jared.

Jared nodded. "You don't know how much," and Bue laughed.

"Get him everything, tell Penny it's for him in case she kicks off."

The other boy made for the hatch. He took a tray from a stack to the right of the serving window and approached the disinterested looking woman. She lazily shifted her eyes in his direction as he walked up.

"What do you want?" she growled as the boy stood grinning brightly in front of her.

"A portion of your best stew and vegetables and one of your delicious puddings please Miss Penny," Makeo said keeping his forced smile plastered to his face.

"You've already eaten you greedy little twit!" She fumed, her grip on the ladle tightening and what looked like steam erupting from her nostrils as she snorted loudly. "Do you want me to call Madame?"

The boy's smile slipped only fractionally and he continued beaming as he replied. "It's not for me Miss, it's for that new boy." He turned around and pointed to where Jared sat, the object of everyone's attention. Anticipating what Penny might say next he then added, "he's a guest of Madame Veer, he's not a pupil here."

Penny took a wooden plate, separated into various compartments for different portions and snorted again. "Well, I don't see why he can't come and get it himself. I work here all day and it would be nice if I was introduced to a guest occasionally," she grumbled. Penny used the ladle to scoop up a portion of a meaty stew and then putting it down took a spoon and put some mashed potato on top of it. The she put an assortment of vegetables in the slot next to it and finally a sweet dish next to that in the remaining compartment. "Cups are over there" she gestured to Makeo, who smiled brightly and turned around. His smile dissapeared as he grimaced and grabbed a metal cup from the stack near the trays and made his way back to Jared and Bue.

Bue was holding court, the other kids around him silent as Bue probed Jared with questions.

"So you're not from here? Where are you from?"

Jared paused, not sure what to say. "Errr, a long way away."

Bue didn't seem fazed but pressed on. "So, how do you know the Caracalic? You know he's the Queen's bodyguard?"

"Err, yeah I was told."

Another boy piped up. "How long are you staying for?"

"Not sure, maybe just tonight."

Bue looked up at Makeo, hovering over them with the tray.

"Here you go mate, dig in. It's not the best but it's not bad either."

Jared could smell the stew and saliva instantly sprang into his mouth. He was so hungry and couldn't remember the last time he ate. Grabbing the fork next to the segmented plate he stuck it into the meaty sauce and pushed the food into his mouth quickly. It was hot and he had just enough self control left to remember to chew before swallowing it. He shovelled in another mouthful and then tore off a strip of bread from the cob Makeo had brought him. He continued to wolf down the stew, thinking he'd never tasted anything so delicious in his life.

Bue and the other boys watched him and Bue chuckled. "Steady on mate, you'll do yourself an injury."

Jared barey heard him and continued to eat. He devoured the stew and bread and then started on the vegetables, the like of which he'd never seen before. One was purple and spiral shaped, another looked like a cactus but the spines were soft and bendy as he cut through them with his knife.

When he'd finished the vegetables he noisily sloshed down several gulps of water from the cup that Makeo had filled for him. The other boys still watched him in silence as he started on his pudding. It was like the sponge puddings his grandmother used to make but when he bit into what he thought were sultanas, they momentarily fizzed in his mouth.

Finally he finished and sat back, pushing the tray away and wiping his mouth with a serviette from the stack in front of him.

Bue smiled. "Enjoy that?"Jared nodded.

"Yes, lovely. I was starving."

"Really, I wouldn't have guessed." Bue replied clapping Jared on the back.

"Well boys, he likes the grub. Guess he passed the first test"

The othed boys laughed and one of them extended his hand across the table. "I'm Bolla"

Jared shook his hand and other boys came up to say hello. The names were many and Jared knew he wouldn't be able to remember them all.

"Stone," one fat boy said, squeezing Jared's hand in a friendly but too-hard grip.

"Declain," another said.

"Jerean," said a third.

When the introductions had stopped Jared noticed that most of the boys had gone back to their own conversations, only the group around him still appeared fascinated by him.

"If you're only staying one night you must be being protected from something," a thin boy with shoulder length black hair sitting opposite him said. "We know the Takoba brought you here. You in trouble?"

"Yes, but...I can't say," Jared said feeling embarrassed.

The boy looked at Bue. "Nice to see a new face though, don't you think?"

"I'll say" Bue replied, putting his arm around Jared's shoulder. "Tell me Jared, you any good with a bow?"

"Like archery?" Jared said surprised. "My father is a member of a club, I've had a go a few times."

"No, no." Bue said shaking his head. "Not the giant's toothpick, a crossbow."

Jared paused for a second then said, "err...no can't say I have."

"Well my friend we'll have to teach you."

A bell suddenly rang loudly and the boys stood up, picking up their trays and cutlery. They noisily scraped their leftovers into a large bin and put their trays into a rack near the hatch. Penny ignored them and was busy sorting out her own area.

As Jared passed the hatch he looked at her. "Thank you, that was nice."

Penny froze and looked up at him, snorting loudly and snapped even louder. "WHAT did you just say?"

The boys near Jared froze and looked at him and then the floor. They began to edge away quickly, a space clearing around him until he was on his own.

"Err...thank you for lunch. It was really nice," he repeated, blushing slightly.

There was a pause where you could have heard a pin drop while Penny stared at him, the deep dish she was holding in both hands looking more like a weapon with every passing second.

Suddenly Penny smiled and put the dish down. "Why thank you young man. So nice to be appreciated occasionally. So few young men your age have any manners any more."

The boys around him breathed out heavily and as Jared was about to move away Penny reached to the side of the hatch and beckoned him towards her.

As he cautiously approached she handed him a paper bag. "For you young man. I'm sure you'll be hungry after your travel here." Jared looked in the bag. Inside were two cakes, square with red and black icing on the top.

"Thank you," Jared said smiling and Penny smiled back, humming a little tune as she continued to clear up.

Bue was waiting for him by the door. "See you made friends with Penny," he chuckled looking back to where the hulking figure was smiling to herself while clearing up.

"Just being polite, don't think she's used to that." Jared whispered following Bue's gaze.

"Come on, it's sports time," Bue said enthusiastically. "You can't miss that."

"I'm not very good at sports, I prefer a game of chess"

"Of what?" Bue said looking puzzled then beamed broadly. "Come on, let's get to the range. I'm going to show you how to fire a crossbow."

Jared submitted to the persistent pull on his arm and followed Bue and the other boys down the corridor. They cut across the open space near Madame Veer's office. Jared noticed that no one stood on the grass, even by accident and kept to the path as they herded into a large hall. At one end were four round targets like Jared had seen at his father's archery club. They were made of compacted straw and appeared quite large, even at a distance of what seemed about fifty metres. The biggest difference to the targets Jared had previously seen was that they didn't have any markings on them, they were just bare straw. On one side of the room was a serious looking man of about 60 with a mane of shaggy hair. He looked fit and athletic and was wiping a crossbow with a rag as the boys entered. As they milled about he put down the bow and barked. "FORM UP!!!"

The boys moved into lines, one behind the other until there were three lines of three and Jared forming an odd line of four. The man looked at him and smiled kindly, beckoning him over. As Jared nervously moved forward the man turned him around so they could talk more privately. He said quietly, "hello Jared my name's Leppard. I know you're probably still nervous but don't be. I know Takoba Mordalayn and he's explained that we need to look after you. Just try and relax. This is the fun time of school for the boys so just join in ok?"

Jared nodded and the man turned round with Jared and in a loud voice barked. "Right you lot. This is your fun time today. Don't spoil it and it'll stay that way. Where's Blautin Nola?"

A boy with brown hair and a scar on his cheek raised his hand. He was blushing as if anticipating trouble.

"Ah, young master Blautin," the man said smiling and shaking his head. "I think you know why I've called your name?"

The boy looked at the floor.

"While you may have very strong opinions about the janitor the rest of us don't wish to read about them, especially in letters two feet high."

Blautin opened his mouth to speak but the man raised his hand for silence and the boy shut it quickly.

"Don't waste your time denying anything. A word of advice for you. Next time you wish to deface orphanage property don't do it in front of the door keeper. It's not like it's got anything better to do than spy on people."

The boy mumbled something but still gazed at the floor.

"So, you can help the janitor for the next two hours, cleaning a latrine or two. Off you go"

The boy mumbled. "Yes Master Leppard," and sloped off and the man then grinned brightly at the boys.

"So, anyone else done anything they thought no one saw? Be easier if you tell me now than if we find out later?"

The boys just looked at him and one or two shook their heads.

"Splendid! Not a guilty conscience amongst you. That's the spirit. Now, we have a guest with us today so we're going to introduce him to the fine art of the crossbow. Master Bue, step forward please."

Bue obediently stepped forward and stood in front of everyone.

"Now, while our young master may be someone who needs a new personality, he currently holds the record for the most accurate with a bow amongst you lot, don't you master Bue?"

Bue smiled and bowed slightly before replying. "No, I'm the most accurate anywhere."

"Oh we are modest aren't we?" Leppard replied, feigning shock. He turned to the bow he'd been cleaning when they came in and handed it out to Bue. "Well come then young master. Show our new guest how it's done."

There was suppressed giggling amongst the boys. Jared guessed this was a ritual that they'd done at least a few times before.

Bue smiled and stepped forward, reaching out for the weapon then theatrically drew his hand away. "But sir, I do declare that you doubt my prowess with a bow" he said, the twinkle in his eye the only thing betraying the mask of seriousness he was attempting to maintain.

Leppard replied solemnly. "No master Bue I don't believe you are as accurate as you claim. Would you like to prove yourself before us?"

"I do indeed sir" Bue replied and with a flourish pulled a red and gold sash from his left breast pocket. "I wager my badge as the best shot against it. If you can beat me sir then you may wear the badge."

Leppard smiled and held the bow out to Bue. "Your challenge is accepted. Let us see who is worthy."

Bue took the crossbow and hefted it. Leppard picked up another and they moved forward to face the targets.

Jared watched intently and whispered to the nearest boy to him "what are they going to do?"

"They've got three shots each," the boy whispered back. "They have to hit all the targets. But not only that they have to do it faster than the other."

"If they're as good as each other how will they know who hit the target first?" Jared queried, puzzled.

"The targets aren't for shooting AT, they just catch the arrows," the boy replied.

"Hush boys, silence now," Leppard said, turning round.

He took up position next to Bue facing the target on the left. The boys formed a long line to watch what was happening. No one spoke and the only sound was the creak of the strings being cranked back on the bows as both figures began hauling hard on the grips either side of the tough twine. As they locked into position with a loud click they both smoothly placed a bolt into the firing grooves.

Jared watched and without warning the light in the room dimmed gradually until it was just a bare glow. He waited puzzled, wondering if the reduced light was some form of handicap to make the task more difficult. Both figures stood rigid, not moving, the bows held at waist height.

The sound of breathing was the only thing that could be heard now.

The seconds dragged on and suddenly light flashed in two places, very close together at the end of the hall. Jared winced against the sudden flare and from the bright blue radiance two huge creatures emerged. Except they weren't real. They were made of light. Both appeared to be some type of huge pig with tusks like a warthog and hugely powerful forelegs. They were yellow and then blue and then red, the colours changing as Jared watched transfixed. They were like moving holograms, snorting loudly and stamping their feet. They looked around as if getting their bearings and then focused on Bue and Leppard and snarled loudly, throwing their heads back and roaring. Then they lunged forward, charging at the two figures who stood stock still in front of them. Both Bue and the teacher raised the bows and fired, seemingly simultaneously. The bolts passed through the transparent shapes without slowing and hit with a double thunk into the straw boards behind them. The pigs squealed as the bolts passed through them and suddenly vanished, fading in a second as if nothing was there.

"Master Bue, I believe you have that one." The teacher chuckled as he reloaded his bow.

"That I do sir." Bue smiled back, copying the man's motions.

When they were reloaded they stood facing the targets again and there was the previous expectant hush. Jared watched fascinated.

The lights flashed and this time it was the see through spectres of two armoured soldiers that appeared before them. As the light faded the soldiers glanced down the hall and saw the two bow men. They roared in challenge and screamed in an unintelligible tongue. Neither Bue nor Leppard raised their bows. The holographic warriors shimmered from blue to red and then stayed that colour, the tone brightening until they were both bright crimson. They drew the short swords from their belts and wihout any further hesitation suddenly charged, their feet slapping noisily on the floor as their sandals pounded down.

Both figures then raised their crossbows and fired but Bue's was slightly off mark and passed by the shoulder of his opponent before hitting the safety board. Leppard's went through the running man's face who stuttered in his steps and then vanished abruptly as the sound of the bolt thudding home echoed round the hall. The ghost soldier continued to charge at Bue who stood facing it, his bow unloaded by his side as the figure raised its sword and brought it down towards Bue's head. Jared wanted to shout a warning but as the sword flashed down, the same light that had given birth to the man claimed him and he vanished; his scream echoing and then fading away.

Bue turned to Leppard. "Good aim sir, a fine shot"

"You're too kind young master Bue," the man replied smiling, "but now is our real test."

The other boys edged forwards to see what was going to happen next. Jared, already spellbound by what he'd seen, wondered what could beat the previous two challenges.

As Bue and Leppard stood after cranking their bows and loading them for a third time there was another dual flash of light and a loud squawk as if a flock of birds were in the room.

Jared looked towards the end of the room and saw what seemed like a dozen large crows wheeling in spirals from the light points towards the silhouetted figures. They screeched loudly, their cries carrying and one behind the other wheeled crazily down the hall. Jared could see that there were at least six racing towards each figure in identical groups. They swooped around wildly, green eyes burning bright and huge claws extended. Like the soldiers they became a brighter and brighter shade of crimson as they hurtled down the hall, spiralling around in a twisted, looping charge of ruby and sapphire.

Leppard raised his bow and fired and his bolt passed through one of the murderous flock facing him. Almost simultaneously Bue raised his and hesitated a fraction of a second before triggering. His shot passed through the lead bird which screamed loudly and then vanished. Leppard's birds however continued to streak towards him malevolently until they all seemed to hit an invisible barrier. One by one they vanished into a shower of bright sparks just a few inches from his face. He stood there without flinching as the birds screeched into oblivion. Bue smiled triumpantly.

The lights in the room became bright, the only sign of the epic demonstration were the bolts embedded in the targets..

"Well young master, it seems you have earned your sash," Leppard said smiling and reached into his pocket, taking out the red and gold cloth and handing it back to the grinning boy.

"Thank you sir, you are a fine shot."

Leppard smiled and winked at Bue then turned to the boys. "Now then, form up. You know the drill, two lines."

Bue walked over to Jared still grinning. "Pretty good eh?" he said.

"How come you won that last one?" Jared asked, confused. "You both hit a bird and his bolt hit before yours."

"Ah ha." Bue replied pointing his empty bow at the targets and looking back down the hall. "It's not that you have to kill any bird. You have to kill the leader. I did, he didn't."

Chapter 8

Jared lay back on his bed couldn't sleep. His mind was still racing over what he'd seen in the past day. Despite reassurances he was worried about his family and knew they must be frantic with worry. He pulled the thin blanket up to his chin and looked across the room. Bue was already fast asleep, his cheek resting on his clenched hand. He snored quietly as he slept. Around them the other eleven boys lay in bed, most sleeping. Only the odd grunt or cough punctuated the dark silence in the dorm room.

Jared finally felt his eyelids slowly close and his last, sleepy thoughts were of the charging hogs he'd seen Bue and the bow instructor face in the hall.

Challandra hummed happily to herself as she set about taking in the dry clothes from the boiler room. The big wooden basket she was carrying was heavy but she hefted it easily. She had been concerned for the new boy when he arrived but from what she'd seen he'd fitted in and had even made friends with that rascal Bue. She smiled to herself as she thought of Bue. Orphaned three years ago when his mother and father died in a boat accident on the Solitary Sea. He was totally uncontrollable for the first six months. Only Madame Veer had been able to reach out to him but even her efforts took time. Finally his grief and rage had subsided and the gentle boy beneath the surface had begun to emerge. His father had been a keen huntsman and Leppard's prowess with a bow had been something that Bue respected and was even in awe of. Within a year he'd become the finest shot with a bow that anyone could remember, rivalling Leppard himself. Leppard had seen the boy's pride in his ability and had fed the passion that Bue approached the sport with. He challenged him seven months ago to a competition with Leppard's Sharp Eye sash as the prize. Bue had lost the first few attempts but kept coming back, practising every spare moment that Madame Veer and Leppard would allow. The boy's reaction to finally gaining the prize had been moving to say the least. True to form Bue had played it down, trying to act like it was no big deal and rarely talking about it unless asked. Challandra was happy to see that he'd taken the new boy under his wing.

She whistled to herself as she placed the last of the dry clothes in the basket and opened the door. As she stepped into the corridor a huge hand clamped over her mouth stifling any sound she could make.

"Don't struggle and don't try and scream," a deep voice whispered clearly but with deadly sincerity. She dropped the basket with a clatter, the clothes spilling out. The figure pulled her into the darker recesses of the corridor. Her hands tugged on the iron fingers over her mouth and she saw glimpses of metal and armour. Flashes of yellow and silver. A bearded man turned towards and glared as the figure pulling her came to a halt.

"My apologies for this miss. My friend will take his hand away now, but if you scream or try to move he will kill you. Nod if you understand."

Challandra nodded slowly and the vice-like grip relaxed and the hand withdrew. She turned around and there appeared to be many armed men in the darkened space. They were near the caretaker's lodge and she was glad the old man and the other day staff had gone home.

"Now miss," the voice said with the same chilling menace. "The boy who was brought here. Where is he?"

Challandra's heart was racing as she swallowed and answered quickly. "Where do you think? He's with the other boys."

The figure was silent for a moment then said, "is the Caracalic with him?"

"No, he left this afternoon."

"Good. One more question miss and then we can get about our business. Is there anything else we should know about?"

Challandra knew straight away what he meant. "No, if you've got this far then the magic won't hurt you."

"That's very good miss. While we fetch the boy you're going to stay with my friend. If I find you've lied to me I will come back. Is there anything you feel you'd like to tell me before it's too late?" His voice was still a harsh, cruel whisper in the shadows and Challandra's mind raced.

"No, there's no security here. We've never needed it before."

Without further conversation the soldier grabbed her roughly, again clamping a hand over her mouth to prevent any noise.

"Right" the leader whispered. "We get the boy and leave. Anyone gets in the way...well, I think you know what to do."

The men chuckled and slowly withdrew their swords which rasped from the scabbards. Challandra went wide eyed with fear and struggled against the grip but the man held her tightly.

The leader signalled to her captor and then quietly began to move his group off down the corridor in the direction of the boys' room.

Jared lay in the darkness and finally felt sleep descending. His mind and body were exhausted from the day's events and he wished nothing more than to get some rest at last. When he closed his eyes he could see Mordalayn standing on the dock. His sword flashing as he knocked down the mercenaries. Jared yawned and as he did so a hand clamped down over his mouth, stifling the shout of protest that rose up in his throat.

Challandra watched the armoured figures move off down the corridor and counted them. Six in total. *There isn't much time,* she thought. She had to do something, anything to alert the boys and the other staff that something was wrong. She knew that the man holding her would probably kill her if she struggled. She saw the last of the men walk off round the corner and decided to try one last, desperate method. She suddenly went limp. The soldier swore and whispered angrily. "Stand up curse you" he hissed as she flopped in his grip. He tried to haul her back up but she hung as if lifeless. With a string of whispered cursing, he released the grip he had on her mouth and lifted her under the shoulders.

As her lips were freed Challandra whispered softly. "Kohelo aspaharn folehol." At first nothing happened but then from the very walls of the building a low growl emerged, almost inaudible at first but rising in volume.

Jared squirmed as the hand held him and suddenly Bue whispered in his ear urgently. "Shut up! Quiet! Something's wrong." He slowly released his hand and put his finger to his lips. The boy on the next bed stirred and looked up, raising himself up on his elbow and looking through sleepy eyes at them both. Bue turned around, keeping his finger on his lips and the other boy frowned.

"What's the problem?" Jared whispered back, feeling scared.

"Footsteps in the corridor, no one should be around this time of night."

Jared strained to listen but could hear nothing. "Bue you're imagining it, go back to sleep."

Bue looked defiant and anger flashed in his eyes. "I know what I heard, get out of bed. Get your trousers and shoes on" he whispered harshly.

Jared blearily complied and stuffed on his socks before shoving his feet in his trainers. Bue looked anxiously at the door and then back to Jared. "Come on" he hissed as Jared stood and reached for his jacket. He opened the window over Jared's bed and the ancient hinge creaked as the heavy frame swung out. "Be quiet and follow me" Bue whispered and pulled himself up, straddling the cold sill. He swung both legs out and then dropped the small distance to the darkened courtyard. Jared peered after him and saw that the room looked out on to the sports hall. "Come on!" Bue hissed urgently, the worry clear on his face. Just then they heard a moaning noise start and Bue looked sickened. "Come ON!!!" he yelled. As Jared was about to follow him, the other boys all awake now, the door of the room burst open and two armed men stood hulking in the doorway, their blades shining in the dim light from the courtyard.

"Stop!" the nearest one shouted and made to lunge at Jared. The moaning noise continued to rise and became louder with each passing second. The soldier hurled himself across the room to try and grab Jared, just as the noise became unbearable. Then something extraordinary and utterly horrible happened.

Challandra felt the soldier's grip on her relax as the moaning sound reached a climax that hurt the ears. He released her and Challandra kicked free, piling up against the wall and away from the stricken man. He reached out to grab her but then clamped his hands over his ears as the horrendous wailing continued. Just as it seemed the sound would become even worse it stopped completely. The soldier glared at her, reaching for his sword.

"Despicable witch!" he shouted. "What did you just do?"

As he tried to draw his weapon a monstrous shape appeared behind him in the shadows blocking out what little light there was, grabbing him tightly, pinning his arms to his sides. The man screamed and thrashed violently but was unable to break the grip. The figure that held him was hugely vast, misshapen and irregularly formed. It was grey and stood around three metres tall with huge eyes and a wide, blunt nose. The nostrils flared as it angrily yanked the wriggling soldier into the air. As it grunted the sound seemed to resonate from every part of its body.

"HELP ME!!!" the soldier screamed as the hulking figure stepped backwards. Challandra remained motionless, staring frightened yet reassured by the sight of the immense creature. The figure took another step backwards and, as if it was entering a vertical pool, the stone of the wall parted as its body made contact, the rock rippling slightly as if made of water. The thrashing soldier screamed louder still as the creature holding him continued to step backwards and with a final motion they dissapeared inside the wall, the man's horrible screams suddenly cut off. The corridor was empty, save for Challandra.

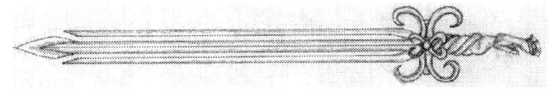

The soldiers lunged at Bue and Jared but Jared dropped down next to the young archer and winced, clapping his hands to his ears as the moaning reached its zenith. The boys were all similarly trying to shut out the noise, one or two whimpering in fear as they curled up on their beds.

The noise was painful and seemed to scratch right within your soul. Then it stopped and with a triumphant smirk the nearest soldier yanked Jared's bed out the way, the wooden legs grinding on the floor and tried to climb out after the two boys. Bue jumped the few steps back to the open window and brought his fist into the man's face, punching him square on the nose. The man fell back cursing and his partner leapt up to the window frame just as a figure appeared in the doorway, a horribly enormous figure that looked like some sort of clay monster with massive fingers on each hand. It lumbered into the room and surveyed the cowering boys, one at a time, steam erupting from its nostrils as it weighed them up. After a moment its gaze turned to the two soldiers and the one Bue had punched momentarily forgot his bloody nose and exclaimed:

"What in the love of chaos is THAT?!!"

Bue grabbed Jared by the sleeve of his jacket. "Come on!!" he yelled and pushed him towards the sports hall.

In the room the two soldiers looked at each other, then at the creature and both made for the window. One was still punch drunk from where Bue had hit him but the other leapt for the open window. His feet scrabbled successfully for purchase as he heaved himself up and out. The remaining man tried to climb out but the monster loomed up behind him.

"Wait!!!" the man pleaded to the soldier outside who simply gazed blankly back at him.

The huge creature tottered towards the remaining man, scooped him up in its arms and pinned him in a crushing grip. With a furious growl the creature then stepped backwards into the corridor and simply stepped into the wall. The thrashing soldier's legs kicked madly and his feet could momentarily be seen protruding, making ripples in the grey stone. Then they were gone.

122

Bue and Jared ran to the door of the hall and burst through it with the soldier sprinting after them.

"STAND FAST!!!" a figure shouted and Jared found himself staring at a loaded and primed crossbow.

"Leppard, it's us!" Bue shouted back and Leppard hesitated before lowering the bow and then raising it again when he saw the soldier running up behind them. The man veered off and hid behind one of the pillars in the central courtyard. Leppard triggered the bow and sent the long bolt in his direction, the shot whistling through the air and dissapearing into the woods.

Jared staggered to a stop, panting madly and pulled up in horror as a huge creature lumbered up beside Leppard. He stumbled and fell, his back to the wall. Leppard ignored it and turned to Jared as he lowered his bow.

"It's ok," he said reassuringly, glancing at the creature that stood silently next to him, its shoulders slowly heaving. "It won't hurt you. They only attack trespassers."

"Wh, what is it?" Jared stammered as he finally found his voice.

Leppard closed the door and bolted it, then turned back to Jared. "They are the wall keepers, the final line of defence against attack. We call them the Vagthunder."

At mention of its name the creature glanced at Leppard and then turned around, lumbering noisily across the floor and into the hall. There it stood motionless, looking at the three of them with a blank expression.

"We haven't had to use them for as long as I can remember. Whoever invoked them was clearly frightened."

"You mean it wasn't you?" Bue said looking shocked.

"No young master. Which means it was either Madame Veer or Challandra. Either way we need to check they are ok"

"Too right!" Bue exclaimed angrily. He turned to Jared and took him by the hand, hauling him upright. "Come on, we have to help the others."

Leppard looked at Jared. "Boy, can you remember how to fire a crossbow?"

Jared glared at him and snapped, "my name's Jared and yes."

Leppard chuckled. "OK Jared. Bue, get him a bow and a pack of bolts."

Bue made for a large cupboard at the back of the entrance hall and began tossing items out onto the floor. Then he reached up and with more reverence he moved to a wider cupboard next to it and opening it slowly extracted both his prize, green, patterned bow and another one. He moved back to Jared and handed him the second one. "Look after this, it's the third best one we've got" he said glancing at Leppard who smiled. Jared had no doubts who had numbers one and two.

Leppard turned to them. "Now listen you two. The Vagthunder can't go outside, they only protect the inside of the building. Hopefully we will drive whoever these intruders are out into the open or they will be taken. Now load your bows."

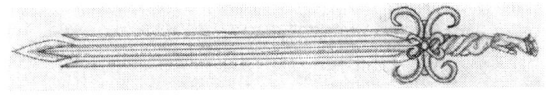

The soldiers outside the dorm room had scattered like leaves in the wind as soon as the creatures emerged from the walls. The leader had heard the intolerable keening noise and knew straight away that the cursed girl had lied about the building's defences. No-one had utilised anthropomorphic defence at any time in living memory and as soon as he realised that the noise was not merely a disembodied voice designed to scare off petty thieves in the night, he'd run back down the corridor, leaving his men puzzled and deafened behind him. Now he was running for his life, his sword having been flung down as he'd rounded the first corner. He'd heard the screams of his men and those he'd sent into the boy's dorm and now only two of them had managed to catch up. He didn't know and had no time to care what had happened to the others. As they rounded another corner a huge lumbering shape staggered forward, roaring angrily and grabbed the middle soldier by his cloak. The man's feet skidded out from under him and he screeched as the creature stepped back into the wall, yanking the man after him, his sword clattering to the floor. The other two didn't spare him a backward glance but hurtled to the main doorway in front of them. As they pounded down the corridor the same monster reemerged alone but looking slightly bigger and with a piercing roar began pounding after them, malformed knees and elbows pumping like pistons. The leader realised they weren't going to make it, the creature was gaining ground at twice the rate they were. Twisting round he grabbed the other man and shoved him into the wall, who crashed noisily as he span, colliding with the stone then stumbled, falling onto his face, his hands flung out to break his fall. He screamed, "NO!!"" and with a snarl the creature bore down on him, scooping him up; the soldier's pitiful cries cut off abruptly. The leader raced to the doorway and barged into it heavily, the doors bursting open as he fell through and onto the steps, just as another creature hurtled out of the corridor to the left and stood on the steps, howling with its head back as the man rolled down the steps noisily and collapsed winded at the bottom. He raised himself up and painfully stood, glaring at the roaring creature, steam erupting from both its nostrils as it frustratedly stared at him, unable to follow. The man stood and dusted himself off, breathing heavily and then removed his helmet and wiped sweat from his forehead. It was Galfront Siavy. He glared at the creature and then bowed theatrically before moving away rapidly into the shadows.

Chapter 9

Jared, Bue and Leppard moved past the hulking yet still Vagthunder in the dimly lit hall, bows primed and ready. In the distance they could hear shouts and roars along with the sound of huge feet pounding the floor in a tattoo of terror.

"Be ready and keep your mind clear," Leppard said to Bue whose his lips were held in a straight line of determination.

"How are we going to get into the main building?" Jared enquired. "That soldier is still out there."

"There's always more than one way to get to your destination my b...Jared" Leppard replied. He had clearly dressed hurriedly once the break in had started and had his leather halberk over a loose shirt that was unbuttoned and he was shoeless. He walked to a small stack of shelves at the back of the hall and pulled it to away. Cobwebs stretched and snapped back from it as Leppard pushed it away to the side. There was a small door behind it and he took a key from his pocket. It fitted the door and with a squeak of resistance the bolt moved back as the key was turned and the door opened with a grind of wood on wood. It clearly hadn't been opened for a very long time. Leppard took the unlit tinder he had in his hand and used it to create a burning torch by holding the material into the casing of an oil lamp burning dimly on the wall. The sputtering glow from the light revealed a set of steps that led downwards and to the right, dissapearing into darkness.

"Old way through." Leppard grinned. "No one's used it for years."

Bue snorted. "Found the other end months ago, just couldn't figure out how to get this door opened."

Leppard stared at him for a second and his eyes narrowed. "Well, young master, as you are versed in this passage's steps, you can lead us."

Bue smirked and took the torch from Leppard's hand, stepping carefully onto the first stair and moving forward. "Remember to duck" he whispered to Jared as he moved downwards slowly. As they moved forward Jared could see scuttling shapes of what looked like large spiders moving away into the recesses of the walls and caught a glimpse of one the size of a crab. He shuddered. Leppard was behind them and closed the door, locking it and pocketing the key. Bue moved a large veil of webbing aside with his hand. Above them the muffled cries seemed fainter and less frequent now as if the commotion in the main building was nearing an end.

As they pressed on Bue turned to look over his shoulder. "Which way?" he whispered. "The left takes us to near the caretaker's lodge. The other way brings us up to the dining room near the service hatch."

"Go left," Leppard replied, motioning with his hand. They moved on, bows held in front of them. The surface of the floor was loose with bits of stone and the glow from the torch spluttered in contrast. There was a strong smell of damp in the air. Shortly they came upon another flight of steps and Leppard whispered urgently "BUE! Let me go first."

Bue was about to argue but saw the look of grim severity on Leppard's leathery face and moved back to allow the bow master to pass him. Leppard climbed the stairs quickly and went to take the key out of his pocket.

"You don't need that," Bue hissed. "Just lift the handle and pull the door up and to the left, it'll open."

Leppard smiled and placed the key back. He looked over his shoulder and down the steps at the two boys below him. "Ready? Now, let's go but be careful."

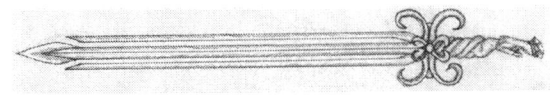

Challandra had remained motionless for a few minutes as the first Vagthunder had grabbed her guard. Partly through fear as she'd never seen these beings before, despite having been told how to summon them and her awe was mixed with a sense of terror at what she'd seen. The men they had taken were gone now, merged with the building and while she felt some pity for them she reminded herself that they had come to take Jared and wouldn't have hesitated to hurt anyone trying to stop them. Her heart hammered in her chest as she took a few deep breaths and placed one hand on the wall and tried to stand up. Just then something hit her in the lower back tumbling her forward. She whirled and stifled a scream only to see the crossbow instructor Leppard facing her with his bow pointed at her. His face creased and he lowered the weapon.

"My apologies Miss," he said looking slightly embarrassed. "Are you hurt?"

Challandra shook her head. "No. We need to check on the boys." Just then she saw Jared's face peering out from behind Leppard and Bue grinning at her.

"Well it's good to see you two are ok," she said with relief. "Although I see you are as always in the heart of trouble Master Bue."

"Just looking out for you Miss." Bue grinned cheekily at her and then stepped out behind Leppard, Jared following him. Leppard reached out his hand and helped Challandra to her feet. The sounds of pandemonium had now stopped, the screams gone and only a soft thudding could be heard.

"Someone needs to check on Madame Veer," Bue reminded them.

Leppard spoke up. "Me and Jared will check on Madame, you and Miss Challandra go and see to your friends. Once you've checked you stay there until we come back. Clear?"

"Crystal," Bue said, already moving forward. Challandra followed him and he moved as if on a hunt, his bow held in his right hand in front of him and his other held slightly to his side and level with his chest, ready to signal to Challandra if he spotted anything. Leppard and Jared moved off in the other direction, moving at a brisk pace and were gone round the corner quickly.

As Bue and Challandra reached the corridor that led to the boys' room a huge figure lumbered into view and stood glaring at them. Bue raised his crossbow but Challandra silently pushed the weapon down. The Vagthunder looked lost, like its purpose had ceased to be and its shoulders drooped as it looked away. Challandra took a deep breath and walked up to the huge figure as it turned slowly to look at her, the sound of its breathing the only thing they could hear in the corridor.

Swallowing hard, Challandra reached out and raised her hand and touched the huge creature gently on its chest. It felt cold. "Thank you," she said quietly, her voice cracking and then swallowed again before whispering. "Emco falhalain merhumkree." The creature sighed heavily and without hesitation turned and walked forwards into the nearest wall. The wall rippled to accept it and then was solid stone, the Vagthunder vanished.

Bue looked scared, his crossbow quivering, then he recovered and Challandra smiled. "They have all returned now. If there were any soldiers left in the building they would have found them."

"There was one in the practice hall..." Bue began but Challandra interrupted him.

"Gone too. That spell sent them back, it's clear now."

They moved to the door of the boys' room and opened it. Bue kept his crossbow levelled as he entered but lowered it as he saw the grinning face of Makeo staring at him from besides Jared's bed, the window now closed.

"Alright there Sharpeye?" The boy beamed brightly "didn't get caught by the monsters then?"

Bue grinned and stepped forward, placing his bow on Jared's bed and briefly hugging his friend, then stepping back. He turned to face the rest of the boys. One or two were still in bed, their eyes frightened. The smallest boy was sitting up shivering, the sheets drawn up to his chin and tears streaming down his face. Challandra moved and sat down, putting her arms around his tiny shoulders and drawing him to her. "Shhh..it's alright," she soothed, and stroked the frightened boy's head. He put his face into her chest and sobbed quietly.

The others seemed ok and Bue made a mental note that everyone was there. "No one hurt?" he asked Makeo.

"Nope, those things dealt with the soldiers. Just what WERE they?"

"Vagthunder," Challandra said from the boy's bed, gently rocking the crying child in her arms. "They are a final line of defense against intrusion to this place. I never thought we'd have to use them. The last time was before I was born."

The boy smiled brightly and clapped Bue on the arm. "Still, glad you made it."

"What happened to the soldier who got out the window?" Bue asked peering through the foggy diamond shaped patterns in the glass.

"Took off just after Master Leppard took a shot at him." The boy chuckled.

"I need to check on Madame Veer with the new boy." Bue said, hoiking his backpack into a more comfortable position on his shoulder.

Challandra sat up quickly. "No, you were told to wait! We still don't know if anybody else is in the building."

"With those things out there? They didn't mess about."

Challandra decided to appeal to Bue's sense of reason. "They've gone Bue and look, if you wander off then Leppard may have to come and look for you, meaning that there will be more problems until he finds you. Just wait here like we said."

Bue mused on this for a moment then decided. "Fair enough," he said, sitting down on the nearest bed. "But if they're not back very soon I'm going after them."

Jared and Leppard rounded the corners cautiously. There was one of the huge creatures in the corridor but, as if reacting to some secret signal, it had ignored them and then walked into the nearest wall and disappeared. The corridor's torches cast a flickering, yellow glow on the walls and Jared was struck by the almost complete silence in the building, after the chaos of only a few minutes ago.

"We need to check her office first" Leppard whispered and motioned to Jared to stay behind him. Jared moved quietly back to a position at Leppard's left so he could still fire his bow if anyone or anything tried to attack them.

As they moved forward a voice suddenly said. "There's no need for that."

They span round to find Madame Veer behind them, her grey hair undone from its tight bun and spilling over her shoulder. She was in a red night dress and held a thin jewelled sword in her hands.

Leppard lowered his bow and exhaled heavily. "Ma'am. I'm so glad you're safe. Is anyone else hurt?"

"They knocked me out," she replied, stepping forward from the shadows to reveal a small cut on her forehead. "Who summoned the Vagthunder?"

"You mean it wasn't you?" Leppard said, his eyes widening. "It must have been Challandra then."

"The girl has presence of mind in a crisis" Madame Veer replied. She placed the sword against the wall, tip down and sat on a chair outside her office. The one usually reserved for errant pupils waiting to face her wrath.

"I feel woozy. Young man, can you take the small black bag from my office and hand it to me."

Leppard moved off down the corridor towards the lodge. Jared glanced worryingly at Madame Veer and then moved, remembering to hold his bow out in front of him as he swung the door open. He glanced around the office from the sputtering light in the hall and spied a small leather bag by the large desk. He bent down to pick it up and then returned outside where the stern principal sat holding her head. She smiled weakly and took the bag from him.

"Thank you Jared," she said before opening it and removing a glass phial. It was like a diamond in shape but contained a dark orange liquid. She removed the tiny cork from the top of the vessel and a smell of pineapples sprang from the neck as she passed it to him. It trembled slightly in his hand.

"Now put one drop only on my cut Jared, please be careful you do not use more."

Jared raised the glass cautiously and looked at the wound on her head.

"But the cut's big, it won't be enough," Jared pointed out.

"Just do as I ask. It will be fine, trust me."

Jared raised the glass and, while trying to still his shaking hand, he ever-so-gently tilted the small bottle and saw the liquid moved to the lip. Madame Veer sat perfectly still, her eyes closed and Jared watched the liquid form in the small neck of the glass before a drop fell from the tip. He was just about to pull his hand back when the drip detached and landed on Madame Veer's forehead, missing the cut. He opened his mouth to apologise when the liquid moved to the wound of its own accord and expanded briefly to fill the cut on her scalp. With no sound at all the cut sealed and closed, the only sign of injury being the blood on her head. Then that contracted in on itself and disappeared too.

She opened her eyes and smiled. "Thank you Jared, very well done. You have a steady hand."

Chapter 10

"We can't stay here now it's too dangerous." Madame Veer said, glancing around the hallway. There was no sign of the recent disturbance and intrusion, the orphanage was peaceful again, the moonlight casting deep, velvet shadows on the floors and ancient walls. Bue shuffled nervously, his crossbow slung and the quarrel back in its quiver. Jared was still astounded by what he'd seen and realised this world had more surprises than he could ever have dreamed of.

Leppard was checking the corridors adjacent to the one they were on. He came back and nodded. "I agree. We need to leave, but it has to be all of us."

Madame Veer tied her long silver hair back with a ribbon from her breast pocket and stood tall. She was an imposing figure even in her night gown. "I can take three with me via Shimmer. The rest will have to walk with you."

"We've got Shimmer HERE?" Makeo said looking flabbergasted. "How come we didn't know?"

"Because you weren't meant to know young man," Veer replied icily.

Leppard spoke to Bue. "Get the three smallest boys and bring them here, tell them to bring clothes, shoes and no more. Tell the others to wait for us in the dorm."

"Where are we going?" Bue asked looking confused.

Leppard was about to tell him to do as he'd asked but thought better of it. "With Madame Veer to the Cherubs. It's the safest place we can think of."

Bue thought about this for a moment then tapped Jared on the arm. "Come on fella," he said grinning and led the way.

Leppard turned to Madame Veer. "Why the walk?" he enquired curiously. "Why don't we all just go with you?"

"The Shimmer won't work with more than four, won't work without me and once I'm gone; can't be used until I come back and reset it. If everyone could use it this world would be in chaos."

"Why not take Jared with you?" Leppard asked, looking confused.

"The smallest boys are too young to walk and the Shimmer's signal may be picked up if Jared uses it."

Leppard smiled brightly. "Fair enough, I could use the exercise anyway."

"You need to take the woodland trails and DON'T use magic unless you have no choice. You will leave a trace that whoever is trying to find that boy will be able to use to track you. You should make it in just over a day."

Bue and Jared returned with Challandra. They had the frightened small child who was clutching Challandra's hand tightly and staring with scared eyes at Madame Veer and the others. The other two children were about seven or eight years old and seemed less upset by the night's events but still uneasy. Madame Veer smiled reassuringly. "Don't worry children, it will be ok. We are going to visit our friends in Cherub mansion. You remember that Mr Cherubsayl came here before as our guest?"

The three children nodded silently.

"Well he's going to look after us now for a little bit. You three are very lucky as you are going to use the Shimmer with me to get there."

One of the boys brightened at this and looked up at Leppard then at Madame Veer. "Cor!" he exclaimed. "Does it hurt when you do that?"

Madame Veer smiled. "No Mispyn, it's just like closing your eyes and opening them again."

"Oh, brilliant. I've never seen one of these before!"

The boys had small leather bags with them with green straps and they were clutching them tightly. Jared glanced at the smallest boy. The child still looked bewildered and was clearly scared out of his wits. Jared caught his eye and winked at him. After a moment's pause the boy started to cry and put his arms round Challandra's waist. She said gently, "it's ok Getruhl" and Jared blushed, grateful no one had seen his unsuccessful attempts at being reassuring.

"Wait here for a few minutes while I get changed," Madame Veer said and moved to a red doorway opposite her office.

Jared looked at Bue. "One day?"

"Yep," Bue replied grinning wildly. "Should be fun with a capital F."

After a few minutes Madame Veer returned. Her hair was tied back in the usual tight bun. She was wearing a black, formal tunic and black trousers with shiny, polished black boots, the type a woman would wear to ride a horse. "*Elegant but also very scary*", Jared thought. Over her shoulder was a larger version of the bags the children had.

"Once we're gone go to the kitchen, grab what food you can for yourselves. Don't be greedy but then don't take too little and make sure you have enough water." Madame Veer said to Challandra.

She turned to the small children. "Ok then boys, come with me," and moved off to a large blue door near the cloakroom they were standing next to and took a key from her pocket. The wood squeaked in protest and removing the lit torch from the wall, she went in. The air was musty and the room smelled like it hadn't been used in ages. "Once we go, lock this door and put the key in my office," she instructed Leppard.

Mispyn ran forward as the door swung open and barely paused to brush the cobwebs from his face and shoulders that had grown across the door frame, before hopping about excitedly.

"This is brilliant, never thought I'd see one."

Jared looked on puzzled. This wasn't a platform like he'd expected with devices to move them individually with some kind of magical control panel. It was just a large, shallow indentation in the floor that was grey and unassuming, like the rest of the room. There were a couple of old, unlit lanterns on the walls and a window, high up on the back wall behind the dish in the floor. The moonlight shone through the grimy glass, casting spattered shadows around the room where the dust span and turned lazily in the air.

Jared looked around and wondered why this room, so boring and basic would have to be permanently locked up and kept secret.

Mispyn was hopping up and down and excitedly shouting, "oh boy, oh boy, oh boy," running around and through the centre of the recessed platform.

Madame Veer took another crystal from her pocket and turned to a small bracket in the wall. It was purple, elegantly engraved and carefully she placed the jewel in a square slot then stood back. After a few seconds the jewel glowed brightly.

Getruhl was staring wide eyed and while appearing less frightened than before was holding tightly to Challandra's hand as they entered the room. Mispyn was still jumping about, his shaggy black hair tumbling over his face.

Getruhl didn't want to leave Challandra and clung on tightly to her hand, crying.

Challandra crouched down in front of him and spoke quietly, "There's nothing to be afraid of Getruhl. I promise you I'll be with you as soon as I can."

Madame Veer looked on saying nothing, clearly realising that being strict would not work now.

The boy wailed and tried to hug Challandra but she gently held his arms.

"No Getruhl. I promise you I'll be there as soon as I can. Please go with Madame now. It's for the best."

She walked with him to the centre of the room. The child still had a tight grip on her hand and wouldn't let go, his face full of pleading. Challandra squatted down and reached up to the clasp on one of her necklaces. She undid it and gently drew the chain free from her shirt. It had an oval green stone on the end encircled with silver. "This is an Aquestan emerald Getruhl. It is a symbol of friendship. I promise you I'll be with you as soon as I

141

can. Wear this to remind you that I am right behind you."

The boy sniffed loudly and tried to smile as Challandra reached up and clasped the chain behind his neck and smiling, tucked the stone under his green shirt and kissed his cheek gently. "I'll be there for you soon, now please. You need to go."

She pulled her hand free and Getruhl stood next to Mispyn. The other two were still jumping up and down with excitement, their ankle length boots clipping on the dusty, hard floor. Getruhl tried to smile and grasped the chain in his fingers for reassurance as he gazed forlornly at Challandra.

She stepped clear and Madame Veer addressed them all. "Now remember. No magic unless absolutely necessary and keep to the woodland trail, not the open roads. Leave as soon as we're gone and lock up. The doorkeeper will be able to tell everyone what happened here."

She grasped the hands of the boys nearest to her. One looked over at Bue. "Beat you to it," he smirked, but not unpleasantly. Getruhl held the other hand of the boy nearest to him.

Bue grinned back and saluted the boy theatrically. "See you soon Jerean. Take care of Getruhl and Mispyn."

Madame Veer closed her eyes and the effect that Jared had seen in the council chamber began again. Large ripples coming in from the corners of the room and converging into the centre. The purple light behind them glowed brighter and brighter until it was too much to look at without hurting your eyes. Jared glanced away and the ripples converged on the group, who started to fade. As the ripples came in on one another in the centre, the group became transparent. Then as the waves completely folded in they spread out rapidly then disappeared.

The purple light glowed even brighter for a second and finally dimmed. It turned a cold grey and the room was lit only by the moonlight coming through the windows.

There was a silence and then Leppard turned to them. "Right, you lot. To the kitchens. We need to get food and then we're off at first light."

Chapter 11

The dorm room was buzzing with excitement as they came back. The remaining boys had no idea what was going on and they bombarded Leppard, Bue and Challandra with questions as they returned to collect them.

"Settle down," Leppard barked as he tried to make himself heard over the ruckus. Eventually the chatter subsided and Leppard cleared his throat.

"Right. We need to leave here. Some bad people came tonight as you are aware but were not successful in their attempt to take young master Jared away with them."

Another excited buzz and Leppard waited until it died away, then continued. "Madame Veer has gone ahead to the Cherubs with the others via Shimmer. We will be walking."

There was a groan from one or two of the boys as this information was taken in. They realised they'd missed using or even seeing the Shimmer working, something only a few of them had ever witnessed.

"However it's nice weather and you could all do with some exercise" he said smiling.

The boys smiled back. They trusted Leppard despite his gruff demeanour and they all liked him.

"You are to all take this with the most exceptional seriousness" he said sternly, his facial expression changing to one of complete sincerity. "You are under my protection and I will not see any of you come to harm. Anyone acting the fool will be punished severely both at the time and when we get back here. Is that clear?"

They all nodded.

"Now, go with master Bue to the practice hall and collect your bows, quarrels and packs. Don't dawdle and when you have them, meet back in the kitchen. You are to take your day clothes, your walking boots and a large pack, nothing more. Now get to it."

Bue led them out the doors, his bow reloaded and held ready for anybody that might spring unwisely from a dark corner.

Leppard turned to Challandra. "Is a day a realistic estimate?"

"Yes, we can maybe make it in less. We have to press on though. They might come back."

"I know" Leppard replied seeing her discomfort and shifting his bow to the other hand he patted her shoulder reassuringly. "We'll be okay. I'm just glad she took little Getruhl and the other two. That boy is scared of his own shadow."

Challandra glared at him and snapped. "He's frightened out of his wits and he's only 5! How did you cope when you were that age?"

Leppard started slightly at her anger and his face creased in embarrassment. "I'm sorry, I like the boy too...it's just..."

Challandra relaxed slightly and blushed. In a quiet voice she said, "I'm sorry. This is too much to take in. I feel guilty about those men. They're dead because of me."

Leppard patted her arm again. "Don't be. They would have hurt anyone they came across. They were brutal men. They would not have shown mercy, to anybody."

Challandra moved towards the door. Turning she looked at Jared. "Come on, we need to get the food sorted."

In the canteen there had been a frantic rush as the boys tried to make for the sweet cupboard until Challandra had screeched at them to get out and wait in the dining area. She sorted the food into bundles and gave each bundle a leg or two of roasted meat, some ham and hard boiled eggs plus a generous portion of green vegetables. Also three or four of Penny's cakes that the boys loved. She wrapped each pile of food up in waxed paper and tied it up in a leather sack with string.

"Penny's gonna kill you Miss when she sees you've robbed her prize puddin's" Stone said cheerily.

"Just take your things and go fill your drinking flask," Challandra said firmly and the boy smirked at her and then walked over to the huge clay water pot at the side of the room.

Leppard and Bue returned from securing all the doors and Leppard coughed for attention.

"Do you all have your bows and quarrels?" he shouted.

The boys took a final cursory glance and nodded in unison.

"And food?"

Again, nodding.

"Right we leave now. We are not going out the front door and we will be absolutely silent. Anyone talking gets my boot up their backside. Clear?"

The boys stood up and Leppard led them out the room and down the corridor. Bue grabbed Jared's arm and passed him his bow. "Here, you forgot this."

"Thanks" Jared said, slinging the bow and trying to buckle the quiver belt while walking. "You ok?"

"Lovin' it" Bue replied cheerfully, his smile threatening to split his face open.

Chapter 12

As the sun prickled the sky the group left the building. Making their way out into the early morning rays of light. The woods at the back of the orphanage were thick and seeing the broken path through the pink and orange light was not easy. Jared was tired and while no longer hungry he wondered if he'd ever get to sleep normally again.

Bue was as chirpy as ever. Nothing ever seemed to upset him or tire him out and he took the rear position behind the group, checking every few seconds around him. His bow held across his chest ready for anyone that might try to stop them. Challandra was in the middle with the main group of boys and she smiled to try and keep their spirits up as they moved silently through the trees. The chirping of birds and the sound of their footprints in the grass was the only thing disturbing the stillness. The trees were tall and their leaves were starting to show the blotches of autumn as they died to make way for winter. The view was beautiful through the long trunks and the path up ahead was overgrown and wound its way around and through the foliage, sometimes disappearing from view completely.

Leppard was at the front and he scanned the area quickly and carefully as they moved on. His senses were honed to spotting trouble from years of hunting and tracking. As the early morning mist lifted slowly from the wood and the sunlight shone on the blades of grass he felt more confident that, as long as the boys obeyed his word and kept to the plan, they would be fine.

After half an hour of walking Jared dropped back to Bue and whispered. "What are we going to? What's the Cherubs?"

Bue finished his current scan of the surrounding area and looked at him. "It's a family, a rich one. They live in a big house in the woods. Them and Madame Veer have been friends for ages. They'll protect us from whoever is coming after us."

It was still light when Leppard called time to rest for the night. Most of the boys were tired and becoming irritable and they gratefully fell on their packs in the long grass to the side of the track.

Leppard set out finding a clear space to make a fire and sent two of the boys off to gather wood. Challandra entertained the others with a few stories and kept the younger boys' spirits up.

Bue was keen to go hunting and Leppard said that provided he could catch something not more than half a mile from the camp then fine. Bue had grinned and promised him a brace of rabbits and three or four birds for the pot when he got back.

He'd taken Jared along and they made their way through the trees, the knee high grass brushing aside as they pushed on. Jared had never been hunting before and he was curious to know the methods. The bright light of day through the trees that they had had since early morning was now making way for a deepening shade of grey. The shadows becoming longer. The noise and chatter of the forest animals was subdued as if they too were turning in for the day. Jared was worried that they would get lost as it got dark but Bue assured him he was an experienced hunter. From all the times he'd been out with his father and lately with Leppard and the other boys. He walked confidently through the forest, his bow held ready for anything.

Jared was about to ask him a question when Bue turned and held his finger to his lips, then pointed further ahead. Jared saw nothing but then after a pause his eyes adjusted and he could see a grey rabbit ahead, nibbling on a leaf of some plant, held between its paws. Bue motioned for Jared to drop down and they squatted, staring ahead. Bue silently raised his bow and steadying his aim he took a deep breath and triggered it. The quarrel shot free from the weapon with a twang and the bolt hit the rabbit with a thud.

"YEE-ES!!" Bue exclaimed triumphantly as the rabbit flew back into the long grass behind it. "Come on, dinner part one" he said grinning and clapping Jared on the shoulder. They ran forward and Bue scanned the foliage. "There," he said and reached down, pulling the body up by the ears. The rabbit was limp and the shot had been clean. He tossed the carcass to Jared. "Cop hold of that, you can carry."

Jared flinched as he caught the rabbit and gingerly held it in his hands. Bue reached for a new quarrel and held it between his teeth as he started to recrank his crossbow.

Suddenly an angry voice said quietly, "what do you think you're doing?"

Jared jumped and dropped the rabbit, Bue had just cranked his bow and he glanced around quickly and then placed the bolt in the firing groove. "Who's there?" he snapped anxiously, training his crossbow on the nearby trees where the sound seemed to be coming from.

"I said WHAT do you think you're doing?" the voice asked again angrily.

Bue and Jared frantically glanced around but could see nothing.

"Come out whoever you are," Bue said turning from left to right with his bow held ready.

"Murdering wretches!" the voice snapped and then a small brown fox stepped clear of a large clump of knobbly yellow plants. Bue looked shocked and Jared stared at it. "You killed him!" the fox said, its tail flicking angrily as it gestured with its head to the body at Jared's feet.

Before either of them could react there was a loud snarling and two bears stepped out on their hind legs from the trees. As Bue turned the nearest one to him swatted his bow from his hands. He yelped as it was torn from his grasp, the mechanism triggering and the bolt firing off into the depths of the woods. "Killers!" The bear snarled, grabbing Bue around the waist and then throwing him down on the earth floor. The other pushed Jared down who shouted in fear. Both bears put one huge foot on the boys' chests and looked to the fox. Its face was full of fury and after a pause it said, "bring them." Practically spitting the words.

"Wh, where are you taking us?" Jared stammered as the bears began to tie their arms and feet with twine from the trees.

"To the conclave," the fox said, eyeing him furiously. "They will deal with you."

The bears tied them tightly and Jared winced as the twine was pulled taught on his legs. Bue thrashed and kicked and tried to stand up. The bear holding him growled menacingly and bared its teeth so he reluctantly went still.

Picking them up and flinging them over their huge shoulders the bears moved off after the fox who walked ahead shouting. "Summon the conclave. Murder in our forest! Summon the conclave!"

After a short journey they came into a clearing and the bears dumped them unceremoniously on the floor. Jared groaned as he hit the damp ground and as he squinted in the deepening gloom he saw, before his eyes, the clearing slowly fill with animals of many types. Badgers, otters, birds, foxes, rabbits and even one or two wolves plus a large boar slowly moved into the clearing and sat in a circle around them. Their eyes staring silently at the two boys and their captors.

As the glade filled, the fox who had found them moved to a large rock on one side of the clearing and a badger detached itself from a group of others and moved to join him. They climbed up onto the rock, facing the gathered crowd. Jared strained to see what was happening and could see only what looked like a zoo of different species. His side was wet where he was laying and he wriggled uncomfortably. He whispered to Bue. "What the hell is this? What did you do?"

The bear above him growled so he went quiet.

The buzz of conversation amongst the animals drifted away as the badger raised its paw and there was silence.

"Human trespassers," the badger said in a loud voice. "Do you know why you are brought before this conclave?"

Bue struggled against his bonds and glared sideways at the fox and badger. "What's your problem?" he demanded angrily. "We were out hunting. That's not a crime."

There was another angry buzz of talk from the animals gathered and Jared whispered urgently. "For God's sake be quiet. You're making them angry!"

The badger held up its paw until the silence returned. "It is here. You are beyond your own lands and in our world now. The rabbit you murdered was a father and a husband; you leave his family without him."

A space cleared slightly to the left of the badger and as the animals rippled apart Bue and Jarred could see other rabbits. A large one and four smaller ones. All were crying quietly.

"You leave this family without its male adult. Kanin was a member of this wood, a loving father and a wise giver of advice to his friends."

There was another buzz of angry conversation amongst the animals with most of them glaring at Bue and Jared, helpless on the floor. Some were looking at the weeping rabbits and then at the two boys, disgust creasing their faces.

"Do you have anything to say for yourselves?" the fox asked above the murmuring.

Bue wriggled and shouted through the wet grass pressing up against his mouth. "Tell this hulking lump to get its foot off me and I'll answer you."

The bear growled quietly but turned to the fox and the badger. The bear slowly removed its huge paw from Bue's chest and dropped to all fours.

Bue took a deep breath and said angrily. "We were hunting, in my land this is OK provided it's for food and not just sport. We didn't know we were in your territory."

"Ignorance is no excuse," the badger answered wearily. "Our laws apply to everyone."

"Secondly," Bue snapped. "Jared was only helping me. He didn't kill the rabbit, I did."

At the mention of the deed the rabbit's family began to weep even louder and the little ones moved closer to the mother, burying their faces into her fur.

Through the last rays of daylight the badger turned a solemn face to them and said. "You have admitted your actions and the fact that your friend did not pull the trigger is irrelevant. He is your accomplice and as guilty as you."

There was an approving rumble of conversation from the gathered animals.

The badger turned to the fox and they whispered for a few moments, occasionally glancing over at Jared and Bue. After consulting they turned to the boys, the crowd of animals once more going quiet.

"You are to be taken from here to the borders of our territory and killed," the badger said slowly and with complete calm.

Jared winced and tried to stand up, the twine around his ankles digging in as he struggled.

There was an approving murmur from the gathered animals.

"Your bodies will be displayed to warn others of the price of killing in our woods."

The murmur was now louder and one or two animals were loudly shouting.

"Unless of course the widow wishes to show clemency. Kirittita?" the fox turned to the crying rabbit who shook her head and hugged her children tighter.

"Very well, take them to…," the fox began as the bears moved to pick Bue and Jared up.

"STOP!" A loud voice sounded in the glade.

All heads turned and in the dimming light Jared saw a path form on one side between the animals and slowly another appeared.

It was a large white stag, with huge antlers. The stag picked its way through the path cleared for it and stood in the middle of the clearing next to Jared, Bue and the two bears, facing the fox and badger. It glanced behind at the boys and Jared saw it had brown eyes that looked old and sad.

"Hekima, our old friend," the badger said surprised. "You are welcome in the conclave."

"That I may be," the stag replied, looking around. "However, I see you have passed a death sentence on these two boys. May I ask why?"

There was an excited buzz of chat and the badger replied. "They killed Kanin, leaving his children orphaned and his bride a widow," the fox replied dramatically.

"I see," the stag replied nodding, "and why did they do that?"

"They were hunting illegally in our sacred woods and slaughtered poor Kanin as he was foraging for food for his wife and children."

Another murmur and the stag then asked. "So what was their motivation for killing him?"

"They are from Alegria and in that barbaric place the killing of defenceless animals is lawful," the fox said, his voice cracking with indignation.

Another angry murmur and the boar shouted. "Kill them!" Its tusks waving from side to side as it angrily shook its head.

The stag asked casually. "Hunting for food or for sport?".

"For food they say, and we have no reason to doubt that. However, as we told them and as this conclave and this wood knows...ignorance is no excuse."

Another murmur of approval.

"I see," the stag said nodding. He glanced at Bue, who was glaring at him and then at Jared who was petrified but unable to look away.

"May I ask you both a question?" the stag said to the badger and fox.

The fox hesitated but then said. "But of course Hekima, your wisdom is always welcome."

"If you kill them, will that bring Kanin back?"

A ripple of confusion and then the fox stammered. "Err...well NO but..."

"So if you kill them what will their deaths achieve?"

"We are going to display their bodies as a lesson to others..."The badger began but Hekima interrupted him.

"You know as well as I do that their bodies will be eaten within a couple of hours by our less enlightened woodland cousins, so I ask you this. As you cannot bring Kanin back and no one from Alegria will learn this lesson you wish to teach...then what purpose will killing these children serve?"

There was a silence in the glade now, the moonlight finally holding sway over the extinguished daylight and everyone's attention was on the large stag.

The badger stared at him, unable to speak but the fox then found its tongue. "Hekima this conclave's laws are just and fair. We agreed them ourselves. These boys..."

"Acted in ignorance without malice or evil intent." Hekima interrupted. "This conclave is young and our laws are not known to all. Their lack of knowledge of our rules is not their fault, hunting has been lawful from time immemorial in Alegria."

"Which is barbaric and should not exist," the fox said quickly, trying to regain control.

"But nevertheless exists, whether we like it or not," the stag said looking around at the assembled creatures. Some were bowing their heads and all were silent.

"If we murder these children just to satisfy our blood lust over their crime then we become worse then they are. Worse I say, because their actions were innocent. Ours would be premeditated and wholly unforgivable."

The stag looked around and every animal in the crowd was now looking at the floor, even the weeping rabbits.

After a long silence the fox said in a strangled voice. "So what do you suggest we do with them?"

"Banish them."

Bue looked over at Jared in confusion.

"Banish them and trust that they tell their people what happened here today."

There was another long silence and the fox said. " Hekima you cannot just..."

"If any animal here believes now that they should be killed then let it make itself known BUT...let that animal take part in their murders if it is so eager to see life taken."

The stag looked around the conclave and none would return his stare.

Eventually Hekima said. "I will take them with me to the border. Let it never be said that we did not treat others fairly and with compassion, regardless of what hurt they caused to us."

The stag stared at the bears and they bent down to cut the bindings free from the boys' hands and feet. Unsure what to do,

Bue and Jared simply lay there, trying to rub some circulation back into their wrists.

"Come." He said gently. "Don't be afraid. Climb on my back. I will take you to where you came from."

Hesitantly and glancing around the gathered, silent animals who stared at them, they gingerly climbed on the huge stag's back and clung on. Bue had the lead and held to the fur on the back of the huge beast's neck. Jared gripped Bue around the waist.

"Now hold tight," the stag said and without hesitation leapt through the undergrowth and the tall grass and into the depths of the wood.

After a short time they came to where they had shot the rabbit. The stag stopped and lowered itself so the boys could get down.

"Thank you," Jared said. The stag looked at him with its sad, old eyes and after contemplating him for a moment it replied.

"Don't come back here. Do you understand? If you do you won't leave alive."

"We understand," Jared said quickly. "We're sorry about that rabbit…"

Hekima interrupted him. "Your words are meaningless. What's done is done. Learn that not everything is the same wherever you are."

In the distance they could see the fire of the camp, maybe one mile distant.

"Farewell children," the stag said and turned and bolted into the woods, never looking back.

Jared watched the plants and leaves wave in its wake and then whirled as he heard Bue squawk triumphantly and pick up his precious bow from the undergrowth.

"Found it," he exclaimed. "Come on, let's go." He looked at Jared grinning, patting his jerkin pocket to show he still had his quarrels.

Moving together they made their way back to camp.

Chapter 13

They sat or lay around the fire. Leppard had listened carefully to what Bue and Jared had said and then told them not to tell the others. His concern was clear and despite his initial anger that they had been gone so long, he softened when he realised why.

"The lands beyond our borders are unusual sometimes," he noted gravely and they had made do for supper with what little they had brought with them. Plus some mushrooms that Challandra had found near the old path.

The fire was warming and Bue sat with his knees drawn up to his chin and looked across at Jared. "Something we don't know is exactly why you're here. Where do you come from?"

Everybody turned to look at Jared who shifted uncomfortably, the orange glow from the fire casting shadows across his face. After a pause he looked at them. "To be honest I don't know where YOU come from."

There was more silence and he realised he would have to continue.

"I'm from Warwick in England. I was in hospital visiting my cousin a week ago when I disturbed some kind of blind, scruffy guy who was trying to hurt a girl named Sophie who's in a coma. Mordalayn came and stopped him and then threw a bracelet onto me that I couldn't take off."

He paused and saw that the group were listening intently to what he said. "Then when me and my parents were about to fly to Malta for our holidays these creatures attacked me. Mordalayn appeared and stopped them, I think he killed them but then he took me and the next thing I knew I was here. One minute I'm on the runway of Heathrow airport and then the next I'm face down on a muddy farm field God knows where."

"What's an airport?" one of the boys whispered but he was shushed by another.

"Why would Takoba Mordalayn bring you here though?" Bue asked puzzled. "Your land is obviously far from here...wherever err, Warrik is."

"I don't know, he said something about people wanting to hurt me and Sophie."

"Who's Sophie?" Bolla asked and a few others murmured their curiosity.

"Mordalayn said she's the ruler here, he called her Our Lady."

There was a gasp of shock from everyone, including Leppard.

"Sophie is the Queen of Alegria?!!" Bue said, clearly astonished.

"I, I guess so." Jared replied.

Bue whistled and there was excited murmuring amongst the others. He turned to Jared once more. "What happened to her?"

"She was hit by a car." Jared saw the confused looks and tried again. "A road vehicle." There were nods of understanding. "She's been unconscious for about three months now."

Leppard then interjected. "The light of this kingdom has slowly faded in the last year. We wondered why such a great loss of power had befallen Alegria. Most believed the queen had gone and deserted us, but now you tell us that she is hurt. That explains it."

There was a silence and Jared asked;" Has she always been the queen here?"

162

Leppard laughed. "No my boy. Not by a long shot. She is the second ruler of Alegria in my lifetime."

"But, how…what do…how does she get to be queen here?"

"That I cannot tell you because I do not know. There are many secrets in this world."

There was a long silence and then one of the other boys spoke up. "We've heard stories about Anghofio. That King James wants to invade us. Is that true?"

Leppard looked around and said, "We believe so yes," and there were shocked murmurs in response. "But I am not privy to the knowledge any more. My days as a soldier are over."

"Did you fight alongside Takoba Mordalayn?" Declain asked excitedly.

"I had that honour yes," Leppard replied smiling.

"Cor! What's he like?"

The others started firing questions at the old bow master.

"Yeah, why'd he leave to be the Queen's Sword?"

"Is he scary in battle?"

"Did you see him kill anyone?"

Leppard smiled and when the excited buzz had died down he replied. "Takoba Mordalayn was a general in the Enlightened Army. I had the privilege of serving alongside him. Our army has not seen battle in hundreds of years but I have seen him fight."

He paused. "The only threat to Alegria now is our own sense of safety. Our army is small and we have little or no real ability to stand our ground in the face of a direct attack. Our queen is powerful but now she is gone…well, the future is uncertain."

The boys were all watching him intently in the firelight.

"Takoba Mordalayn is an honourable and noble warrior. Our only threat in my time in the army was from the velvet forests and forces from over the Sea of Glass. Mordalayn is indeed an awe inspiring and terrifying sight. Only King James himself is said to rival him as a swordsman. Mordalayn is someone whose blades you want to protect your back, but never facing you."

"Why did he leave?" the same boy asked.

"Something awful happened to him. I do not know the details but it was apparently terrible. In the aftermath he volunteered to be the new queen's bodyguard when she was crowned. The ruler of Alegria is always a child and always chooses their own Sword. Many wanted the role but Queen Sophie selected Mordalayn."

The boys were silent, intently hanging on to Leppard's every word.

"She has ruled for just over twelve years, but this past year no one has seen her. We pray to our gods that she will return but we do not know what the future holds for the Emerald Queen or Alegria."

Beevor suddenly burst from the trees about ten metres back from the camp fire and screamed "HELP!" and ran past Leppard and the others to the other side of the fire. They all whirled round to where he was standing, knees shaking and pointing terrified at the trees he'd just come from.

"What's wrong?" Challandra said concerned, jumping to her feet.

"L..l..look!" the boy stammered and at that moment the undergrowth scraped noisily and the branches of the nearest trees bent outwards. A huge fat creature emerged from the darkness. It was a pale grey colour and hugely flabby and obese.

It had legs like lobster claws, at least four on each side and it chittered in a noisy clicking pitch. The boys all jumped up, yelling. The creature waddled forward, its body sagging against the ground and antennae on its head waved.

Leppard grabbed his pack and bow, Bue the same and they were trying to crank them while moving back to the other side of the fire.

"Get behind me!" Leppard shouted to the frightened boys, who were scattering like leaves on the wind. The creature chittered again; the sound high and threatening. It moved forward, the screams of the boys ringing in the air as they made their way either into the overgrowth or behind Leppard and Bue.

Bue succeeded in cranking his bow and was fumbling for a bolt when a voice shouted:

"WAIT!"

Challandra turned and shouted over the noise. "It's cold, it's attracted to the fire, it means no harm."

As the monstrous creature shuffled towards the campfire Challandra turned and grabbed a large burning branch and turned to face the intruder, waving it in front of her.

She stepped forward and the creature chittered in fear and with a noisy rustling of foliage managed to back off into the woods behind it. Challandra pursued it slowly as the frightened beast backed away. Then it turned and with lots of crashing and crunching of vegetation manoeuvred itself off into the dark depths of the forest, chittering loudly.

When she was sure it was gone Challandra lowered the flaming branch and walked back to the others. Frightened eyes peered at her along with the shocked and surprised eyes of Bue,

Leppard and Jared. She placed the branch carefully back in the fire and looked at Bue. "You can lower your bow, the animal is gone."

Hesitantly he did so and said, "what, what was THAT?."

"Slythid" she replied. "They live in the forests. They are harmless herbivores." She looked up. "It won't come back now, you can relax."

Challandra sighed in relief and slowly the boys returned to the fire and sat back down, most looking over their shoulders into the darkness beyond the trees.

After a few minutes one of the boys said, "so tell us more about Takoba Mordalayn please," and the others relaxed, looking eagerly to Leppard.

Leppard looked up and surprise registered on his face. Then he smiled and said, "I think you can ask him yourself."

There was a crunch of leaves and twigs and the boys turned to see Mordalayn emerge from the shadows between two large trees. He was dressed as he was when he left Jared and his huge sword was sheathed. He looked around the group and then moved forward. "My apologies for the unannounced return," he said to Leppard. He looked across at Jared who smiled nervously, unnerved by the warrior's silent return.

Leppard extended his hand which, after a moment's hesitation Mordalayn shook. "It seems we need to sharpen our ears somewhat Takoba, you came just after the right time I think," and gestured for the Caracalic to sit down next to him. "Please join us, we have food and water."

Mordalayn did not return the smile but said, "I have my own rations, yours you should keep for yourself."

Leppard looked around at the ashen, shocked faces of the boys. "Very well, but I believe Master Blautin was going to play us a delightful tune on his flute was he not? Nothing like some good music to aid the digestion." He glanced at the boy who beamed proudly and reached for his backpack. Inside was a silk cloth which he withdrew with tender care and unwrapped slowly to reveal a polished silver flute.

"Yeah, go on Blau," another boy said. "Play us a tune."

Blautin blushed and after carefully inspecting his prize instrument with eyes and fingers he raised it to his lips and began to play.

Jared was impressed with the tune and the boy's ability. The music was sweet and uplifting. Despite their tiredness and fear of the last day or so, they felt their worries fade slightly. As if the music was massaging their spirits. He played well and after a few minutes stopped to applause from the others, Challandra was smiling happily.

The little lad smiled back, raised the flute to his lips and began to play once more.

Chapter 14

As they began to bed down for the night Stone spied that Blautin hadn't put his flute in his backpack. He made a snatch for it and Blautin span round.

"Give it back," the younger boy snapped angrily as the older child grinned and held on to the flute, dangling it out of reach of the frantic swipes of its owner.

"Come and get it," Stone said, jumping up and dancing around. The others barely took notice but then Blautin stood still and started to cry.

Stone didn't stop and instead started to laugh. "Hey, what are you? A little…"

"ENOUGH!"

Everyone jumped and looked at Mordalayn who was sitting opposite the two boys across the fire. There was a horrible silence and Stone stared at the warrior, embarrassed and scared. Blautin stopped crying and wiped his wet cheeks with the back of his sleeve.

"Give it to him," Mordalayn growled.

"I was just messing…" Stone began but was interrupted.

"You are a bully and bullies are despicable," Mordalayn said with limitless menace. Everyone was looking at him. Challandra was scared, knowing the Caracalic's reputation. Leppard glanced from Mordalayn to the boys and then back. Stone handed the flute back to Blautin and then sat down, his cheeks burning with shame. He hugged his knees and looked away.

After a long pause Mordalayn spoke again. This time more softly.

"Bullying is vile. Would you have liked it if he'd taken something you loved?"

Stone shook his head mutely. Blautin sat down, putting his prized flute in its silk cloth and wrapping it carefully before putting it in his pack. He sniffed the last of his tears away and looked at Mordalayn, at the same time frightened and reassured.

The Caracalic had everyone's attention and he spoke calmly and quietly, the only other sound in the forest the crackling of the fire.

"To make someone weaker than you a victim only for your own pleasure is beyond vileness." He glanced around slowly at everyone as he said this. No one could meet his eyes, even Bue and Leppard lowered their gazes.

"Recently I saw this."

Mordalayn had been shadowing Jared for four days in Warwick. The spell he'd placed on Queen Sophie would prevent their enemies from finding her now. However, she was still vulnerable and as long as Jared was trackable they could, if they could get to him before she came out of her death sleep, use him to find her. Mordalayn had followed him and his parents this night to a house where a woman holding a baby had answered the door. The house was in an area that Mordalayn had not explored before. He looked around. The sun was going down and he glanced at his wrist band. The crystal was still a murky shade of green. He needed to eat. He'd smelled food about quarter of a mile east from here and decided to break off to find rations. Drawing his hood over his face and pulling his robes tight around him, he leapt from the roof he was on to the adjoining one and then shimmied down the drain pipe to a path between two houses. Behind them was some coarse ground and he vaulted the fence and ran along the edge of the copse of trees, keeping to the shadows. Shortly he came to a junction and turned right keeping his back to the walls. Leaping up again he climbed silently and fluidly to the roof of a detached house and ran soundlessly across the tiles to the peak. He knew the stores here would certainly have bins out the back for disposing of unwanted food that he could forage for. He was about to move along the roof when he looked down and something caught his eye.

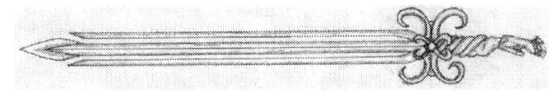

"Oooh sissy dolly," Aiden snapped at Maria nastily.

Maria was scared. She'd gone to the shops to buy some milk for her mother and Aiden was there. She didn't like Aiden. He was older, bigger and bullied her and the other small kids at every chance he got. The shops were only round the corner, she could see the front garden of her house from here. She hoped someone would help her but there was no one around.

Aiden grinned at her, his smile not even remotely reassuring and held out his hand.

"Give it to me and let me look at it."

Maria gripped the doll even tighter and shook her head. She knew that if she gave it to him, even for a second, she'd never see it again or he'd break it.

Aiden moved forward, backing her up against the wall and looked both ways in case any adults were around or that nosey Community Support Officer who occasionally wandered round the estate.

"Let me hold it for a second and I'll let you have it back," he said.

Maria was on the verge of tears and didn't want Aiden to see her crying. "Let me go Aiden," she pleaded. "My mummy will be wondering where I am."

"Best give me the doll then you stupid cow," he said trying to snatch it from her.

Maria bolted and ran and Aiden followed her laughing. "Go on run little cow!" he whooped, easily catching her up in about three steps.

Maria screeched as Aiden tripped her up, pushing her down on the paved slabs outside the shops. She skidded and fell, the milk carton going flying and bursting open.

Aiden reached down and grabbed her doll in his grubby hands. She screamed as he tore it free from her grip and shook it in front of her triumphantly.

"See what happens when you don't do what you're told?!!" he shouted at her.

Maria had skimmed her knees as she fell and she started to cry. Aiden grinned and grabbed the head of her doll and pulled hard.

"No!" Maria screamed at him as the head came free with a pop. Aiden laughed and dropped it on the floor and put his filthy trainer on it, stamping up and down on the plastic body and twisting his foot.

Maria bawled loudly, looking on helplessly as Aiden ruined her toy. The doll was a present from her nana, who had died last year, and it was her favourite. Giving the doll one last twist with his foot Aiden turned around and walked off laughing.

Staggering to her feet Maria looked around and ran wailing into her home, shouting for her mother.

Aiden walked down the alley between Maria's house and the precinct of shops. Whistling a happy tune with his hands in his tracksuit bottoms he failed to notice the cold, furious eyes that watched him silently from a rooftop across the square.

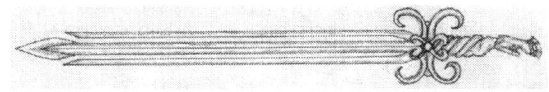

When Aiden got home his mother was in front of the huge plasma screen TV in their lounge. She turned as he came in, her half smoked cigarette clutched in her fingers. "Get yourself some dinner, there's microwave corned beef hash in the freezer."

"Whatever!" Aiden said disinterestedly and slunk off upstairs, leaving his mother in a cloud of smoke watching television.

He went up to his room and opened the door with the sign, "Aiden's Den. Keep Out or be Dead," on it with a black skull and crossbones.

He switched on the TV in his room and turned on his games console. He fell back onto his bed and picked up the control pad while a war game started to load. As the game began he became engrossed in the action, not noticing the squeak on the stairs that meant someone was coming up.

As his door opened he hit "pause" on the pad and cursed loudly. "Mum! I told you to knock when you...." then looked up and his voice trailed off abruptly.

Mordalayn stood glaring at him in the doorway. His rage at what he'd seen the boy do to the little girl was barely controlled as he silently closed the door.

Aiden stammered. "What, wh..who are YOU?"

Mordalayn moved forward and stood towering over him silent and terrifying, his hood thrown back to reveal his face. Aiden gulped, the game controller forgotten in his hands, his eyes flicking over the huge sword on the stranger's back and the figure's cat face, whiskers bristling angrily. Glancing around the room Mordalayn saw the chaos of a young boy's bedroom with old sweet wrappers and magazines on the floor amongst old clothes. He looked around slowly and his eyes finally rested on Aiden.

"The necklace you're wearing. Give it to me," he said flatly.

Aiden's hand went up to the chunky, gold necklace he wore. It was a present from his father for his tenth birthday. "What? No way. Get lost!"

He scrambled to his feet and made for the door but Mordalayn grabbed him by the collar and hauled him back, clamping his gloved hand over Aiden's mouth to stifle the boy's yell of fear. He tugged hard at the necklace which snapped free with a jerk, two of the links clattering to the floor and Aiden yelped.

Casually placing the chain into a pocket of his robe Mordalayn tossed Aiden back against a pile of dirty clothes in the corner of the room. As he reached for the door handle Aiden found his voice.

"Don't take that. Please! My dad gave me that." He started to cry.

Mordalayn paused for a second then turned. He glared at Aiden and his green eyes narrowed. "You laughed at that little girl's tears today," he said slowly. "Remember how this feels." Then he opened the door and closed it behind him. He lithely crept down the stairs and walked past the lounge doorway, Aiden's mother was still engrossed in her TV show and never noticed as Mordalayn made for the open kitchen door and vanished into the back garden.

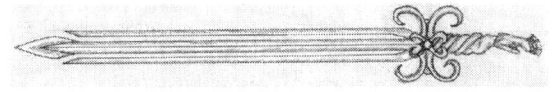

Maria's mother Sylvia kissed her forehead as she slept, heartbroken about what had happened. She'd disinfected Maria's grazed knees and cuddled her while she cried herself to sleep. *"That boy Aiden is utterly vile"* she thought, but the police either couldn't or wouldn't do anything about his behaviour. Each time they either failed to return her calls or simply sent that useless community support officer round to deal with it. The officer had tried to visit Aiden's home to discuss the matter with his mother but she had simply screamed at her to go away. The only advice the police were willing to give now was "tell Maria to keep away from him."

She stroked Maria's hair and pulled a stray lock away from her face, tucking it behind her ear. Sighing, she stood and pulled the door half closed, the landing light casting a subdued beam into the room. Taking one last look at her sleeping daughter she went downstairs into the kitchen.

Making for the rubbish bin Sylvia pulled the white bin liner free and checking there were no holes in the bag she tied the yellow string tightly at the top and opened the kitchen door. She walked the ten or so yards to the large wheelie bins on her driveway and opening the nearest one she tossed the bag inside. Before she could close it a thick voice spoke quietly. "Don't be frightened but please don't turn around."

Sylvia jumped with fear. "What do you want?" she stammered. "I haven't got any money on me."

"I'm not here to hurt you," the voice replied. "I just want to give you something." Sylvia twitched her head but there was only a shadow behind her, the low light on the driveway was not enough to see by. She closed the dustbin lid and rested her hands on it. After a pause the voice continued.

"The boy who hurt your daughter today will never do that again. He is sorry and he wants you to have this to make up for his actions."

Sylvia glanced to her right as a paper bag was placed on the lid of the wheelie bin next to her. The gloved hand withdrew and after a long silence she slowly turned round. The driveway was empty. Breathing out heavily she placed one hand on the wall to steady herself. Then she delicately picked up the bag and walked into the kitchen to see what was inside.

Next morning Maria came downstairs for breakfast bleary eyed and grumpy. She was still upset and was surprised to see her mother making pancakes at the cooker, singing softly to herself. As Maria came in she smiled broadly.

"Hello my little angel" Sylvia said, wiping her hands on a tea towel, hugging Maria then kissing her cheek.

"What's the special occasion mummy?" Maria asked, looking confused and taking her seat at the breakfast table. They only usually had pancakes on special days like Shrove Tuesday or sometimes on a Sunday.

"Well my sweet, today is a special day because your grandmother has bought you a new doll."

Maria thought about this and even though she was only 7 she wasn't stupid. "Mummy, how can nana buy me a doll?"

Sylvia smiled again, barely able to contain herself. "Look in the bag darling," she said, nodding to the white paper packet on the table.

Creasing her face in confusion Maria leaned over the table and took hold of the packet. She placed it in her lap and opened it. Reaching inside she pulled out the contents and gasped.

Inside was her doll, but different. It had golden, curly hair down to its waist. which shone in the morning light from the window.

"Oh mummy, it's beautiful," she exclaimed, holding it up and smiling. Sylvia put her arms around Maria and laughed. "Yes my dear, it's lovely," She saw her daughter's face light up with joy and wondered who had been the one who'd put things right.

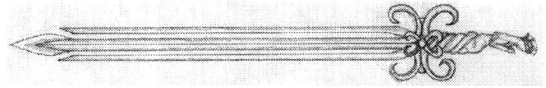

"So, remember when you tease or bully someone else you cause them pain that can usually not be taken back."

Stone, who'd taken the flute, bowed his head in shame and after another long silence Leppard said, "I think we all need to try and get some sleep now. We have an early start in the morning."

The boys began silently arranging their packs as pillows. No one spoke and no one would look directly at Mordalayn in case they met his steel gaze.

Chapter 15

The foliage swept past him as he leapt clear, the leaves clinging briefly to his chest and face as he grunted with the exertion, grabbing the tree branch for leverage and then hauling himself on. Him and his three fellows knew only one of them might make it out but none cared who it was. Their mission was far too important for petty self preservation.

The dogs snarled in the background and cries from the men pursuing them echoed around the vast gardens of the castle estate. They had done what they were sent to do and now at least one of them needed to get back to give that precious information to their leaders.

Kulkrain sprang over the low wall that bordered the sanctuary and sped on. Hereth, Dexan and Javohl were behind him. All four were grimy and exhausted after the gruelling mission but, after days of discomfort and the loss of two of their number they finally had what they wanted.

As they ran across the circular courtyard facing the king's bird sanctuary and pounded through the tall maze of hedges a soldier appeared in their path and raised his crossbow. Before any could react the man triggered the weapon and the bolt caught Dexan in the throat. He flew back and landed lifeless, spread eagled on his back amongst the thousands of tiny black stones that made up the courtyard. Kulkrain reached the man before he could reload and chopped brutally with the side of his hand and then flung him aside. The man went limp and they ran on, none of them sparing a backward glance for their fallen comrade.

They ran to the side gate, the wall surrounding it overgrown with clinging vines and vegetation, the stone work old and ancient. The gate was a portcullis like all entrances and exits in the royal palace and as Kulkrain and Hereth ran through there was a grinding noise. The spiked gate flashed down in a split second, trapping Javohl. Kulkrain and Hereth whirled, their dark skin shining in the moonlight. Breathing heavily Javohl looked back. "Go my brothers. I will hold them as long as I can," he gasped without hesitation.

Kulkrain reached through the gate and grasped Javohl by his forearm. "Strength in the next world brother", he said quietly and Hereth silently reached through and grasped his friend's arm too.

Javohl reached to his belt and drew a long dagger. "GO!" he shouted and turning he ran back the way they'd come, the sounds of dogs and men much closer now.

"COME ON!!!" he shouted loudly as the first soldiers appeared and ran straight at them. Kulkrain and Hereth ran on, not seeing him take down two soldiers before they could even raise their bows. Javohl snarled and drew the sword of one of the dead men at his feet and whirled, taking the head of another man who strayed too close. Then one of the huge dogs leapt at his sword arm and bit down hard. Javohl fell and in seconds it was all over as the soldiers and dogs engulfed him.

Kulkrain and Hereth hurtled on. They heard the distant shouts of someone shouting for the gate to be raised and ran along the path that led to the river. As they passed the eastern keep a shout went up. They ran to the trees and under the shelter Hereth grabbed Kulkrain's arm and whispered.

"You have more strength left than I brother," he gasped. "Go now, I will lead them the other way."

Kulkrain saw the soldiers emerge from another gate on the far side beyond the keep. "Strength in the next world," he whispered and turned and ran. Hereth ran back to the main path and pounded along it. The soldiers shouted and made to follow him.

Kulkrain cut through the trees, his instincts and the moonlight helping him through the thick, twisted ground. The boat was maybe two hundred yards beyond where they were. If he could make it he could be out onto the protected waters in minutes.

He clubbed and fought his way through the branches and finally saw the white rippling of the moon on the water. Without pausing he lurched forward to where the small boat was moored and hacked the rope in two short strokes, jumping into the rocking vessel.

Shouts behind him meant that Hereth's diversion had failed. He frantically heaved the oars into position and pulled hard, trying to get out of crossbow range as fast as he could.

He twisted to see a squad of ten or more soldiers appear howling on the bank. Two or three pointed and some tried to shoot after him but the shots splashed into the water. Not slowing down he continued to haul hard and knew that unless they pulled a miracle he was now clear until the far side of the lake. There he could ditch the boat and move back to land, where they would never find him.

The captain of the guard knew the mission had been a partial success. Of the six spies they'd caught, two had been killed upon discovery, one in the courtyard and another by the dogs at the gate. The final two had nearly made it but one had tried an unsuccessful diversion. He knew also that King James would be looking for someone to blame if even one got away and it would almost certainly be him. He glanced over his shoulder as another soldier; huge and bearded appeared from the trees. The man's shoulder insignia signified he was a marksman.

"Can you make the shot Tobias?" he said indifferently.

"Did you need to ask?" the figure said in a rumbling voice and raised a huge and sleekly designed bow to his shoulder. After interminable seconds he pulled the trigger and the cord twanged. The bolt whistled out across the glimmering, velvet water. After a second there was a thud and the silhouetted figure pulling so urgently on the oars was flung forward, tumbling from the tiny boat and into the water with a splash.

Nodding satisfaction and silently thanking his personal gods, the captain turned to Tobias.

"Good shot," he said nodding his approval.

Tobias grunted and stared out where the empty boat continued to drift away.

"Right! Back inside. There's a mess to clear up. Find out who was on guard duty." He barked to his men and they melted back into the trees, heading towards the castle.

Kulkrain waited until he could no longer see any sign of movement on the shore and then painfully hauled himself back up into the boat and lay flat on his side. The bolt had pierced his left shoulder and gone clean through. When he was sure that no one would be able to see him any more he sat upright and winced as the pain lanced up his side. Stripping his shirt he rolled it up and tied the soaking material around his shoulder, the fabric turning crimson where it touched his wound. When he was certain he had staunched the blood flow as much as he could he slowly pulled on the oars and made for the far side of the lake.

Chapter 16

At dawn the next day the boys woke. Mordalayn had remained awake all night keeping watch and as they silently ate a small breakfast they made no attempt to engage him in conversation. Once everyone had eaten they put out the fire and made their way onwards. The Cherubs was on the other side of the woods and the few boys who had been to the house before were excited, telling the others about the wonderful garden that the owner, Maximo Cherubsayl had cultivated over many years. With talking plants, flowers in every colour you could imagine as well as a little farm of animals. Not to mention the fairies.

They walked on as the huge sun rose in the sky and after a few hours the trees thinned and in the distance they could see a house. "First!!!" Blautin shouted in excitement as he pointed to the building in the distance. It looked like a farm building to Jared and appeared to be a bungalow. A thatched roof of tight weaving adorned the house and to the left was a second building that Jared guessed was used to keep animals.

The boys started talking excitedly and hurried their pace, Mordalayn at the back checking around constantly while Leppard and Challandra were at the front.

"Never been here before, looks pretty good," Bue said to Leppard who smiled.

"As I recall you were not allowed to visit last time due to being confined to the orphanage as a punishment"

Bue shrugged and ignored the comment. "Big house, how many people live there?"

"Just Mr Cherubsayl and his wife. They are old friends of Madame Veer."

As they walked on to the house, people began to notice their arrival. The front door opened and a big man appeared. From behind him the three boys who'd gone ahead squeezed past and ran down the path to the front gate. The man stepped out and Madame Veer appeared beside him.

The other boys started to run and soon they were at the front gate, hugging their friends. As Jared walked up he could see that the formerly petrified Getruhl was now smiling and had lost his shyness. The boy was pointing back to the garden and to the house, talking excitedly.

Leppard and Mordalayn stepped forward to greet Maximo. He looked middle aged and his head was a mop of shoulder length, black hair. Big but not fat with a big black beard he appeared to be somebody who had worked his life in the country and had a big, red, happy face. He looked pleased to see everyone and as the boys ran up to him he squatted down and hugged a few while shaking hands with others and clapping a few on the back.

"Blautin, hello son. Still good with a flute I hear."

"Jethrul, hear you're getting along well these days."

"Stone, you seem to have grown a foot every time I see you."

The boys laughed and were clearly pleased to see Maximo who greeted most by name and made some friendly comment or other then turned to Jared.

"And you must be the young man I have heard so much about," he said kindly and took Jared's hand in his huge one and shook it hard. "Such a pleasure to meet you."

Madame Veer then spoke up. "Boys, your attention for a moment."

They paused in their excitement and she continued. "As you know we are here because of the danger that befell us. Most of you know of Mr Cherubsayl's house and the others have heard stories."

There was a buzz as the boys murmured their agreement.

"You may relax here and enjoy the grounds and the gardens with Mr Cherubsayl's permission BUT you are still under my authority and absolutely no one is to break house rules or leave the grounds for any reason. Is that clear?"

The boys mumbled their understanding and then another woman appeared next to Maximo. She looked about the same age, and was small framed with blonde hair down past her waist, flashed with streaks of silver. She smiled at the boys and said hello.

"Hello Mrs Cherubsayl," they said back and she looked to Maximo.

"I'm sure the boys would love to explore the gardens with you Max," she suggested. "Why don't I take our guests inside and you show them around."

"Good idea!" Maximo beamed. "Who'd like to see the gardens and my lovely animals then?"

There were loud shouts of approval and even Madame Veer smiled. "Good, good. Right, drop your stuff in the hallway then come back."

They did so and assembled in front of him. Mordalayn, Leppard and Challandra moved towards the door. Jared made to follow but Mordalayn said quietly. "No Jared, you go with the boys. Have fun. This meeting is not for you."

Jared looked up confused but saw Mordalayn's expression was friendly and handed the Caracalic his pack and then moved to the other boys. Maximo led them off to the garden, all of them chattering excitedly.

Near to the house was a small garden of tall flowers, like sunflowers nodding in the gentle breeze. As they walked up to them one of the flowers turned its head "Hello young people, such a pleasure to see you," it said in a lilting voice

Jared and the others jumped and one boy squeaked in fear. Maximo chuckled "Now, now. Don't be frightened lads. This is the whimsical sunflower. Why don't you say hello?"

Jared stared at the plant, still not fully comprehending how this world could constantly surprise him. The flower turned slowly, its head passing along all of them. Its mouth was just below the centre of its orange face and it appeared to be smiling. Slowly it extended one of the leaves from its mains stalk like an arm and looked at Jared. "You are not of this world are you?" it said. Its voice was lilting and soft, female and reassuring. The sort of voice you could imagine reading little kids a bedtime story.

"Shake hands Jared," Maximo said kindly.

Jared held out his hand and grasped the large green leaf which tightened slightly as it wrapped around his fingers. "Such a pleasure," the plant crooned. Its voice was ever so soft and Jared felt sleepy just listening to it. The other children gazed at it. Some of them had seen it before but they all still seemed amazed. The plant turned its face to a neighbouring flower and in a whisper said, "Serena, we have visitors. Surely you would wish to say hello."

The other plant raised its dial to look at them and gently shook it from side to side as if waking up. "My, my. Little men, young Blautin you have grown" Serena said. Blautin giggled and stood still as the plant extended one of its leaves to tickle him under the chin. Other plants nearby, maybe ten in all turned to gaze at the visitors and Maximo chuckled at Jared's confused expression.

"Not used to this are you?" he said,

Jared shook his head. The sunflower he had been introduced to turned to him "You must excuse me now young man. It is high noon."

Before Jared could reply the flowers all straightened as tall as they could go and raised themselves up. They were stock still and their dials were turned to the sun, high above in the sky. A soft song, like a birdsong but sweeter and more melodious came from the plants and Jared again thought he would doze off. The plants swayed slightly to the rhythm. "Come," Maximo said "it is the plants' time to pray."

Jared and the others walked away, glancing over their shoulders as the sleepiness lifted. Watching the plants, tall and beautiful in the bright sunlight.

Further down was a small pen with a fluffy green animal in it, about the size of a Labrador puppy. It jumped about excitedly as the boys and Maximo approached it and yipped loudly. As they got closer, Jared could see its face was more or less hidden by the tumbling green locks of fur. Just a small, pink snub nose stuck out from the middle of the pea green curls. It jumped up and down and rubbed against the bars of its wooden cage as the group came near.

"And this," said Maximo, sliding the bolt on the top of the cage, "is Terka." As Maximo raised the hatch the animal launched itself at the hole and cleared it, landing on Jared who grabbed it as it scrabbled around chest level and when he had a firm grip, began lapping his face with a slobbering wet tongue.

"Hmm…likes you," Maximo said amused and a couple of the other boys laughed. The creature had tiny paws that scrabbled for purchase on Jared's arms and after slobbering over his face for a few seconds more it put its head on his chest and began to purr contentedly. To Jared it was like holding a big ball of fluffy cotton wool with a face. He stroked its head and the creature snuggled up against him. Maximo reached over and took the creature by its collar and gently lifted it away. It made no attempt to resist and as Maximo placed it back in its cage it began excitedly yipping at the boys. "I see you make friends easily young Jared," Maximo said with a smile.

"Err…actually, no not usually," Jared replied.

They then rounded another corner and a group of small flying figures buzzed round the corner to meet them. Jared jumped again and saw that he was facing about six or seven little people, about twelve inches in height each with tiny clothes. They had wings on their backs which beat too fast to see. They stopped in front of the group, hovering and looking expectantly at Maximo.

"Ahhh, children and let me introduce my friends the fairies," he said turning to the boys. The fairies flew down to the children and began chattering excitedly.

"Hello young sir, how are we today?" one said to Blautin. Another made a beeline for Bue and hovered next to his left ear.

"Hello there, may I accompany you on your journey round our house young fellow?"

Maximo laughed. "They are very friendly to people and like to help," he said brightly. "Tell me Keran, have Kloee and the others come back yet?"

"No master," one replied looking serious. "I think they are still collecting for you as you asked."

"Good, good," Maximo said nodding. "Well, I'll leave you with my winged friends for a while." He walked back to the house.

"Want to play a game?" a hovering fairy said in a high voice.

Jared looked around, the other fairies were nearby, their faces expectant and wings beating fast.

"Err..sure," he replied. "What do you have in mind?."

"Brilliant!" the fairy said clapping its tiny hands together. "We're going to play Phase."

"Phase, Phase!" the other fairies shouted darting around the shoulders of the children in weaving patterns. Two giving each other a high five and then looping the loop, sparkling dust spilling around them.

"Come on, I'll show you," the fairy said beaming and flew into the back garden.

When the boys got there, there was a fairly large swimming pool with wooden cages either end. Both were big and looked sturdy. The fairy turned to him and buzzed down low.

"My name's Jeejoh," he said conspiratorially and winked at Jared. "I'll be your keeper for this."

Jared glanced over his shoulder and saw the other boys coming up behind them. The fairies were flitting around excitedly amongst them and darting in wild circles and loops.

Jeejoh flew on ahead, down the slope to the pool.

Just then Maximo stuck his head out a window and shouted. "Hey! You are going to play beginner's rules on this I take it?" Jeejoh turned round and flew up to him and Jared saw them have a short conversation before Maximo nodded approvingly and shut the window.

Jeejoh flew back down and Jared. "What was that about?" he asked.

The fairy giggled and pointed to the pool. "If you are good at Phase it can be a bit dangerous. The master just wanted to make sure we were playing a nice game with you all."

The boys reached the pool's nearest edge and another fairy, this one a plump female, addressed them.

"Hello my name's Indira," she said in a high voice. "Now, who knows how to play Phase?"

One or two of the boys raised their hands, Bue amongst them.

"What level?" she said to Bue.

"Twelve," he replied looking proud, to a gasp from one or two of the fairies.

"My, my," she said nodding. "You HAVE had some experience. OK, you can be the captain of your team. Jared can be the other. Now choose."

They quickly selected team mates, Jared not having a clue what was going to happen, then the fairies split off to hover behind the right shoulder of a boy each.

"What do we do?" Jared said to Bue who raised a finger to his lips and grinned his gap toothed smile.

"Now," Indira said clapping her tiny hands for attention. The buzz of conversation died down. "Last man standing, no substitutions. Clear?"

Everyone murmured their understanding, except Jared who was still confused. The boys stripped down to their shorts and jumped in the pool. Bue nudged him and grinned. "Don't worry, it's fun. Trust me," and jumped in with a splash, swimming over to the far side. Jared hesitated but looked up and saw Jeejoh hovering, a friendly smile on his face.

"Don't worry young friend, you'll be with me," he said winking and once Jared was in the water and swimming to his side with his other five team mates Jeejoh addressed them all.

"Right, normal sized missile. No curving and no aiming for the face. Clear?"

Everyone except Jared murmured understanding and then the fairies suddenly glowed with bright orange light and one by one the boys rose in the air, some giggling, one or two kicking their legs and rose to about four metres above the water. Jared felt himself rising and fought the panic in his chest. "It's ok, just relax," Jeejoh said quickly.

Once everyone had arrived at the same height Indira flew up to join them and floated in the middle.

Jared glanced around. There were five people on his team and a short distance away, facing them were Bue's. They were all floating in the air, dripping wet. The fairies at their shoulders glowed brightly, the orange light casting bright patterns on the boys' backs. Jared was intrigued as to what would happen next.

Indira waved her tiny hand and a hexagonal shape of light appeared next to her. It glowed then flashed red and blue, faster and faster. She looked at Bue. "Call."

"Red," he replied quickly and the hexagon blurred so it was impossible to see when it was one colour or the other, then suddenly stopped…on red.

"Get in!" Bue said laughing as the hexagon vanished. Indira glanced down and extended her arms to the pool. A ripple of activity disturbed the surface and a ball of water erupted from it and made its way up. It slowed and paused, hovering near to her and she gently moved her hands in a circular motion one over the other. The water formed a perfect ball and then moved towards Bue who held out his hands and it hesitated just beyond his fingertips.

Jared watched puzzled.

"Your call Bue," Indira said and took a tiny whistle from her blouse pocket and put it between her lips. She blew it and a high, shrill note fluted out over the pool.

Bue looked at Jared and grinned. "Now to show you how it's done" he shouted and drew his arms back over his head then hurled towards Stone, next to Jared. The ball of water followed the motion of his hands and then launched straight. Stone yelled and threw out his arms, but a second too late. The ball of water hit his chest and exploded, soaking him. The light from the fairy died out just after the ball hit and he plummeted downwards. As he reached the surface of the water Jared winced expecting a splash but instead there was a brief flash of bright yellow light and the boy vanished. Jared looked around dumbfounded.

He glanced behind him and saw the large wooden cage had Stone in it, dripping wet and waving madly. "Thanks Sharpeye," he yelled at Bue. "You wait till next time."

Bue grinned back and yelled. "In your dreams;" and Indira blew her whistle.

"One to…what name do you want for your team?" she said looking concerned.

Without hesitation Bue replied. "Sharpeye's Shooters."

Indira nodded approvingly. She turned to Jared's team. "Five points to Sharpeye's Shooters. What do you want your team to be called?"

Jared thought for a minute while the remaining four players on his team threw out suggestions.

"Alegrian Amphibians," one shouted.

"Aquarate," another said.

Jared listened and then smiled. "We're Jared's Javelins"

Bue laughed and one or two others too. Indira turned to Bue again. "Your point, your turn to launch."

For the second time she drew a ball of water from the large pool and sent it spinning to Bue who stopped it by raising his hands and this time passed it over his shoulder to Jethrul.

"Cop this" he said to the other boy. "Give 'em what for."

"You got it," Jethrul responded enthusiastically and raising his arms hurled the ball of water as hard as he could at Jared.

Jared yelled and hurled up his arms. He fully expected to find himself falling, but after a pause opened his eyes and saw that the ball of water was paused, rotating slowly just beyond his fingertips.

"Well caught mate," Bue shouted and turned to his team. "Ok, spread out, don't bunch together. Make it hard for him."

The fairies beat their wings and the boys were pulled along as they relocated to a wider spread. Indira watched and waited until they had stopped moving. "Enough? Good. When you're ready Jared."

Bue's team paused and Jared brought his arms above his head like he'd seen Bue do and launched the ball at Jerean near the front. The boy caught it effortlessly and smiled at Bue as he raised and lowered the ball as if bouncing it.

"Any one you'd like to see fall skipper?", he asked Bue as the fairies on Jared's team spread out and then paused.

"Save Jared for me," he said with a laugh and the lad hurled the ball at Bolla who, with a howl deflected it back with a curving sweep of his arm. The ball shot back at Jerean, who barely had time to register his astonishment. It smacked him full in the face and then he was falling to the water below. Like before, he blinked out of existence just as he reached the water's surface and reappeared in the team's wooden cage a split second later. He was shaking his head and wiggling his finger in his ear.

"Five points to Jared's Javelins," and the fallen boy's fairy flew to the side to watch the game.

Another ball of water was summoned up from the depths of the pool and before Jared could try and reach for it he found himself rising up.

"Five metres, any quitters?" Indira asked and paused for only a split second before she turned to Jared. "Your throw young man."

Jared watched the boys opposite him and trying not to look down he hurled the ball at Bue who simply leaned out the way and the boy behind him caught it. He tossed it sideways to the lad next to him who then threw it as hard as he could back at Jared's team. The lad it was aimed at caught it, revolved the ball rapidly between his hands and then threw it back. It caught Mispyn in the stomach. He pulled a face of annoyance as he fell then burst into light and materialised in the cage.

"Ten, five. Your throw Jared," Indira said flitting between the teams.

As the ball of water appeared Jared tossed it over his head to the boy behind him who caught it, weighed up his targets and then hurled it straight at Blautin next to Bue. The lad caught it easily and threw it up and sideways to the boy on his right who tossed it to his neighbour. After four or five passes the final boy hurled it at Jared who frantically ducked and the ball smacked into Getruhl behind him. The team were down to three.

Once again the players rose another metre. "Six metres, any quitters? No? Good," Indira remarked and some of the boys looked down and began to get nervous. The height was looking more and more fearsome.

Bue had the ball in one hand. He grinned as he looked at Jared. "You ready?"

Mordalayn, Madame Veer and the other adults sat or stood in Maximo's large kitchen.

"Whoever attacked you was trained well," Maximo said as he made tea from an enormous, black kettle. The smell was sweet and little green herbs floated as he poured in the hot water.

"They were going to kill anyone who got in their way," Challandra said solemnly. "The Vagthunder stopped them."

Maximo started handing out mugs. Mordalayn shook his head at the one offered to him.

"What's so special about this boy?" Maximo asked curiously.

"It is best you do not know," Mordalayn replied curtly.

Maximo looked puzzled. "Who were the men that attacked you?"

Leppard spoke up. "They had no markings that I could identify. Most likely hired mercenaries from Flintor. Two got away, the rest were caught."

"They knew the boy was with us," Madame Veer said. "As he had only arrived hours before we can assume there is a traitor in the higher reaches of Alegria's council."

"Until Our Lady returns to us, he is to be kept out of harm's way," Mordalayn said.

"He can stay here as long as you need him to," Maximo replied. "My house has protection, the plants and flowers are able to detect and subdue intruders."

"I appreciate your generosity Maximo," Mordalayn said. "Let us just say that this boy must be protected at all costs."

They were down to two players each at seven metres and Jared's stomach was doing flips and somersaults. He dodged the ball aimed at him and Bolla caught it then shouted "CATCH!" Jared fumbled it and the ball fell, spreading out and pattering as water droplets into the pool below.

Indira blew her whistle. "Free shot to Sharpshooters."

A blob of water rose up and Bue reached down to grab it. He grinned wickedly at Jared. "Time to go mate," he said and hurled the ball at him. Jared tried to throw up his arms but the water hit him full on and he felt himself plunging down. He opened his mouth to scream but suddenly the world flashed white and he was in the team cage with the others.

"Hey, hey! Told you you'd be mine," Bue said looking down at him and laughing. As the ball rose up he squared up to the one remaining boy on Jared's team. "Your time too Makeo," and span the ball at the lad.

The lad contemptuously caught it and then hurled it back almost too quick to see. Bue caught it at chest level and plunged down, blinking out and then reappearing in his cage.

"In YOUR dreams Sharpeye," he shouted and prepared to take on the last lad facing him.

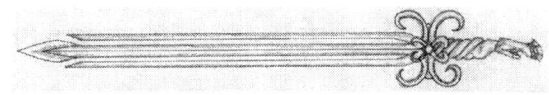

When the game was finally over the boys made their way smiling and breathing heavily to the house, still dripping wet and carrying their clothes.

"Fun isn't it?" Bue said to Jared, clapping him on the back.

Jared smiled. "Yeah, that was a lot of fun. Can we do it again?"

Makeo interrupted in a loud whisper. "Wanna play when it's dark? We can go out after midnight and have a go if you want."

A few boys giggled. Maximo appeared on the doorstep of the house and smiled as they came back. "Are we having fun boys?" he asked in his deep, jolly voice.

"Great," one or two of the lads replied.

"Good, good," he said, clapping his hands and rubbing them briskly. "Let's get you all dried off and then we can get you something to eat."

He made to walk back into the house but then turned and stared at Makeo. "You will NOT be sneaking out to play a game or two tonight. Phase is dangerous in the dark. Do I make myself clear?"

Makeo blushed. "Yes, sorry."

Maximo nodded and went back inside, the soaking wet boys following him.

They headed back to the house. Passing more flowers and a group of what looked like chickens but with exotic rainbow colours on their feathers. They were happily pecking away at seeds on the ground.

"Lunch might be in order I think," Maximo said to the boys. There were murmurs of approval to this as they looked towards the open front door of the large house. Smoke was already coming from the chimneys and some of the boys could feel their stomachs rumbling in anticipation of food.

Chapter 17

The four fairies were arguing. Again. Kloee, Muttley, Mary and Garf were unable to be together without squabbling it seemed. While they said they were best friends they quarrelled all the time.

Sometimes they argued about what colour the sky should be. Other times they argued about how much sugar you should put on porridge. They had even been known to argue about whether you should sleep with your eyes closed.

Today they were arguing about which path to take to get to the clycinth flowers that their master used to make his famously tasty palopud pudding. Kloee had found a path that she said led to a big crop but Muttley argued that they should go another way where there were more. Mary had sided with Kloee and Garf had sided with Muttley.

"Don't be silly!" Kloee said, hovering in front of Muttley, her little wings beating fast as she pursed her lips and placed her hands on her hips.

"I'm not being silly," Muttley replied, equally as obstinate, his pointy ears prickling with indignation. "This way is obviously better, there has been more rain this side of the wood so there will almost certainly be more flowers." He pointed to the ground around him.

Kloee snorted and shook her head, sparkling dust flying out and gently falling to the ground. "Muttley you are so....oooh!" she stamped her foot in mid air and turned to the other two. "Tell him!"

Mary and Garf were too engrossed in their own conversation about who of the other two was right to hear her and continued loudly shouting at each other. Silver and gold specks flying in a storm as they gestured their arms about wildly.

Kloee shrugged and turned back to Muttley. She shifted her tiny leather pack over her shoulder.

"Well I'm going this way. You can go your own silly way!" she said with finality and flew off in the direction she had intended, her wings beating an angry buzz.

"Master said we should stay together!" Muttley shouted after her, then turned to Garf and Mary, who had stopped arguing about who was right and had started to argue about if they should follow Kloee.

"Guys, guys!" Muttley said, holding up his small hands and getting their attention. "I'm going the way I know is best. If you want to come with me you can."

"But we can't leave Kloee on her own. Master said not to," Garf pleaded, his little face creasing in concern.

"When she can't find anything she'll come back," Muttley replied and flew off down the path to the right of where Kloee had gone moments earlier.

"I think we should go after her," Garf said to Mary.

Mary glared at him. "WHAT about Muttley? We can't leave him either!"

"Not my fault, don't yell at me," Garf snapped.

And they started arguing once more.

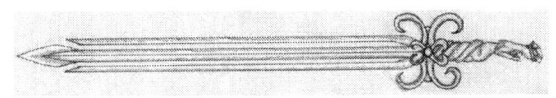

Kloee was cross. She found the flowers like she had said she would. She was pulling them free from the earth, putting the white and red-spotted petals into her little bag and pushing them down to make certain they wouldn't shake loose when she flew home. *The other three were stupid,* she thought. They could clearly see she was right but they were just being stubborn to upset her. Well, she'd show them. When she came home with a big collection of petals for their favourite dessert, the master would be really pleased with her. She'd get a bigger helping than anyone else. Then the others would be sorry they'd argued.

She tugged the petals free and stuffed them down into the leather pouch. These parts of the woods were safe from predators but sometimes you got wolves or other animals coming down if they hunted. No one could catch a fairy in flight and Kloee knew that provided she kept her wits about her and her ears open, then no one could sneak up.

Still cross at the silly behaviour of her three companions she tugged on a particularly stubborn plant which was rooted very firmly. She took a good grip around the stalk with both of her tiny hands and, straining with the effort, her wings beating madly, she tugged and heaved. Suddenly the plant tore free. Not expecting the sudden release she shrieked in shock and flew back, somersaulting into the air. Clearing the high grass clump behind her she span, sparkling fairy dust scattering around her crazily. Managing to regain some self control she calmed her erratic flight pattern and hovered in the air, holding the plant in front of her. The green stalk was covered in clods of earth.

"Silly plant," she tutted and was about to start plucking the petals free when the grass behind her moved and a man's face appeared. Dirty, bloody and bare chested, his shoulder bound with a grimy cloth he staggered towards her and fell, his hand reaching out, imploring for help. Kloee shrieked in fright as the man collapsed on top of her, bringing them both crashing to the ground.

Kulkrain had made it to the shore in his boat and had waited till dawn to start his journey on foot. As the last one alive he knew he had to deliver his message but also knew that the wound in his shoulder was probably fatal. His training allowed him to shut out the pain but no training could give back what had been taken. He grew ever weaker as he fought his way on through the dense woodland. He'd managed to staunch the blood from the wound which, luckily, was clean. Then he'd washed it with fresh water and bound it as tightly as he could. His exhaustion was now like a fog before him and only his willpower kept him moving. *"A soldier of Alegria never gives up in the name of keeping the light,"* he repeated to himself over and over, silently, like a mantra as he ploughed on. He had only his knife now and knew that if he met a predator he would not be able to defend himself.

He climbed a short rise in the earth and grasped a protruding tree root to haul himself up. As he made the top of the climb his foot slipped and he fell backwards, landing heavily. Moaning in pain as the wound reopened in his shoulder, he felt the blood seep through his clumsy bandage. The curtain of exhaustion began to descend upon him and he shook his head to clear it. "For Alegria," he said through gritted teeth. Summoning the last of his energy he struggled upright. Taking a deep breath he hauled himself up the small rise and this time made it to the top. As he moved forward, stars began swirling before his eyes and he cursed his body for proving so useless at a time when he needed it most. As he tottered forward he saw beyond a large clump of tall grass a tiny figure suddenly lurch up into the air. Gold and silver particles danced around as it squeaked and bobbed about in front of him. As his weakened mind and body started to close down he lurched towards it and raised his hand, imploring for help. Then there was darkness.

Kloee's muffled squeaks came from under Kulkrain's body as she struggled to free herself. At twelve inches tall she was lucky he hadn't crushed her as he fell. Fortunately he hadn't landed completely on top of her. After much grunting and shoving she finally managed to get her head free and hauled herself out, dragging her satchel behind her. The petals were all crushed and she indignantly hovered above the prostrate form, wings beating furiously, as she dusted herself off. She glared at the silent form beneath her.

"What did you want to do that for?" she shouted indignantly. "That was a silly thing to do."

Kloee was cross. Not only had she been very frightened, she'd also been trapped and was dirty. Not to mention her prize petals being ruined by this careless person.

"Well?" she said angrily. "Haven't you got anything to say for yourself?" brushing some specks of dirt from her arms and out of her blonde hair.

Kulkrain lay there unconscious and as Kloee stared at him she saw the blood seeping through the torn bandage on his shoulder. Her anger vanished in an instant as she realised something was seriously wrong. "Oh…my," she stammered and flew down to his head. "I'm sorry I shouted at you, I really am. Are you hurt?"

Kulkrain moaned quietly but didn't stir or open his eyes. He was laying facing away from her and Kloee lowered herself to the earth and looked frantically at his face. His skin was pale and he was clearly in need of urgent care. "I'm so sorry," she said again and reached for the tiny water bottle on her belt. Uncorking it she poured a little bit into his lips. Kulkrain murmured, but still did not move.

Replacing the bottle Kloee decided what she must do. Flying off to the place she'd left the others, she knew they had to get help.

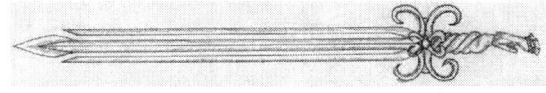

Kloee came across Garf and Mary still squabbling. She flew up to them as they argued, fairy dust littering the floor and the air around them as they shouted and waved their arms around.

"Garf, Mary, a people's hurt!" Kloee shouted as she hovered next to them. They ignored her and carried on arguing over who they should have followed. "HEY!!!" she shouted again and they both stopped and glared at her as she stood there with her hands on her hips.

"Oh, very stroppy aren't we!" Mary said and was about to continue when Kloee shouted.

"There's a people hurt back there, he needs our help!"

Mary and Garf looked at each other and back at Kloee. Their expressions instantly changed and Garf said, "I'll fetch Muttley" and flew off up the path. Within a minute he was there too and, their animosity forgotten they sped to where Kulkrain was lying.

"Poor people," Kloee said, her voice full of concern. "We need to get him to master." She hovered over Kulkrain's injured shoulder and then looked at the others.

Muttley nodded. "Ok, let's do this the way we were told ok?"

Without any discussion they each moved to hover above a foot or a shoulder and, looking at one another Kloee counted to three and then they all glowed bright orange. Kulkrain lifted off the floor, rising slowly, his eyelids fluttering in his deathly white face, his arms lolling to the side. Then, with as much care as they could give, they gently flew home with Kulkrain between them.

Chapter 18

As Maximo and the boys approached the front door he turned to them.

"So I think we should get you all dried off and there's some lovely food waiting for you....," he continued when suddenly there was a high pitched voice that shouted:

"Master!"

Maximo turned quickly to the sound and Jared was astonished to see four small fairies with light glowing around them like oversize fireflies, flying around a man who was shirtless and bloody. He appeared to be unconscious and Maximo ran, surprisingly quickly for someone his size, to intercept them.

The fairies gently placed the man down on the floor on his back and the orange lights around them gently faded. "What happened?" Maximo said, feeling for a pulse on the man's neck. Jared and the boys crowded round.

"Found a people in the woods master!" Kloee replied. "He fell on me when I was collecting for you."

Jared remembered the first aid course he'd been told about when he went rafting with his father the summer before. He looked at Maximo. "Roll him on his side, the opposite one to his bad shoulder. He could choke on his own tongue."

Maximo looked at him confused for a moment but then moved forward and after some twisting and gentle pulling he rolled Kulkrain onto his side. Mordalayn emerged from the rear door of the house and strode quickly to where they were gathered. "Move aside," he said in a low but clear voice and without hesitation a path was cleared for him. He looked at

Kulkrain and saw the tattoo on his right arm. "Alegrian brotherhood," he noted, crouching to check the wound on the shoulder. "He's badly hurt; we need to get him inside."

Maximo turned to Kloee. "If you four would be so kind as to take this poor man into the house, to my bedroom and lay him down. We will deal with his wounds."

"Of course master!" Kloee said eagerly and once again her and the other three hovered over Kulkrain and drew him up in the air, the orange glows from their bodies shining brightly as they took him into the house. Mordalayn cleared a path of open doors and when they reached Maximo's room they laid him gently on the bed. Maximo's wife came running into the room and Maximo removed the grimy shirt from Kulkrain's shoulder. The wound was messy. He turned to his wife; "get me hot water and bandages and ointment for this. He appears to have lost a lot of blood." She scurried from the room. Maximo then turned to the others. "Everyone else please wait outside," and pointed to the door. Jared and the boys left and the fairies flittered silently out the room. Maximo closed the door, leaving him and Mordalayn alone with the injured man.

Outside Kloee turned to Jared. "You're very clever young master" she said blushing. "I didn't know about putting the poor man on his side."

Bue looked at Kloee hovering above Jared and smiled. "Oh, think she likes you mate, when a fairy finds a human it likes, you can't get rid of them."

Kloee frowned at Bue and hovered next to Jared looking at him adoringly. "Young master's lovely," she purred as they moved down the corridor.

Chapter 19

Makeo held his finger to his lips and gestured for the others to follow. Silently they crept out into the corridor and made their way to the back door that led to the garden. Stifling giggles, the smaller boys gripped towels and held their shoes in their hands. The light from the fairies lit the way, giving them just enough illumination to see by. The fairies grinned broadly. Being mischievous was part of their nature. As they reached the back door Makeo turned and was about to speak when a harsh voice boomed. "AND WHERE EXACTLY DO YOU THINK YOU'RE GOING?"

Makeo jumped and Getruhl yelled in fright. Kloee squeaked in terror and flew behind Jared's shoulder, sparkling dust flying up in the air in her wake. She timidly peeked out behind his neck at the owner of the voice.

Maximo had appeared from nowhere and was stood in front of the doorway, the lamp light casting deep shadows on his thick face. He stood with his hands on his hips, his fists balled. He glared at Makeo, then at the others. He was still dressed in his day clothes and had his shirt open and his waistcoat unbuttoned. Makeo silently cursed himself for not waiting till later when Maximo would have been asleep before he'd excitedly arranged this midnight pool trip.

"I said WHERE do you think you're going?" Maximo shouted, his voice sterner still.

"We just wanted to…"

"Well you know what 'want' did, don't you?" Maximo snapped at him.

The other fairies were hovering over their charges. Jared and Bue looked sheepish. For all Bue's cheeky behaviour, he knew this was wrong.

"I gave you AND your Madame gave you, strict rules about your conduct in my house and you act like this?" Maximo said, rounding on Jared and Bue.

Makeo said quickly. "It wasn't their fault Master Cherubsayl. It was my idea."

Maximo thought for a moment and looked at each one of them. Kloee and one or two of the other fairies were still scared and peeped timidly out over the boys' shoulders, tiny auras winking in the light.

Maximo finally relaxed. "There are rules in this house for a reason. I do not impose them just to make you unhappy. Do you understand that?"

Makeo looked at the floor, his cheeks burning with embarrassment.

The hovering fairies also bowed their heads and Jared felt awkward. He glanced over at Bue who shrugged.

Maximo's face softened and he turned to Makeo. "You are a good boy Makeo but you need to learn. The pool is dangerous at night."

Makeo nodded, still looking at the floor. "I didn't mean any harm Master," he said, tears welling in his eyes.

Maximo placed a reassuring hand on his arm and gestured back down the corridor and smiled. "Come. Let's go to the kitchen. I will make some hot chud and tell you a tale."

In the kitchen they sat round the large oak table while Maximo stirred the a thick, light brown liquid into mugs and handed them out. The fairies had gone, back to their own quarters and once everyone had a cup in front of them they began to drink. It was hot and reminded Jared of toffee fudge.

Then Maximo told them a story. The story of someone who had only meant well.

"Many years ago in Alegria there was a family who took over a big house when a rich aunt died and left it to them. She loved her family and they loved her and the house was so big and so full of things that it took weeks to get everything sorted.

The attic of this house was enormous. Full of exciting things and the children of the family loved to go up there and see what treats and surprises and treasures they could find in boxes, sometimes dusty, sometimes old, sometimes broken but always captivating and interesting. Their curiosity knew no limits.

One day they were clearing the attic when the youngest sister found a statue of a little boy. It was elegantly carved and made of a beautiful creamy coloured marble. The boy had his eyes closed and appeared to be at peace, his hands clasped in front of him. The statue was small, maybe four feet tall but heavy. They thought it was very lovely and their father got the servants to bring it downstairs and put it in the girl's room. She had it placed near her window and the next morning when she woke up she found the statue had come to life. The sunlight through her window had warmed it and it was a little boy who said his name was Nakal. She ran and told her father and family and they welcomed the smiling, magical, happy boy. He said he'd been asleep in their attic for over 50 years and was so pleased to see them.

At first hesitant of this magical imp, the family soon warmed to his friendly nature and his constant joyful energy. He just wanted to be friends and all day he was with one or more of the children playing games and if they went out he went with them, laughing and singing the whole time.

Soon it got around that Nakal was living with them and more and more people wanted to meet him. He was a creature of joy. He lived only to be happy and to make others happy. Wherever he went he made children smile and the joy he brought was felt by all.

One day the children went with their family to the lake and as Nakal was popular a lot of other children came along to be with him.

They played games on the shore, they swam, they had food and then Nakal was so happy that he had made so many wonderful friends after so long sleeping, that he started to sing. He sang on the shore, his arms raised and thanked life for being so good to him. As he sang the lake responded by making waves, sending him the message that it too loved him.

Unfortunately Nakal didn't know when to stop and as he sang the waves got bigger and the water got rougher and the children further out were frightened. Those nearer to shore scrambled back and those near to Nakal pleaded with him to stop.

He couldn't hear them though, he was so caught up in his own happiness that he sang. His eyes were closed and the song while beautiful, caused a storm that threatened to drown some of the children.

Finally he stopped and looked around dreamily and only then did he see the fear and terror he'd caused. One boy was pulled out from the water unconscious and had to be revived.

Shivering and scared the frightened children left, their normally friendly faces looking at Nakal with distrust and fear for the first time.

Nakal was confused and couldn't understand why people hated him when he'd only been singing to show how much he loved them all.

The boy's father approached him and shouted angrily that he must never EVER do such a thing again and Nakal cried, not understanding what he'd done to make everyone so angry.

When he finally came home, his eyes were red from crying. The oldest brother, who knew in his heart that Nakal was not evil, approached him and took him for a walk. His anger gone, he looked kindly on Nakal and they sat in the garden and he said.

"Do you know you could have killed that boy today?"

Nakal sobbed and the brother put his arm around his tiny shoulders.

"I am so sorry," he wept "I never meant to hurt anyone. I only wanted you to love me."

The brother hugged him and said, "I know that. We still love you Nakal but what you did today was foolish. No one thinks you did it to be horrible but it was a silly thing to do."

Nakal looked up at him and smiled. "Thank you," he said and wiped his eyes with the back of his small hand.

"Come and see my sister," the brother said brightly. "She will be pleased to know you're back."

"Could you bring her out here to me?" Nakal asked. "I don't wish her to see that I have been crying."

The brother wiped Nakal's cheeks with his hand and smiled. "Sure," he replied. "I'll go and get her."

"Thank you," Nakal said quietly and as he watched the brother go into the house, he closed his eyes and clasped his hands.

When the brother returned a short time later with his sister, Nakal was a statue once more. His face looked peaceful and he was the same way they had found him.

They both cried for the poor creature, who had wanted only to be loved and they returned him to the attic, hoping that one day he would come back."

Maximo looked around the table at the boys. There was silence and Bue stared at him, his chud drink unfinished and cold.

Maximo smiled and looked at Makeo. "Whatever love you have in your heart. Don't be so blind as to think that your actions from that love will only be loving."

He walked over to Makeo. "Do you understand?" he asked kindly.

Makeo smiled. "Thank you Master," he said and Maximo laughed and ruffled his hair.

"Now, off to bed with all of you. We have another big day tomorrow."

Chapter 20

Kulkrain awoke. The fire in his shoulder was gone and he felt the tightness of bandaging around it. He realised he was in a large bed and as he tried to sit up the dizziness hit him like a hammer and his head fell back on the pillow.

"Just rest, you are hurt," a deep voice said from the darkness.

Kulkrain turned his head and as his eyes adjusted to the gloom he saw a figure in a chair near the window.

"Takoba Mordalayn," he murmured. "Thank the sun I found you."

Mordalayn stood up and walked to the bed, taking a jug of water from the cabinet and pouring a mug for the injured man. Kulkrain tried to raise his hand to take it but the Caracalic shook his head. "Relax, you are lucky to be alive and have lost a lot of blood." He placed the mug to Kulkrain's lips and tilted gently. After he'd drained the contents he lay back.

"Thank you."

Mordalayn nodded and placed the mug back on the cabinet then took his chair and moved it to the side of the bed. "What happened?"

Kulkrain paused before replying. "There were six of us, we were sent to infiltrate Anghofio castle. After your report of the attempt on the queen the council realised that they knew more than we ever believed." He paused to cough slightly.

"Take your time, don't rush," Mordalayn said, knowing that he needed to know whatever secrets this man carried with him, but that he had also come within a hair's breadth of dying.

After a few seconds Kulkrain winced and continued. "We made it and lay low for two days. Yesterday we finally found what they knew. It...it is devastating. I was not aware of the full extent of the Emerald Queen's true origins."

"You were never meant to know," Mordalayn replied. "What you don't have cannot hurt you or be taken from you."

Kulkrain managed to smile weakly and then said "Takoba, this news is shattering. My comrades are dead. Only I made it through."

"What are they planning?"

And Kulkrain told him.

When he'd finished Mordalayn paused for a moment and then stood. "I have been by your side since they found you. Your loyalty will not go unrewarded Kulkrain, you have my word. Sleep now."

As he went to leave Kulkrain spoke. "What will happen now? Do we have the ability to stop this?"

Mordalayn turned and looked at him then said "I don't know my friend. Alegria has become complacent. We never thought anything as terrible as this could ever happen."

Stepping outside he saw the anxious faces of Maximo and his wife, Leppard, Madame Veer and Challandra. He closed the door and turned to them.

"Anghofio are now more than a potential threat," he said, iron faced. "I need to leave now and Jared needs to come with me."

Madame Veer looked concerned. "What did he tell you?"

"That is something I cannot say," he replied, "But the news means we cannot wait."

Mordalayn turned to Maximo. "Do you have enough power to Shimmer us?"

Maximo beamed and replied. "Yes of course. We rarely use it but we have enough for you."

"We leave now, fetch the boy," Mordalayn said and Challandra moved off down the corridor.

She returned with Jared and nearly all the other boys, excited by what was happening and wanting to know what was going on. Bue was particularly keen and it took Madame Veer shouting loudly to quiet the noisy chatter in the cramped corridor.

"Jared and Takoba Mordalayn are leaving now. This is urgent and will not be discussed," she said, her voice and stare as tight as the bun her hair was in. "You will all remain here until such a time as I deem it safe for us to leave. Is that clear?"

"Can I come too? Jared's my friend. I can protect him," Bue protested, looking hurt.

"No Bue," Madame Veer replied tight lipped. "You stay here and set an example to the other boys."

There were murmurs of understanding and Mordalayn looked at Jared. "We leave now."

Maximo led them down the corridor and opened a door at the end. Behind it was a flight of steps that led down, winding to the left. Jared clutched his small pack and walked down nervously. The Shimmer was like at the orphanage, a small concave dish in the centre of the room. Maximo held his flaming torch up and turned to them. "When I tell you, step into the centre and do not step clear until you arrive."

Jared stepped to the edge of the dish, with Mordalayn at his side. Maximo inserted an orange crystal into the mechanism like

Madame Veer had done before. It shone brightly as it locked into place. Jared nervously looked around. Mordalayn stepped forward first and again Jared was reminded of seeing ripples in a pond. Around the huge cat man they appeared and he faded away and vanished. Maximo looked at Jared. "It's alright my boy. Just walk on." Jared hesitated and finally plucked up the courage. Just as he was about to step forward there was the sound of feet on the stairs. As he and Maximo turned, Bue emerged holding his pack and crossbow with Leppard chasing him,.

"You're not going without me," Bue shouted and ran forward, grabbing Jared's hand and pulling him into the centre. As Leppard tried to pull Bue back he tripped and fell into the dish. Before Maximo could react they all rippled and faded away.

The dish was empty. The room silent. Maximo removed the now clear crystal from the mechanism and sighed deeply. There were tears in his eyes as he turned and hurled the crystal against the wall where it shattered. He recovered after a moment and said quietly to himself. "May the gods forgive me for what I have done."

Chapter 21

Jared woke up. His arms hurt, something hard was digging into them. He shook his head and tried to clear the fog that held him. Last thing he remembered was being at the Cherubs and stepping into the Shimmer. Now he was in a dark room and he felt scared and disoriented. As his eyes adjusted to the gloom he squinted up and saw that his wrists were tied with some kind of metal bracelet with chains vanishing into the darkness above. He looked around in the dim light and saw Bue on his right. The boy was stirring, groaning and shaking his head groggily. Jared looked to his other side and saw Leppard restrained too. Jared looked around frantically and tried to see over his shoulder to check if anyone was behind him, but couldn't turn in the painful position he was in. Bue shook his head and looked at Jared. "What the...?" he exclaimed and pulled in annoyance at the chains holding him. "Where are we?" The links held tightly and he began to thrash louder, squirming against the bindings.

Leppard snapped back at him. "Be quiet! We are prisoners," and Bue stopped struggling. Jared looked around and saw that they were standing on some kind of huge, round, engraved floor. The rounded area finished some way ahead of them and the poor light there was in the room was coming from a doorway that looked to be about twenty metres away.

Jared groaned and his head jerked up as he realised he was trapped. He struggled briefly with his restraints before glancing at Leppard. "Is everyone alright?" he asked, straining to look around.

"We are prisoners in Anghofio," Leppard said quietly. "I never thought they'd be so bold as to openly declare war on Alegria like this."

"H..., how do you know where we are?" Jared asked, frightened and bewildered.

Leppard stared straight ahead and answered "The Shimmer was rigged. Only King James would need to do this. Ergo, we are in his kingdom."

All three were now wide awake and their eyes adjusted to the murkiness in the room. There was no telling how big it was as the darkness above them was absolute and no one could turn around. The doorway gave some semblance of reassurance that they were in fact trapped within a normal place.

"How did they get us?" Bue said, still struggling against his bonds.

"The jump was rigged. When we Shimmered we came here where they were waiting, simple as that. That we are still alive proves that they want to talk to us. Otherwise none of us would still be breathing."

"Why us, we don't know anything?" Bue said, the fear in his voice showing.

"We have all been with Jared, it is him they want and need but they are clearly taking no chances." Leppard informed them.

The door ahead of them suddenly opened with a loud grind and bright light flooded into the room. They all winced and squinted at the glare as three figures emerged from the yellow light that bathed the room and walked towards them. As their eyes adjusted Leppard whispered loudly "James!"

As Jared's vision finally adjusted he saw that there were two guards escorting another man. They were standing in front of them, where the normal floor met the round area he and his friends were imprisoned upon. The other man was thin and tall with a black shirt and silver clasps on the sleeves. He had cropped, black hair and a long, slanting scar that ran from his left cheek to his forehead. His face was split by a big smile, but it was far from friendly. His eyes were black, like a crocodile's. Cold and unfeeling.

"That's King James or "your Majesty" to you, let's not forget our manners shall we," the man replied to Leppard. "My, my what a mess you've got yourself into!" he exclaimed with mock concern. "One moment playing with the fairies, the next caught like a rabbit in a snare."

He looked at Bue and Leppard. He stared at Jared. "You must be the young man we've spent so much time looking for. A pleasure to meet you dear boy." He smiled again and Jared squirmed under the malevolent gaze.

"What do you want?" Bue snapped loudly.

"Dear oh dear" the king tutted theatrically. "What I want, you rude little boy, is something you cannot give me."

"To the hells with you!" Bue snapped and spat at him. The king pulled a face of disgust.

"Charming little orphan," he mused then looked at Jared again. "Now then…Jared isn't it? These people around you. Would you consider them friends?"

Jared looked around frantically but could find nothing to help him.

"Well?" James asked again.

223

"Yes...they are my friends. Please let them go. If it's me you want I'll help you."

The king glanced at his accompanying guards. "Such a good lad eh? Willing to save his friends," he said in a jolly tone.

The guards laughed nervously.

King James nodded to one and the man grabbed a lever on a panel next to him and pulled. The floor they were on suddenly began to grind and move. With a grating crunch the circular platform started to retract, triangular sections appearing with their points in the centre, where before it had looked like solid stone. The pieces slowly moved back and the three prisoners then sagged painfully where the floor had been, their feet treading into nothing. Bue yelled in pain as did Jared as the iron bracelets on their wrists dug into their skin. King James waited until the stones had fully retracted and then stepped forward. The guard threw a coin from his pocket into the yawning abyss. No one heard it land.

The king then raised the large object he was carrying. It was big and had a velvet cloth over it. He pulled the cloth free and it revealed a glass cage, an oval dome like a bird cage with a handle on the top and a wooden base. Inside was Kloee, looking extremely annoyed.

"I take it this is a friend of yours too?" King James asked Jared. "We found her hiding in your pack when we caught you. Didn't we little one?"

Kloee glared up at him and her wings beat furiously as she pounded on the glass with her tiny fists. James chuckled at her futile attempts to break free and then turned back to the three prisoners.

"You are now standing above a drop that no one's ever measured…mainly because it's too deep to do so," the king said in an offhand tone. He looked at Jared again and his tone changed to one of menace. "Now Jared… you will answer everything I say or I will drop your friends one at a time into that hole. Do you understand?"

Jared nodded, ignoring the pain in his wrists and straining to look down. There was only blackness beneath his feet.

Bue glared at the king but said nothing. Leppard gritted his teeth while trying to ignore the biting pain in his hands.

"Let's begin shall we" the King said, his jovial tone returning. "I want you to tell me everything about the Emerald Queen that you know. If you lie to me I will know and one of your friends will die each time you do so. If you leave something out I will know. Do you understand?"

Jared gulped, petrified.

"First of all, where is she now?"

"I don't know," Jared stammered and then continued quickly. "After that monster tried to kill her at the hospital they moved her but I don't know where."

The king smiled, clearly believing him. "Where is she likely to be?"

"I don't know where another hospital is like that. They're everywhere. She's probably guarded now anyway."

The king laughed at that and waved his hand dismissively. "Let me worry about that Jared. Why have our oracles been unable to see her since our first attempt?"

"Again I don't know," Jared replied almost in tears, knowing that his answers were crucial to keeping his friends alive.

"Mordalayn poured something on her when he stopped the monster."

King James glanced from Jared to the guards. "A masking spell. Very impressive." He continued. "What is the problem with her?"

"She's in a coma. She was in a car crash about three months ago." The king looked blank. "She was hurt and fell asleep and she can't wake up."

The king looked thoughtful. "So this is why Alegria didn't simply elect a new ruler," he said, more to himself than anyone else. He chuckled again. "Who would have thought it. For all Alegria's plans and magic they never considered their monarch could become trapped in limbo."

"One more question Jared," the king said. "Is she likely to wake up?"

"Again I don't know," Jared replied desperately. "She's been hurt for a long time. Maybe."

"Thank you Jared, you've been most helpful." He turned to one of the guards. "Tell them to signal our men in Alegria." The guard bowed and ran to the door. The king paused for a moment and turned to leave. Then, as if remembering something he turned to Bue. "Oh and I don't like being spat on by fatherless brats," he glared at the boy and then turned to the other guard. "Drop him."

Kloee gasped and silently shrieked "No!" behind the glass. Bue thrashed frantically against his chains and Jared's heart leapt into his mouth. The guard grinned cruelly and reached for one of the mechanical levers at his side.

"Wait!"

226

The voice carried not just pleading but also a tone of command. The guard hesitated and looked at King James who was staring at Leppard.

The old bow master cleared his throat. "This boy is young. He has his life ahead of him. If you have to kill someone, please…take me."

King James looked at Leppard with surprise and a little admiration. He paused then smiled kindly. "Courage and self sacrifice, two qualities to admire in a man." He shook his head and clapped his hands. "I applaud your gesture. Very well." He turned to the guard. "Drop him instead."

Bue screamed, "NO!" as the guard pulled the lever.

The chains holding Leppard detached from the bracelets.

He fell. Silently.

Chapter 22

"I'LL KILL YOU, I SWEAR ON MY MOTHER I'LL KILL YOU!" Bue screamed at King James, tears streaming down his face.

"Yes, yes. Very dramatic," the king said irritably and turned to Jared. "I think you can see now that I mean what I say. I will return in one hour. Use that period to think of everything you can about your time over here." He turned and walked away holding Kloee in her glass prison and the guard followed him.

Jared stared and then nodded his head slowly, utterly terrified.

"I'LL KILL YOU!!!" Bue screamed after King James, his voice cracking as he stared down into the abyss below them.

Jared was too scared and bewildered to feel anything. The king had, with not even a trace of anger, murdered Leppard. The old tutor had bravely given his life for Bue's but the king hadn't even seemed to care. Instead it appeared to be amused him to take one over the other.

The door ahead slammed and they were in gloom again. The floor ground its way back towards them. The triangular pieces arrowing to the centre where they locked with a crunch.

Bue was sobbing uncontrollably, his head bowed against his chest. Jared craned to look at him. "Oh God," he whispered. "What do I do now?"

Leppard lay at the bottom of the pit. He couldn't remember how long he'd fallen for but it had seemed a long time. He could feel nothing in his body and above him, no larger than a star in the sky, was the light from where the boys were still kept prisoner. As he watched the light winked out and he guessed that the floor had been closed again. There was no pain which frightened him and in the pitch darkness he could see nothing, only hear a slow dripping coming from somewhere near.

He was scared at the thought that death meant spending eternity at the bottom of this hole. He silently prayed for Bue and the others and hoped his sacrifice would lead Bue to have a long and happy life. The lad was like a son to him and he knew deep down Bue was a good boy.

As he finished his prayer a bright light suddenly appeared from ahead of him. He squinted against the sudden glare and as he watched there was a scuffling noise and a small blue creature waddled towards him. He looked down and saw his own smashed body in the light the creature was radiating. He winced and stifled a cry of fear.

The creature was incredibly short but with huge feet, like paddles with black claws on the ends. It looked like a cross between a rat and a kangaroo. As Leppard stared in shock at the creature it smiled and said:

"Don't be frightened Leppard. I am your chaperon."

Leppard stared at the creature, unable to move and stammered, "Gryphoid?"

The creature smiled. It's eyes were a deep, limpid brown and its skin was baby blue. Its too-short arms were folded across its chest and its long, wide blue tail was curled around its feet.

"Yes." The smile was serene like a mother to a baby.

Realisation hit Leppard then. He was dead. This really was it. The Gryphoids came for you when you died, or so the legends spoke. Only those who had been brought back from death had ever seen them and told of it. Now he knew it was true.

He noticed the dripping noise had stopped and the air around him seemed to be static.

"Time has stopped for us, for a while," the Gryphoid said by way of explanation and sat on a portion of its own tail, adjusting itself to get comfy. Its skin glowed with the baby blue and sensing Leppard's fear it spoke reassuringly. "Don't be frightened. You are a good man and you have led a good life. Let me tell you of all the good things you and your life have achieved for others, some that you will remember and some that you never knew of."

The creature began to talk. It told Leppard of all the things he'd ever done that had helped others from when he was a boy until now. It reminded him of the things he had done that had made others happy. It said that there were people whose lives he had saved or forever changed by his generosity and self sacrifice. It reassured him that while many of his gestures had been forgotten by both him and others, some people had never forgotten his kindness towards them.

Leppard began to weep as he heard these things. Not with sadness but with joy and for what seemed like an incredibly long time the creature talked. By the time they had finished and Leppard's soul moved on, he felt more joyful and at peace than he had ever felt before.

Chapter 23

Jared was thirsty, tired and his wrists ached. He could take most of the pressure off his arms by standing on tip toe but the bracelets cut into his wrists harshly. Bue was still crying quietly, his screaming and thrashing having ended after exhaustion took over. Jared knew King James would come back soon and to stop him killing another friend he had to remember everything he had seen, both at home and here. He had no doubt that they would be killed anyway. If only there was something they could do. He was downhearted at the sight of Bue imprisoned, a soul he thought could never be caught. Leppard's chains hung limply.

Jared racked his mind to think of what had happened since he had stumbled into Sophie's room in Warwick hospital. He remembered the fear and chaos at Heathrow airport and the futile struggling against Mordalayn's iron grasp. He thought about the removal of the tracking sigil and the horror as it had fought the exorcism. He remembered the soldiers on the dock and the poor man who'd been taken by the lake's guardians for his attack on them. Then his thoughts turned to the runaway thief in the dusty streets that Mordalayn had saved and then....

His head snapped upright. Oh God, what was the man's name?

He racked his brains for the little scruffy man's name and then it came to him.

Taking a deep breath Jared went, "Scious, Scious, Scious, Scious....Scious."

He looked around, half expecting the room to dematerialise in front of them and for them all to wake up back at the Cherubs. But...nothing.

"Worth a try," he said to himself. "Might have guessed..."

There was a loud crack and ahead of them the air split open as if cut with a sharp knife. A brief, millisecond of blue light spilled from the slash and suddenly a man burst forward from it. He was flung forward and staggered as if coming to a sudden stop after running and looked around bewildered. His hat flew from his head and he grabbed it back.

"My oh my," he said and patted his pockets then his arms and legs as if checking they were still in one piece. "Who calls Scious away from his supper?" He looked at the imprisoned boys in front of him and a look of concern crossed his features. "Dear oh dear, you poor people. Hello young man," he said addressing Jared. "Never thought you'd need the help of one such as I."

Bue had snapped alert and he stared at the newcomer. "Can you release us?" Jared asked quickly.

Scious scratched his head. "Of course, of course, of course. Anything for my friend," and looked around. Seeing the mechanical levers near to him he looked at the boys. "Does this release you?"

"Yes, but be careful. The one on the far left retracts the floor," Jared replied.

Scious tutted and pulled the levers one at a time. The chains detached from the bracelets and one by one they were released. Bue and Jared fell to the floor and collapsed. They rubbed their sore wrists and shook their numb hands to get the blood flowing again.

"Now we need to get you out of here so we do," Scious muttered, scratching his head under his hat again. "It really is most inconvenient you summoned me while I was eating. Had to quickly grab my hat, never go out without my hat you know."

"We need to find Mordalayn," Jared said and Scious smirked.

"The warrior? Your friend? Of course, he stopped those horrible men from hurting me. We must indeed find him."

"How do we get out?" Bue asked, his eyes still swollen from crying and his voice croaky from where he'd been shouting.

Scious looked around the gloomy room. "Stand next to the door," he said.

Bue and Jared followed his suggestion and he stood next to the levers and then yanked hard on the one to open the pit. With the same deafening grind the triangles retracted into the surrounding floor. Scious ran and stood next to the boys. Within a few seconds they could hear a key being frantically turned in the other side of the door and as it swung open two guards ran in.

The guards ran to the empty chains and the open floor, confused. As they ran forward Scious pulled Bue and Jared through the open door and slammed it, turning the key in the lock smirking triumphantly. The two guards thudded into the door on the other side and began pounding on it, shouting furiously. Scious raised the large bunch of keys then placed them in a large pocket in his coat.

"Come, we have to go," he whispered and moved up the corridor, the guards still hammering on the door.

Jared looked around. The table next to the room they had been in was bare. Only a flagon of wine and a couple of mugs plus a crude dice game. Light flickered in the stone corridor from lanterns on the walls. The place was dank and gloomy, moss in scattered patches on the floor and walls. The corridor ended just beyond the door to their former prison. No one else was about.

"We need to get out of this place now," Scious said as they moved away. "People will be coming soon."

"No, we have to find Mordalayn we can't leave him here," Jared replied. He turned to Scious and looked imploringly to the little man. "Can you help us find him?"

Scious bowed. "But of course, of course, of course my young friend. Your friend is a friend of Scious's too so he is. It would be my honour and my pleasure."

"Where would they have taken him?" Jared asked, glancing left to right to check no one was coming.

"I would suggest that the king would have taken him to the games."

"Games?" Jared asked confused.

"This isn't just a prison," Scious said frantically. "This is also the place where the king has his sports. Nasty sports though they are."

Jared still looked concerned. Bue said quickly. "They've taken him to the arena?"

"Would say so young master, would say so," Scious answered, bobbing his head again, the feather in his hat waving madly.

Jared paled. "We have to get him out of there. Can you do it?"

"Like I said, always happy to repay a debt, but my debt is for one repayment only. Scious takes all of you or some of you, but I do not come back once I go."

Bue spoke up. "Show us the way," and gestured for Scious to lead. He scurried on ahead, the shouting and pounding on the door becoming fainter and fainter until it faded away. The corridor was narrow and now there was no sound apart from their own foot falls on the uneven stone.

As they passed a small closet in the wall Bue shouted. "Wait!" He reached inside and pulled out his prize bow and the quiver belt, still full of quarrels. Inside there was also their backpacks. "Our stuff," he said unemotionally and began tossing out the packs to the others. Jared saw Bue's face was grim and cold.

As they reached the end of the corridor Scious raised his finger to his lips, gesturing for them to be quiet. "We mustn't make a noise but I can get us out of here." He reached down and withdrew the big bunch of keys. He squinted at them and after a moment grunted. He inserted a big rusty key into the lock of the wooden door. After a few seconds of fumbling he cackled triumphantly and grabbed the handle, yanking it and the door swung open. Peering round the frame cautiously he beckoned the others to follow him.

They stepped into a more brightly lit but still relatively gloomy hall with tall cylindrical stone pillars supporting the roof. The light filtered in from above from a huge round window in the ceiling and from various doors that led off from the main area. Scious looked back at them and whispered to them. "There is one guard here but he's asleep. Make no noise."

They slipped out the door and crept slowly past the snoring guard. He had a tankard in his hand and nearby was a flagon of wine, nearly empty. His helmet was on the table next to him and he snuffled as they tiptoed past him. They froze as he stirred but breathed a sigh of relief as he simply slumped into a more comfortable position and carried on snoring. Scious led them to a door on the far left past the guard and after checking they were all present he opened it very quietly and they all went through. "We need to get upstairs," he said, shutting it behind them. He tapped the side of his nose with his index finger and winked at them, "Scious's nose knows," and tittered at his own joke.

As he went to move on Bue grabbed his sleeve. He had loaded and cranked his bow. "Where does this go?" he whispered.

"To the next level young master, where the games are held so they are." He gestured to the room they'd just left. "The other doors lead to the rest of the jail. You were in a special room. We needs to get past the guards on the next floor."

"Can you do that without us being seen?" Bue asked him looking doubtful.

Scious looked hurt. "Oh yes! Sneaking is one of my better things." He moved up the spiralling staircase, his feet falling silently on the steps. Bue and Jared looked at each other then moved to follow Scious.

Chapter 24

"Not so close to me!" Harrod whispered angrily as the frozen figure of the priest crinkled into immobility in front of him.

His partner grunted and returned the jewel to his pocket. The old priest who had stopped them as they were about to enter the hub was now swathed in ice. Harrod waved his hand in front of the old man's face, looking a little concerned.

"You're only supposed to stop them not kill them Crow. We need them later. No one else knows how the magic here works." He tutted, a frown creasing his brow.

"He's not dead," Crow answered crustily. "Although he might have a cold when he wakes up."

Harrod stared again at the eyes of the iced man in front of him. They were frozen open in a shocked expression. He shrugged. "Whatever. Now…let's get this done." He beamed brightly, his carefree demeanour returning.

Crow winked at him and they both drew the hoods of their priestly robes over their heads and Harrod knocked loudly on the door with the tip of his staff.

"Open in the name of the queen and all that is joyous in Alegria," he shouted in a high tone.

"Don't overdo it," Crow hissed as the locking bolt was pulled on the other side.

The door opened a crack and a pair of suspicious eyes peered out. "Yes?" a voice croaked quizzically. "What do you want?"

"Tidings to you errr…exalted brother of our most beloved brethren," Harrod said, grinning brightly, his pearly white teeth showing. Crow nudged his arm as the old man on the other side peered doubtfully at him. "We bring grave news of Our Lady and must speak to the Prime Guardian immediately."

"Oh really," the old man said, his eyes tightening even further. "Well, in that case you need to tell me the daily password don't you."

Harrod's smiled slipped a fraction then he beamed again. "Brother of our most wonderful and precious world of loveliness, in our haste we forgot to find it out. Please bring us the Prime Guardian so we may deliver him this most urgent and pressing of messages for his exalted ears only."

There was a pause and the eyes narrowed again. "There IS no daily password. Nice try!" The door slammed again and the lock was shoved in place. Harrod scowled and they could hear the sound of running feet plus muffled shouting.

Crow pushed him to one side. "Trust you to gild the lily" he hissed and drew another crystal from his robe. Stepping back he spoke a few words and with a whoosh the crystal glowed and the door vanished into dust.

They stepped forward, the powder from the disintegrated door making them cough and saw several scared priests gawking at them. All were dressed in white and gold robes and all stood around a huge tower, squat at its base and rising up and up into the ceiling high above where it tapered to a finer and finer point before vanishing. It glowed a dark green at its base and as Harrod and Crow strode nearer the priests started to scatter.

"Gentlemen we come in peace, we leave you in pieces," Harrod said brightly, then adding to himself, "I've always wanted to say that." Crow removed a third crystal from his pocket and turned, dropping it in the open doorway. It expanded sideways and then flashed upwards. Looking like some bright form of shiny, grey chewing gum it completely sealed the doorway. Then he took his other stone and turned to the nearest priest who raised his hands in shock. Blue light flashed from the crystal and the man was frozen, immobile. His hands were still raised as if in surrender.

"Deal with them I need to find the Prime," Harrod yelled as the priests shrieked and scattered while Crow started to stalk them round the vast room, immobilising them one at a time.

Two priests stood in front of a wooden door, ornately carved and although terrified were clearly not going to move without some form of persuasion.

"Now gentlemen," Harrod said calmly. "Let's be reasonable."

They shook their heads and he sighed. "CROW!!"

With the other priests despatched, Crow made his way over and without hesitation turned his crystal on them.

"Thank you kind sir," Harrod said and with a shove, pushed the immobile forms aside. They hit the ground with a bump and tinkle of loosened ice chips.

The door opened. An old man with a white beard and a robe stood there, fearless and composed. Crow and Harrod hesitated and the old man looked at them. "What is it you want? I am no threat to you."

Harrod beamed again. "that's good to know. We need you to activate the summons signal for your absent ruler. If you would be so kind."

The Prime Guardian stepped forward. Crow took his arm and pulled him to the marble barrier that encircled the huge grey pillar. At one section was a stone tablet, held in place in a horizontal frame. Crow pushed the priest up against it roughly and Harrod tutted. "Now, now Crow there's no need to be so...pushy. This gentleman is here to help us. Aren't you?"

"Our Lady is unreachable now," the Prime Guardian informed them calmly. "Even if I activate this, there's no guarantee that...."

"You let us worry about that, there's a good chap" Harrod said patting his shoulder.

The old man swallowed hard and placed his hands over the tablet. The lines of writing etched into the stone began to glimmer and then flow, mingling and merging, criss crossing in patterns.

The priest softly spoke a few words and the words stopped weaving and formed together. The base of the pillar changed from dark to bright green. Light sped up it and within seconds the whole thing glowed.

"Forgive me My Lady," the priest said, closing his eyes.

"I'm sure she will old chap," Harrod assured him jovially and turned as Crow brought out his crystal once more. There was a crackle of energy as the priest was encased in ice.

Harrod rubbed his chin thoughtfully. "Now...how do we get out?"

Chapter 25

Mordalayn was restrained, tightly and with no possibility of free movement or struggle.

King James had ordered way before the Caracalic came through the Shimmer, that the warrior was to be securely clapped in irons from the moment they had hands on him. Now he was in a tiny one man cell. Iron bracelets secured his wrists and ankles and the chains attached to his arms were retracted into the walls, pulled to the limit of their reach. His legs were manacled together and his neck was secured by a collar with two chains either side, also running into the walls. The cell was almost pitch black. Mordalayn made no sound and his face was impassive. He gave no sign that he was in discomfort. His tri-blade was gone as was his pack. He waited, his mind concentrating on being serene. The news from the messenger had to be taken back to Alegria immediately and as only he had heard it he had to remain calm if he hoped to ever get out of this place.

The door in front of him suddenly opened and the light flooded into the tiny space. He did not squint against the brightness.

"Ahhhh, the Queen's Sword," King James said in a mocking tone. "Caught like a fish in a net."

Two guards were either side of the king, looking nervous as their monarch approached the imprisoned warrior. As the king moved forward they quickly moved, to flank him. Sidestepping to remain slightly ahead, hands on their swords, ready to defend their ruler.

The king sensed their unease and chuckled. "Calm down my good fellows, this warrior has lost his teeth." He walked up to the imprisoned figure, who glared at him silently. He held up Mordalayn's sword in its faded, red leather sheath, the straps dangling. "You won't be needing this any more. However as I'm sure you're aware, one of my guards lost a hand trying to withdraw it from the scabbard."

Mordalayn smiled thinly.

"Booby trapped swords, what will you little Alegrians think of next," the king shook his head and tutted. "And to think you look down on others with your supposed peaceful pacifism."

Mordalayn looked at him and spoke for the first time. "Next to every peaceful ruler there needs to stand a warrior of steel."

King James smirked and glanced at his guards "That's very good. My, my...such eloquent poetry from a hired thug. Did your little queen think that one up?" Adjusting his grip on Mordalayn's large sword he snapped to his guards. "Come!" he barked and clicked his fingers. The guards backed away, not meeting Mordalayn's relentless stare and backed out the door, gratefully slamming it behind them.

King James moved up the stairs from the cell and turned to one of his guards. "Are the other prisoners ready?"

The guard answered quickly. "Yes your majesty, we have the traitors ready. Plus those that were on guard duty in the inner chamber when the spies breached our defences."

"Good, good," the king said absent-mindedly then grinned. "Well, there's not a second to lose."

He walked quickly up the wide marble steps to a much bigger set of double doors. Two guards bowed as he approached and the doors swung open, inward. King James walked into a private balcony and two of his counsellors were there. They turned as the door opened and bowed their heads. He walked past the lavishly ornate, golden chair. As he stepped up there was a roar of cheering. He stood and raised his arms, then slowly lowered them to rest his hands on the cool black marble in front of him.

Below him was a circular floor completely covered in a vast metal grill. Surrounding the floor was a tall wall about eight metres high, curving to enclose the entire area. Seated behind it in curving rows of stone benches were around four hundred men in armour. They cheered loudly as the king greeted them and with a crash of heels they stomped their heavy boots on the floor. On the fourth stomp shouting as one voice "KING JAMES!!!."

This was King James's private amphitheatre. Only his most trusted and favoured subjects got to watch spectacles played out here. The king grinned and lowered his arms. The room slowly fell silent and after a pause he addressed his assembled audience.

"Loyal soldiers of Anghofio. Tomorrow we march on Alegria."

There was another loud and prolonged roar of approval from the men. The king waited until it had died out. "For years we have lived in Alegria's shadow but now the queen has forsaken her realm and Alegria is weak. No longer will they be there to gloat and look down on us. Soon we will have Alegria for ourselves!"

He raised his voice on the last sentence and there was an even louder roar of approval from the assembled men. They wore the black and orange cloaks of the elite King's Daggers and all were bearded. His most loyal and highly trained men.

"As my gift to you all," the king said loudly. "I give you a spectacle you probably thought you'd never see." He gestured with his right hand and through some unseen mechanism a hole opened in the floor and slowly Mordalayn rose up into the arena. After a moment's pause the men screamed louder than ever, all standing to roar with delight at the prisoner displayed before them.

As the platform Mordalayn was on reached the surface it stopped with a loud clang and he glanced slowly from side to side, his face betraying no emotion.

The king signalled for silence and the clamour gradually died away as the excited mob of men sat down again.

"Behold," king James said in a mocking tone. "The queen of Alegria's sword. Caught like a common street rogue."

There was much laughter.

"Now I present him here for your pleasure, as my loyal soldiers." King James gestured again and crossbow men appeared on the wall, their bows primed and pointed at Mordalayn. One by one they took up position. There were twenty in total, fingers over their triggers. Then a portcullis opened with a grinding noise and four guards came out at a quick march, their black cloaks flapping behind them, their swords drawn. They nervously approached the Caracalic and proceeded to unlock his chains. Mordalayn knew he could take at least two of them before the snipers could loose a shot but he also knew he had to remain calm for the time being.

As the last chain was released, the guards stepped back, swords still pointed at the huge figure.

"Now my friend you will not be alone," King James told him. There were sniggers amongst the seated crowd. The king shouted loudly. "Bring out the rest."

Another iron grilled gate ground slowly upwards. Mordalayn glanced back as around twenty men, some frightened some defiant, were pushed and herded into the arena. When they were all in front of him King James addressed them directly.

"Those of you who betrayed my trust, you have one chance to redeem yourselves now." The guards used long staffs to push the men into the centre of the grilled floor which was rusted and menacing looking. They prodded the prisoners, some of them their former equals, towards the centre of the room. They were placed in groups of two, facing each other. As a guard approached Mordalayn he bared his teeth and snarled at the man. The guard blanched and swallowed hard and instead gestured to the Caracalic to take up his position. He stood facing a man of average height. The man's face betrayed no emotion as he looked the huge figure up and down. He instead looked over at where King James stood waiting patiently for the men to be partnered off, his face lit by a wicked smile. When the pairing was finished Mordalayn mentally counted the number. Twenty one in total, one man stood alone, looking relieved but also frightened.

The buzz in the room was powerful. Everyone could feel the excitement and the gleeful anticipation of the audience. After waiting for a few moments more King James spoke again.

"Those of you below are there for betraying your king or for being enemies of Anghofio. You now have one chance to receive the king's mercy." He paused at this and the room was silent, all attention was on him. He continued. "The floor you are standing can be either lethal or benign, depending on where fate has decided to put you." There was subdued laughter at this and the king paused again. "Those of you on benign platforms have to defend them. Those of you who are not will need to steal one."

Some of the men in the arena clearly knew this and had already seen this game played before. The others looked terrified or angry and glanced around frantically for ways of escape. There were none. Mordalayn slowly scanned the arena and saw that of the men assembled here maybe half were hardened soldiers. The others simply looked bewildered and scared. Normal men who had earned the wrath of an evil king.

"Before we begin...a few rules," King James said raising his voice and again the audience cheered. "If you are not on a benign platform when the bell strikes its third tone, you will die. If you try to share a platform with another, you will both die. If you refuse to fight...you will die. Whoever is left at the end will be granted Our mercy. Any questions? Thought not."

Guards came forward from the open portcullis gates clutching crudely made, short swords and King James spoke clearly. "Do not pick these up until the first trumpet sounds. Anyone who tries is a dead man." The guards unceremoniously dumped the blades at the feet of each person, with the exception of Mordalayn who was left without a weapon. They retreated rapidly through the open gates, the portcullises slamming down as they stepped through. A trumpet sounded a high note through the room and the men bent down to retrieve their weapons. King James sneered. "The mighty Queen's Sword will fight unarmed. Let's see if this haughty warrior can show us all how he earned his status with the odds a little fairer to his opponents."

Mordalayn glanced down and around the arena floor. The grill was vast and covered nearly all the circular space beneath them. The platforms beneath the grills were about one metre by one metre, large enough for two men to stand over but also big enough to defend by allowing a defender free range of movement. At another signal from King James the metal platforms beneath them began to slowly move around with a grinding noise. They scraped underneath the grill in unpredictable patterns under the feet of the men above. The man who had no partner suddenly dropped his sword and shrieked "NO! This isn't fair!" and tried to run for one of the portcullises in the wall. He got to make three strides before four crossbow bolts thudded into him. He fell heavily to the floor, dead before he made contact with the grill. There was more laughter from the assembled audience and several could be seen making bets as to the outcome, many pointing with enthusiasm at Mordalayn.

"One more thing," King James said, rising from his ornately carved chair once more. "Feel free to change partners at any time." Still more laughter and a loud cheer went up from the audience and they leaned forward, elbows on their knees to watch the spectacle below. With a grinding crunch the circular metal platforms locked into position under the floor and as Mordalayn glanced down he saw his partner had the safe point. The man looked at him. "Think I'll change if it's all the same. See you in the final," he said quietly. As the trumpets blew loudly to signal the start of the contest he leapt sideways at the man next to him and grabbed him by his collar, yanking him back and hurling him against the arena wall. The man cursed and scrambled to his feet as his usurper took a defensive stance, ready to repel any attempt to reclaim the position.

All around men began struggling, no one in the arena knew how many safe platforms there were but they all knew there would be less than the amount of men alive there in that moment. No one came near Mordalayn, content with easier possibilities and amidst much shouting and grunting they tried to shove one another over the exposed metal of the grills, swords clashing together. Mordalayn quickly looked around in every direction, primed to defend his position but the desperate men around him knew their best chance was against each other and not against him.

To his left an inexperienced man, not used to sword play fell to the more prolific moves of his opponent. With a silent glare at the man who had beaten him he slumped forward onto the floor. A cheer went up from the men watching and in a couple of places coins began to change hands. The victor in that round stepped back into the central spot of his platform and glanced from side to side quickly in case anyone tried to flank him.

One or two men on the outer edges of the group were not being bothered by the others, most of the fighting was in the centre where only Mordalayn was left unchallenged. King James watched the spectacle intently, his hand resting on his chin as he watched the Caracalic standing unopposed.

The first bell began to toll and the men who had safe positions checked where they stood once more to make certain they were safe, swords held ready. Two men were down and as the second bell tolled the victor of the second fight frantically grabbed the body of his beaten opponent and pulled it clear of the platform and onto the grill. The third bell sounded and all the safe points had been claimed, there was no one left to fight in this round. After what seemed like a horribly long time the final bell tolled. Suddenly with no further warning, blue flame shot from every place in the grilled floor except for the safe areas blocked by the metal plates. The flames were three metres tall and as the audience cheered enthusiastically and the men in the arena looked on in horror, the bodies of the two losers and the man who'd tried to run, vanished. Just as quickly as they had come the flames disappeared and there was no sign the men had ever been there except their fallen swords.

The survivors looked around at their fellows and as the cheering in the arena died down the plates underneath the grill began to move again with a strained grinding. "Well done and welcome to the second round gentlemen," King James said, clapping theatrically. With another clang of finality the plates locked into positions beneath the grill once more and the trumpet sounded for them to fight again.

Chapter 26

Crow and Harrod peered round the room but strangely there was indeed no other way out. The frozen priests stood glistening in the pulsing green light of the huge cone tower in the centre of the room.

"Errr...you can get us out of here can't you?" Harrod said, his cheerful demeanour slipping only slightly.

Crow grunted and removed the crystal again then walked to the shining, fat grey wedge blocking the door. He spoke a few words and the barrier slowly sagged in on itself, collapsed and finally crumbled to dust. Harrod cautiously stuck his head out and looked up and down the corridor. There was no one.

"This is weird" he said to Crow. "We've just walked into the most secret place in the whole of Alegria if not the world and there's no one trying to stop us any more."

Crow glanced at him. "The Alegrians became lazy. When you have so much power for so long you forget what it's like to be powerless."

Harrod shrugged and the two men edged down the long, dark corridor, checking in shadows and making their way to the main doors. Harrod was fully expecting a squad of Alegrian guards to jump out on them at any moment. There was no one and as they made it to the main doors, to this most secret and precious of Alegrian chambers he shrugged. "If they'd known it was going to be this easy Siavy wouldn't have paid us so much," he mumbled.

Crow placed the crystal back in his pocket and they took a final look down the corridor then strode through the doors. The winding staircase behind wound up and up and after many steps they arrived at a second taller and more slender door. Both pulled their ceremonial robes firm and drew their hoods over their faces. Crow placed his hand in a carved recess at the side of the door and it glided open silently. In front of it was a huge statue in brown and black speckled marble. There was just enough space to squeeze out one at a time into the huge hall. Harrod went first and the door closed behind them. They moved off, blending into the traffic of people around them. No one paid them any attention.

"Praise be to Alegria and all who..." Harrod began as a group of priests came near to them but Crow nudged him again and he went quiet. As they walked out the main entrance of the central hall, Harrod muttered to himself. "It really shouldn't have been THAT easy."

Chapter 27

Jared, Bue and Scious made their way through the tunnels of the dungeons. In the distance they could hear the faint sounds of cheering and what sounded like fighting. Scious led them up snaking corridors, lit by sputtering torches. There were no sentries left in this level, the two they had trapped and the drunken jailer seemed to be the only ones left. As they moved onwards they saw a curved wooden doorway ahead. Scious turned. "This leads to the main games room," he whispered and motioned for them to wait. Bue glanced at Jared who looked nervously at Scious as he tip-toed forward, his spindly frame reaching the doorway. Adjusting his hat he cautiously touched the door handle and pulled slightly. The door moved and he peeped out. Turning back he whispered to them. "It's ok, come on." As they reached him the clashing of metal, the roars and shouts were louder. They faced a curving corridor that appeared to be encircling the arena. Unbelievably there was no one around.

"They are over confident" Scious said softly and beckoned the others to follow him. They crossed the passageway swiftly and reached a recess in the curved wall. Scious looked anxious. "I can take you now if you want but if you want all of you, you MUST be together. My debt is good for one boon only. I will not make two trips."

Jared glanced at Bue before he answered. "We need to get Mordalayn out of there."

Bue pulled a face. "You can't. By the sounds of it there are hundreds of people in there."

"Well then, we'll have to sneak up on them won't we," Jared snapped angrily. "Where's the entrance to the arena floor?"

"This way," Scious replied "but you won't make it more than a few yards." He smirked again. "I have a better idea."

They moved around they hallway again and towards a row of steps that led down. The sounds of mayhem from the arena rose and fell deafeningly.

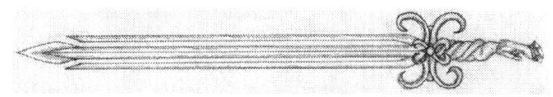

Three men down and the survivors squared off once more. Now down to eighteen men the plates had reduced to twelve. The screams of excitement from the soldiers seated on the stone benches was almost thunderous as those before them threw themselves at their opponents. Again there was some who were left untouched as the six vulnerable men picked their opponents. They twitched nervously, their swords held ready. There was a scream as another man went down to his opponent's blade. Mordalayn again had a safe point and stood unarmed and ready. Although in the first round no one had tried to fight him, they knew that he was not someone to try and face in the later stages. He whirled as a man tried to attack him from behind. With a snarl he dodged the stab aimed at his ribs and swept his elbow up into the man's face. The attacker was dashed back into the wall. There was a roar of approval from the spectators and coins again changed hands. The man groaned and staggered to his feet, shaking his head and squared off to the Caracalic once more.

Mordalayn knew there was no point in trying to reason or negotiate. They were both being forced to fight to the death and he admired the man for his bravery. His foe looked up and their eyes met. Mordalayn's gaze was cold. He adjusted his stance to prepare for another attack and the man hurled himself forward, swiping the sword in a classic attacking move. Two actions from side to side as he lunged, followed by a thrust that would have gutted anyone in front of him. Mordalayn was no longer in front though. He stepped behind the man and grabbed his neck with huge hands. "You are brave my friend," he whispered and after a moment's struggle his rival fell limp. Mordalayn pushed the body to one side.

Again the audience bellowed loudly in appreciation and Mordalayn glanced around rapidly for other challengers. Four men were down and the remaining eight fighting for space struggled on. Looking up to the gloating face of King James Mordalayn silently prayed for both a miracle and vengeance.

Scious and the others made their way to the door at the bottom of the steps. While Bue held his crossbow ready Scious opened the door and peered in. Inside was a darkened room that curved with the space it was built around. A blast of hot, damp air sprang through the gap and Jared could see what looked like copper pipes twisting and winding around. Scious again lifted his finger to his lips and they cautiously moved into the stifling, foetid room.

Inside were two small, damp, sweaty figures. They were green in colour and hunched over various knobs and levers. One was barking orders at the other. "No, no!" it snapped irritably. "You keep the gauge at sixty until the third trumpet call! Have you listened to anything I've said?"

The other figure snapped back. "I kept it at sixty, just my hand slipped is all."

"Your hand slipped?! YOUR HAND SLIPPED?!!!" the other one shrieked. "It'll be more than your hand that'll slip if you ruin King James'ss fun today."

The second creature snorted and wiped sweat from its forehead with an equally sweaty sleeve. It had a large, scaled nose that occupied most of its face. "Why don't you do the plates and I'll do the flames. Happier then?"

"NO!" the other snapped. "You do as I tell you and I...." His voice trailed off as he saw Bue's crossbow aimed at his face.

Scious spoke up. "Switch off the flame and raise the portcullis nearest to us."

The creature hesitated and tried to move but Bue jerked, moving his bow. His expression was furious and the creature decided not to argue. "The...there are HUNDREDS of soldiers up there" he stammered, trying to get some semblance of control back into his little world.

"Just do it," Bue told him.

The creatures gulped and the littler one reached for a valve.

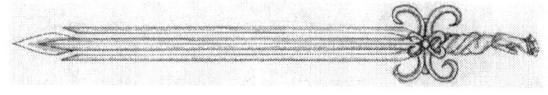

As the first trumpet sounded there were five men down. Those who were safe constantly checked for threat while the remaining fighters struggled on. Panicking, the man who held the safe point flung himself at his adversary and managed to knock his sword away. It arced against the marble wall and clanged to the floor. The man's momentary joy was short lived though. The other took advantage of his distraction and grabbed his sword arm by the wrist and proceeded to grapple with him, trying to pull him clear of the plate.

"GET OFF!!!" the man shouted, terrified as the second bell tolled. Others around them winced, knowing full well the price for having two on a plate at the end of a round. The two men thrashed madly, knowing only one could survive but neither strong enough to dislodge the other. The third bell tolled with cheers from the spectators as they waited eagerly for the blue flames. Silence fell as expectation reached its peak and then…nothing happened.

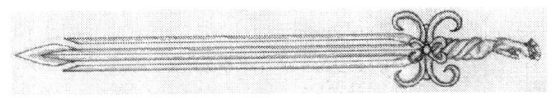

King James stood, furious as his pleasurable diversion was halted. The two struggling men finally halted and let each other go. The others looked around, unsure if this was part of the games or not. There were jeers and booing from the audience. King James turned to his nearest advisor and snapped angrily, "Find out what happened down there. I want whoever's responsible in the arena with them!"

The advisor gulped and moved to the doorway behind him. King James looked at Kloee, trapped in her glass coop, and grinned as she hovered inside, hands on her hips, glaring furiously at him. "Don't worry little thing," he chuckled. "You'll see your friends soon enough." He eyed Mordalayn's sword and his mood abated somewhat. Regardless of having his fun spoiled, the boy would be ready to spill everything he knew by now and the victory against Alegria was nearly complete.

The creature killed the flame control. "The arena is now safe," he said. There was a grinding noise as the plates again began to rotate and murmurs of confusion could be heard from the soldiers seated above. The creature grabbed a handle and pulled down hard. The grinding stopped, the plates frozen once more.

"Raise the maintenance portcullis on the right of this room," Scious said.

The creature stared at him with petrified eyes and pleaded. "Could you erm…make it look like we tried to stop you? We Chupateen will end up in there too if King James even imagines we didn't at least try."

"My pleasure," Scious said beaming, "Now, open the portcullis."

The creature moved to a set of glistening steel valves on the wall and began to twist one hard. Bue and Jared moved to the small open entrance to the arena floor. As they turned there was a couple of thudding noises and groans. Scious smiled, wiping his hands briskly, the Chupateen unconscious behind him. "Call the Caracalic over, he has one chance to make it so he does," he whispered. "There are bowmen all around the walls, yes bowmen."

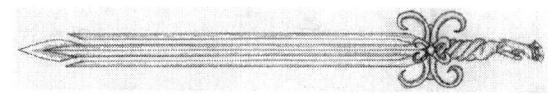

As the hubbub increased and the King glared angrily around him, the combatants looked about anxiously. A few still believed this was part of the games to torment them, but others realised something had gone wrong. The crossbow men lined on the walls had lowered their weapons and were glancing around baffled. Mordalayn saw Kloee in her glass prison and as he wondered what was happening a small gate rose up across from him. Looking over, he saw Bue's face in the shadows behind it. Bue beckoned to him and then pointed up and around, indicating the danger. Most attention was now on the king as people looked for answers in their confusion. Bracing himself, Mordalayn tensed his muscles ready to jump.

From the angle they were at Jared could just see the royal box with Kloee's glass dome perched on the balcony. He prodded Bue. "Can you break the glass and free her?" he asked.

Bue looked up and his face creased. "I'd rather put a bolt through James'ss neck," he replied bitterly.

"We don't have time," Jared replied. "Can you smash the glass with a shot? Then she can come with us."

"What do you think?" Bue replied and raised his bow.

As King James sat waiting he pondered what might have gone wrong. His prisoners were securely chained, with no access to either their weapons or magic. Those who had embarrassed him would be dealt with accordingly but he knew the system that powered the arena was sturdy and reliable and had existed for hundreds of years. The arena itself had fallen out of use due to Alegria's pacifism and dislike of such spectacles. Faced with a neighbouring kingdom so powerful no ruler of any other realm had tried to continue with such practices. Forever in Alegria's shadow. Well, not any more.

As he turned to look behind him to see if his advisor was returning there was a crash and the glass of the domed cage next to him shattered. Acting on reflexes, he hurled himself back out of his chair and down on the floor, face down with his arms over his head. Kloee flew up angrily from the shattered remains. As the remaining guard moved towards her, she hurled her hands out and a blinding flash of light erupted from her palms. The guard shrieked, temporarily blinded and dropped his spear.

"Nasty, horrid, horrid bully!" Kloee shouted pouting and flew to where Mordalayn's sword was resting. It glowed yellow and she flew up and out over the arena with the huge weapon floating next to her.

"Here! Over here!" a voice shouted and she frantically looked around to see Jared and Bue shouting at her from behind an iron grill in the wall. A couple of crossbow bolts shot past her. The bowmen on the walls were recovering their composure and Jared and Bue ducked down as quarrels ricocheted off the wall and iron bars in front of them. One or two passed into the engineering room to clatter off the walls.

Mordalayn saw his chance and sprang lithely across the floor. King James stood up and shouted to the bowmen. "STOP HIM!!!" As the Caracalic bounded over the grill, bolts sprang from the weapons and whacked into the floor around him. He leapt for the small opening just as Kloee flew through it with his sword and grunted in pain as a bolt thudded into the flesh of his left arm, above the elbow.

He slid through the gate and Scious grinned at him. "Hello there sir, I told you Scious honours his debts."

In the arena every soldier was on his feet and there was a pounding on the locked door of the tiny room. "Hold hands please everyone, you too little miss," Scious said to Kloee who glared at him but hovered between Bue and Mordalayn. The Caracalic snatched his sword from her and threw the strap over his head before taking her tiny hand in his. "Now off we go." Scious gave a big smile and with a flash of diamond light they were gone.

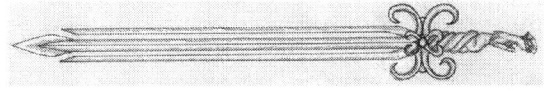

King James strode down to the dungeons, his wary guards at his side. The king was furious and no one wanted to say or do anything that might further provoke his wrath. The two Chupateen who had been operating the arena mechanisms had been found unconscious and it appeared they had been caught by surprise. Uncharacteristically forgiving, the king had simply walked away when faced with their explanation. One they had given while gibbering with fear and rubbing their sore heads. As the king reached the dungeon levels two guards bowed and quickly opened the doors. Marching through he made for the main cell area. Four guards surrounded the terrified dungeon master.

King James looked at the man and then at the guards. "Found him asleep your majesty," one said. "Other two are trapped in the abyss room. The prisoners have escaped and their weapons and belongings are missing."

King James glared at the fear stricken jailer and looked around the room. His eyes bored into the kneeling man. "Were you asleep?" he enquired in a friendly tone

"Errr…no, I mean yes your majesty. Please forgive me."

"But of course I forgive you. Am I not a kind and benevolent king?"

"Oh yes your majesty of course you are."

King James smiled and gently placed his hand on the man's head. "You were obviously tired, we all need a nap now and then. Even those guarding prisoners for their king. How could any man judge you for dozing off like that?"

He turned to his guards. "Assemble the Daggers and send the signal to our spies in Alegria. We march in one hour. Our plans are not hindered by this setback."

He turned back to the jailer. "Now. What shall we do with you then?"

Chapter 28

They appeared in a field, the moon in the sky above them throwing a milky glow over the tall grass. Jared wobbled uncertainly on his feet, his stomach doing flips from the magical jolt. In contrast to the shouting and chaos of the arena, this was peaceful and his ears were ringing in protest after the bedlam of the last few minutes.

They all breathed out in relief and slowly let go of each other's hands. Kloee flew up and perched herself on Jared's shoulder. Mordalayn quickly scanned the field and Bue looked Jared up and down. "You ok?" he asked, looking concerned.

"Fine I guess, you?"

Bue smiled but even in the moonlight Jared could see that the other boy was hurting inside. He reached over and placed his hand on his arm. "He gave his life for you because he wanted to," he whispered.

Bue shook off the hand and turned away.

Mordalayn checked his wound and grunted when he saw it was only a graze. He looked at them and then to Scious. "Where are we?" he snapped at the little man.

"About four miles from Alegria good sir," Scious replied pointing to lights in the distance, sparkling like jewels in the velvet night.

"Could you not have taken us nearer to the castle?" Mordalayn growled.

Scious looked hurt and replied defensively. "I saved your lives good sir, Scious keeps his word so he does, oh yes he does. Had to land here so we did, I'm not an alchemist, can't just take you kind sirs just anywhere. We could have materialised into a building or even a horse. Would sir like that? Being merged with a horse?"

He looked indignant and Mordalayn stared at him for a long moment. "You are right. My thanks little man. Your gesture will not be forgotten."

Scious beamed and then bowed. "I bid you good night gentlemen...and lady," he bowed again to Kloee who narrowed her eyes at him. "Scious will be on his way." With that he scurried off in the direction of the trees and in a few seconds he was gone, only the sound of his feet could be heard, until that too faded.

"We need to move," Mordalayn said. "Alegria is four miles to the east, the castle another seven from there."

He began moving off to the road at the edge of the field, the grass rustling against his clothes, slinging his sword over his shoulder he tied off the sash and Bue and Jared exchanged worried looks and then ran after him. Kloee flew behind Jared and cast a glow in front of him to light his steps.

"For you young master," she said, eager to please. "A light so you don't trip and hurt yourself."

"What are we going to do when we get into the city?" Jared asked confused.

Mordalayn continued walking. "Steal some transport and get to the castle as soon as we can." As he made it to the wooden fence at the edge of the field he vaulted over and made straight for the road, Bue and Jared struggling to keep up with his long strides.

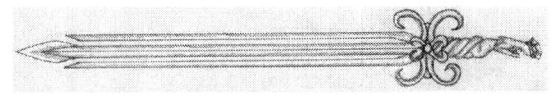

Milus Forsinavue was bored. His master was still busy inside the tavern and he had no doubt he'd have to help him get into the carriage when the time came. The old man was spending more and more of his evenings here and sometimes didn't leave until the tavern closed. The job wasn't so badly paid but the lack of activity dragged Milus down and frustrated him. He looked at the sky and saw that dawn was not too far away. He decided to make certain everything was tidy. His master tended to get irritable unless his private coach was kept in immaculate condition. Whistling softly he jumped down from the cab and walked around to inspect the vehicle. The four horses had been fed and watered and he patted the nearest one as he walked past it. He took a cloth and began wiping the surface of the exterior, lifting off the few smudges and dust streaks that had appeared since the last time he checked.

As he bent down to begin wiping the spokes on one of the large wooden wheels he heard the sound of footsteps. He could see three pairs of legs approaching him through the gaps in the wheel. He straightened up and made his way around to the other side.

"Good evening gentlemen," he said cheerfully, hoping for some conversation to relieve the boredom and then recognised the tallest figure. "Takoba, my respect," he said, touching his hand to his forehead.

Mordalayn stopped. From the tavern there were voices and the sound of laughter. Life carrying on as normal for the people of Alegria. There were very few people about in the dark street, only a woman further up emptying dirty water into the gutter who looked at them disinterestedly and then went back into her house, shutting the door. Further down were a couple of people walking, one supporting the other and both laughing occasionally. In the distance a dog barked then was silent.

"Do I know you?"

Milus smiled. "Oh yes. Milus Forsinavue. Former coachman to the council of Alegria. Recently fallen on harder times...at your service."

Mordalayn paused for a moment as he looked at Milus. "I need your coach. I don't have time to argue and if you try to stop me you will fail."

Milus looked puzzled for a split second then looked at the closed door of the tavern and back at the group in front of him.

"Whatever." he shrugged "I take it this is important if the Queen's Sword wishes to steal a common coach...albeit a very nice, clean and well looked after one."

Mordalayn was silent.

The man shrugged again. "Fair enough, I never really liked this job. I might as well take you. You steal this coach I'm out of work anyway." He looked at the Caracalic's companions. One was a bewildered looking young boy of about 11 who looked foreign. The other was about 13 and had a hard look in his eyes. Slightly behind the younger child was a glowing, hovering fairy who frowned at him as he looked at her.

"Young miss," he said, again touching his hand to his forehead as he acknowledged Kloee, who pouted even harder.

He stepped up into the cab and gestured for them to get in. Mordalayn swung the door open and Bue and Jared struggled on board. Milus turned back and looked through the small hatch behind him. "Where we off to then?"

"The royal palace, stop for no one," Mordalayn replied and Milus cracked the whip. The horses moved off as the first rays of sun pricked the sky.

Chapter 29

The carriage swayed to a stop at the watch tower beyond the bridge to the palace. The bridge was vast and beneath it was a drop of awe inspiring depth that led to the forests and fields far below. Milus cracked his whip and brought the horses to a trot but before they had stopped, the door opened and Mordalayn jumped out. The startled guards at the bridge jerked to attention. "Takoba," they said saluting. He quickly glanced at their uniforms and identified the guard captain.

"I need to see the council now," he snapped and the confused officer cleared his throat to reply but Mordalayn was already walking to the captain's tethered horse. He quickly untied it and swung himself lithely up into the saddle. He turned back. "Escort the passengers and this man to the palace. I will meet you there."

Before the still startled officer could respond Mordalayn kicked the horse with his heels and charged down the long, wide bridge to the palace half a mile away.

The thundering hooves faded. The guard captain looked up at Milus who gave him a half smile and then to the faces of the two boys and the fairy peering at him from the window of the coach. He turned to one of his men; "Ride with them, escort them to the council chamber." The soldier saluted and climbed up next to Milus who cracked his whip again and the horses moved off. As the carriage retreated one soldier turned to the captain. "What was that all about sir?"

The captain shook his head. "I have no idea, but whatever it is I'll wager it's very bad news."

Jared and Mordalayn faced the council. Bue and Kloee had been told to wait outside and Milus Forsinavue was tending his ex-master's horses.

Unlike the first meeting this one was in a large oval room with a large oval, wooden table in the centre. Since the absence of the queen most of the council were living in their designated quarters and had been hastily roused by the palace guard. Messages had been sent to the absent members but as this meeting was not planned it was doubtful any would attend before it was over, even by Shimmer. There was not one tired face amongst them. The urgency was paramount even though the assembled council was incomplete, five chairs sat empty. The councillor Lighvoor went to speak.

"May I call this meeting to order and..." he began but Mordalayn stepped forward.

"We do not have time for pomp and ceremony Lighvoor," he snapped, looking round the table.

Lighvoor's voice trailed off. Then after a pause. "You are right Takoba, please say what you must."

Mordalayn stepped to the far end of the table and placed his clenched hands on the polished surface. "Anghofio have a spy amongst us that knows secrets only the innermost circle of priests, myself and Our Lady are privy to."

There were murmurs of shock and he continued. "Your mission to send spies to Anghofio was a success; they found what we needed to know, albeit at a terrible price."

The murmuring increased in volume then the rat faced general Degrezen spoke. "Forgive us for not informing you of that mission Takoba, there was no time."

Mordalayn did not look at him. "There is no need to explain your actions to me general. I trust this council implicitly and regard all actions and decisions as for the greater good."

"What was the information they found?" the one eyed woman asked in a lilting voice.

"The Anghofians placed spies here. They now know how to summon the Queen. As I stated before, only a handful of people know of Our Lady's true origins and more than half of them are in this room now."

More murmuring and again Mordalayn spoke. "While you all know that this can be done, none of you are aware of how. Which means someone in the priesthood has betrayed us. If they are able to activate the signal to summon her then they can trap her when she arrives."

"What are they planning to do exactly?" a man further down the table asked.

"They failed to assassinate, now they will try to bring her here. If they can bring her through and trap or kill her then her power and the power we rely on will be snuffed out like a candle. Anghofio can invade as we will have no time to find a new monarch. The usual interim for changeover will not happen and we will be defenceless."

There were gasps of astonishment around the table and then someone else spoke. "But Takoba, surely if they bring the Queen here she will be able to help us."

"No! They are fully aware now of her fragile state and will trap her the moment she appears. I am sure you are all aware that the only reason we never tried this method ourselves is that we knew something was terribly wrong. Any attempts to forcibly bring her here might end her life."

Lighvoor spoke up. "The Queen's Sword is correct," he said. "Any attempt to bring the Queen here when she is so badly hurt may cause her permanent or fatal injury. She needs to come to Alegria aware of who and what she is, not wrenched here against her will."

Mordalayn continued. "The summons is used when her presence is needed urgently. There has been no problem with this before...but Anghofio know that by activating it now they will possibly force her here with devastating results."

He looked once more around the table and then to Jared before speaking again.

"I was at her side here when she was hurt. She was frightened, didn't know what was happening and as I reached out to her she faded away in front of me. This council took over as she had planned but Our Lady is in a limbo between three worlds. The normal dreaming world, her waking world and this one. Until she is returned to health we are incredibly vulnerable."

"Doorways exist all over both worlds, linking them. Anyone with the power and knowledge may use them. Luckily very few people have the tools to do so or the magic to make them work. All are inactive now as a precaution in this terrible time."

"Prime Guardian Jacoban is missing." Mordalayn indicated an empty chair. "This in itself indicates that the plot may have already been initiated."

Degrezen spoke again, his nose twitching. "Whatever you need Takoba, the council will grant you." There were further murmurs, this time of approval from the assembled councillors.

"I myself do not know how to access the portal," Mordalayn said. "I need you to grant me the right to do that. I need you to tell me where the inner sanctum is."

There was an uncomfortable silence and then a woman spoke up. "Takoba we don't know either. It was always assumed that as Our Lady's sword you were given all knowledge she had."

Mordalayn stared at her in disbelief. "Power corrupts. I know more than many but there are some things even I was not told. Do you mean that only the priesthood know where the sanctum is?"

There was another long silence and the woman looked away. "I am sorry Takoba, neither us nor our ancestors ever expected such a catastrophe as this."

Mordalayn looked at the empty Prime Guardian's chair and then around the table again. "So much power with no power to fall back on" he said quietly and in the empty, hollow silence that followed there was suddenly a high keening noise of a trumpet being blown, loud and long. A two tone blast of a short and then long note that made everyone in the room look up in shock. After a pause the same two tones were repeated and then again and again.

"What's that?" Jared said looking from the astonished faces of the councillors to the stone hard one of Mordalayn.

273

"The invasion warning" he said grimly. "Alegria is under attack." He turned to the councillors. "You know the protocols, lock yourselves down in your quarters, bar the doors with the spell of stronghold...and Our Lady be with all of us."

They all stood up and without hesitation made for the vast door, running as fast as they could.

Chapter 30

Mordalayn pounded across the vast, round, main hall of the palace as the trumpets sounded. Around him people were scattering like leaves on the wind. The Alegrian guards were trained for such an event as this but as they surged to the main entrance they were bewildered and scared. For hundreds of years the trumpets had only been sounded for ceremonial events or drills. Some were pulling helmets and breast plates on as they assembled in the forecourt beyond the doorway to the main hall. Many thought this was another practice run and were laughing nervously amongst themselves.

Jared and Bue, with Kloee flying frantically alongside them, ran after Mordalayn who had reached the main set of men, roughly two hundred in all. "Where's your captain?" he bellowed over the din of the keening trumpets.

"Other side of the bridge sir," the nearest man said pointing as a small group of riders could be seen galloping towards them in the far distance.

Mordalayn glanced at the man and noticed his scabbard was empty. "Your sword! Where is it?" he snapped and the man blanched in embarrassment.

"Err...it was damaged sir, still with the swordsmith," he stammered back, looking away and blushing.

Mordalayn stared at him in disbelief and then shoved him away and looked to Jared and Bue as they ran up, Kloee hovering over Jared's shoulder.

"You two stay in the main hall out of sight," he snapped then a bright light began to emanate from high above and he turned in shock to the huge tower above them. The vast, multi faceted crystal in the tower was starting to glow. High in the sky the clouds were moving, becoming grey then black as they swirled and merged then broke and merged again above the huge pointed spire. Lightning began to flash in tiny bursts on to the tower's needle point. Mordalayn looked dismayed as the tip began to glow then fade. The crystal pulsed bright white, then green then faded again.

"Our Lady! They have activated the signal!" he shouted and looked on in horror as the crystal continued to pulse and the trumpets continued to sound.

Chapter 31

Miles away King James sat in a field with his most trusted guards around him. He trained his telescope over the towers of Alegria castle and whistled merrily to himself. He could hear the distant peeling of the trumpets, a beautiful sound that had started the moment his troops had cleared the ground and begun the march across the open plains leading to Alegria. As they had pounded through the villages on the outskirts of the city the terrified residents had fled indoors, slamming their hatches and barricading themselves in their homes. Alegria had not faced invasion in hundreds of years and the population were petrified. Over a thousand of the Anghofian army had marched with their king, the elite of his troops, the King's Daggers, and all were proud to be there that day. A day their children and grandchildren would tell wide eyed stories about in years to come. The drummers had beat the marching rhythm for them and every thirty second step they would hit double beats on their drums. Then the whole legion would raise their right fists in the air and shout as one, "KING JAMES", the sound carrying for miles.

Now the king sat and looked at the distant castle and then turned to his nearest aide. The man leaned in instantly with a whispered question. "Your majesty?"

"Send in the Glavers, I want them to know how serious we are," he said amiably and the man nodded and turned to another soldier further back.

"Order the Glavers to attack!" he shouted and the man ran back to the main body of armed men.

"Now for some entertainment" King James said grinning as he again raised his telescope to view the palace before him.

Mordalayn saw the riders jolt to a stop at the foot of the marble steps and run up them two at a time.

The captain looked at him, winded from the sudden exertion and panting. "About a thousand men Takoba," he gasped. "About two miles hence," pointing over his shoulder.

Mordalayn looked grim. "Take half of these men and secure the bridge entrance, the rest can stay here with me." He turned to the swordless man and said with a sneer. "As you are unable to fight you can run. Go and find as many soldiers as you can who are in the building and tell them I want them here now."

The man bowed fearfully, and then ran off into the palace. The captain had separated half the group of men and was now running back down the staircase with them. He mounted his horse and signalled the other two riders and they galloped back to the bridge, the group of soldiers following them at a fast run.

"What can we do?" Jared asked and Mordalayn turned to him and put his hand on his shoulder. "There is a secret room behind the main throne room. It is where the queen appears. They will almost certainly try and trap her there in case she gains power once she is through. The door is directly behind the throne. Push the left eye of the statue of the bird above the throne to open it."

Jared winced as the men around him scrambled to try and form some semblance of order amongst themselves. Above them

278

the crystal still pulsed into light and then dark again, the lightning far above flashing intermittently, thunder cracking loudly.

Mordalayn stared at him and spoke clearly. "No Alegrian can help her until she is here, but as you are of her world you may be able to stop this somehow."

Jared suddenly saw shapes flitting in the sky and his stomach turned. He pointed up. "Isn't that...?" he said and saw Mordalayn turn and then look back in dismay.

"Glavers!" he hissed the words. The hover boards of the cackling creatures that had attacked Jared at the airport were in the distance but this time there were dozens of them.

The shapes flitted back and forth in the sky above the far end of the vast bridge and Bue gasped. "They're going for the soldiers!"

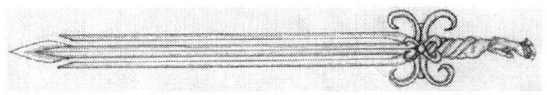

Jared stared in terror as the weaving shapes crisscrossed and then, like an evil swarm of bees, dived down onto the group of running men. The trumpets were still sounding loudly and then ceased. As the soldiers at the palace doors watched helpless, the Glavers tore into the men and one by one they were lifted up, screaming and then dropped over the yawning chasm either side of the bridge. The three men on horses fared better at first but then the Glavers attacked two at a time and wrenched the men out of their saddles and out over the edge. The panicked horses bolted, two back to the palace and the other out and away over the bridge and to the road beyond. Two men who had both courage and skill made a valiant gesture of defiance and stood back to back, taking three or four of the swooping assassins down before they were engulfed and dragged to their deaths.

"It's a massacre," one soldier next to Jared cried out in dread.

Within minutes it was over and the Glavers soared up in the air again and assembled in the sky above the bridge.

Everyone knew what was coming next.

Behind them the messenger came running back. With him were a handful of armoured men and they skidded to a halt.

"Is that it?" Mordalayn seethed at the man who blushed again.

"There is no one else sir."

"Seal the palace, anyone who is not able to fight is to be inside, NOW!!!" Doors and windows began shutting with bangs and thuds and the main door started to slowly close.

"Both of you get inside!" Mordalayn bellowed at Bue and Jared and pushed them to the vast, arched, wooden gates of the palace. As the gap got smaller Bue ran through but Jared tripped and fell, sprawling forwards and then watched fear stricken as the door closed with a loud boom.

Mordalayn picked him up and turned to the troops. "Assemble as close to the doorways as you can," he yelled and started pulling men into lines. Above them the crystal continued to glow, this time brighter, and Mordalayn prayed that they could stop this. He glanced yet again up at the peak of the huge tower. The lightning was flashing faster and faster and the thunder cracked. The swarm of Glavers in the distance bobbed in the air like some flock of malignant crows and then as one began to surge towards them.

Jared stood next to Mordalayn and yelled loudly. "What can I do now?"

"JUST GO!!!" Mordalayn roared back as the black spindly shapes swarmed towards them cackling loudly like a demonic choir of army ants. They merged over and through each other and as Jared stared at the vast number he could see there were at least a hundred of them.

"How are we going to stop them?" he shouted to Mordalayn over the din of the approaching force.

"Just get to the tower and stop them bringing the Queen through," the cat man shouted back. Jared was about to argue when Mordalayn whirled and grabbed Jared by his shirt and belt and before he could say anything heaved him back and then launched him up and into the air. Jared barely had time to register what was going on before he landed with a crunch on the tiled, slanting roof above the main doorway. Winded he breathed heavily and with a start realised that he was slipping back, the loose tiles from his sudden impact coming loose and cascading back towards Mordalayn and the soldiers in a shower of red stone.

Kloee flew up and hovered protectively next to him. She glowed again and his slide abruptly stopped, his kicking feet dislodging a few more of the tiles that crashed unnoticed amongst the men below. "Thanks," he gasped and turned into the gentle pull of her protective light. He flung his arms out to stop the slide and with a grinding noise stuck still and then scrambled up and lunged for the window. More tiles came loose under his feet until he managed to grab the ledge and flung his hands through the open window. As he went to heave himself in he turned round. The sight was stomach-churning. Swarms of Glavers were hurtling towards them as Mordalayn drew his tri-blade. The others with him formed a ragged line against the oncoming black tidal wave of evil and Mordalayn glanced up at Jared.

"Go!" he shouted again. "Get to the crystal room. You are the only one who can stop this."

Jared hauled with arms and pulled himself up and in. Turning he slammed the stained glass window and twisted the latch. The room he was in appeared to be some kind of observation point with only a couple of carved wooden chairs and a wide table in the middle. Making his way round the table he opened the door and looked both ways. The hallway to his right was clear and the staircase on his left was deserted. He darted up the stairs and kept to the wall as the staircase spiralled round.

The Glavers swooped on the hundred or so men with shrieks and laughter. Unlike the bridge though, the men were so tightly packed they could not pick out targets so easily. Mordalayn leapt at a cackling figure that came too close and while still in the air side swiped his huge sword at the Glaver who tried to dodge the blow but failed. He saw two Glavers holding a struggling soldier by each arm and attempting to lift him up. He leapt at them and elbowed one out of the way and brought his blades down on the other, splitting it in half. As the frightened soldier nodded his thanks a third Glaver appeared, grabbed the man around the waist and scooped him up. It flew to the edge of the battlements and glanced over at Mordalayn. Then with an evil grin it dropped the screaming man over the edge, laughing in triumph and flying off.

The others were swinging their swords at the Glavers who were too fast for most. Another man stepped too far from the company of his fellow men and almost instantly a grinning Glaver wrenched him up in the air before dumping him screaming over the edge.

Mordalayn cursed and wondered how they could have let themselves sink so far into useless clumsiness as a kingdom. "Aim for their boards," he shouted. "Cripple their boards!" As a Glaver shot by him he reached up, impossibly fast and again wrenched the figure off. The board ploughed into the closed and barred double doors of the palace entrance. It took a chunk from the oak and then split into pieces. The Glaver looked up with frightened eyes. Mordalayn snarled and threw it down before despatching it with his sword.

The other soldiers were losing their discipline and the tightly packed men were spreading out. Glavers weaved everywhere and men were dragged screaming up into the air. A few tried to run for the staircase but were quickly caught and thrown over. Mordalayn swung his sword in powerful arcs and again and again Glavers fell to his blades. He saw a man being hauled up into the air but too far away to help. He fumbled with his belt buckle and twisted the metal catch on the side. A short, knife came free and he hurled it at the black clad monster. It caught it in the face and the monster skidded off its board, dropping the wriggling soldier and collapsing onto the floor dead. Its board clattered to the ground next to it. Wiping sweat from his brow, Mordalayn whirled and swung at two Glavers who tried to ambush him from behind. One fell and the other arced up and away shouting curses back at him. The soldiers who had retained discipline were now giving the attacking force some problems. Without as much room to manoeuvre as on the open bridge the Glavers couldn't fly freely and had limited range of motion. Mordalayn ran at the group and shouted. "Fight back to back. It's the only way!"

Some of the men heard him and began to heave together. One fell as a hover board caught him in the chin and sprawled at the head of the staircase. A Glaver managed to grab Mordalayn around the waist and he yelled in rage as the spindly, leathery arms tightened. "Got you!" the Glaver cackled but then suddenly shrieked and dropped him. Mordalayn looked around confused and saw the Glaver twitching with a crossbow bolt in its head. He glanced up and Bue saluted him from one of the narrow windows above the door. The boy had found a spot to hide and pick off the enemy at the same time.

The light in the crystal burned brighter and the lightning was becoming more frequent. Fear took hold of Mordalayn as he looked up and realised that unless Jared could do something the plot would work and the queen would be forced through the portal to have her life ended. Grimly he turned and again raised his sword at the buzzing swarm around him.

Chapter 32

Jared was panting heavily as he forced himself up the steps and rounded the corner. The throne room was deserted, the sounds of the battle at the front entrance faint in the distance. Everybody in the royal palace was either hiding or fighting. He looked for the statue on the throne and saw it straight away. A large bird of prey, like an eagle or a falcon. He ran up and was about to approach it when a familiar and grotesque shape lunged out of the shadows and stood in his path.

Skidding to a halt he was confronted by the ghastly sight of Rancidrain. He was still wearing his tattered old blue suit and held out his arms wide as Jared stuttered on his feet in front of him.

"We-ee-ll!!" he cackled nastily. "Seems you can't stop being nosey can you little boy?" and Jared saw he had another rainbow blade in his filthy hands but this time it was a huge curved sword, the lights playing merry colours on the wall.

Kloee shouted in her high voice. "I've had enough of this. Ugly people with ugly souls!" and flew straight at Rancidrain who, caught off guard, tried to swat her with the blade but missed. His grotesque, eyeless face contorted in panic and he staggered back, tripping over the top step that led to the throne. He floundered and fell, dropping the sword on himself.

"No!" he shrieked as the blade pierced his leg. Jared watched him glow the same rainbow colours as the sword and the shriek stretched out and then died away as Rancidrain exploded into little dots of multi-coloured light. The dots slowly drifted apart and spread out across the vast room and up to the ceiling. The sword faded and, like in the hospital, turned into a lump of rock. Jared stared at it and Kloee flew back to him as the final snatches and pieces of colour that had been Rancidrain faded away.

"Nasty, horrid, horrid man," she snapped. Jared ran forward and pushed the left eye of the carved bird. With a gentle swish, a panel behind the throne slid back and he ran towards it. Kloee made to follow him but he turned and shouted; "No! Mordalayn said no one from this world can come in here. I have to do this alone."

She pouted angrily but flew back, looking worried and Jared stepped through, the door closing behind him.

Chapter 33

In front of him was a small room, circular in shape and with many tiny, arched windows on the side opposite the doorway. In the middle was what looked like a huge, clear, glass rose but as if someone had pinned back the petals. Above him was another crystal, a smaller version of the colossal one in the main tower. It was glowing brighter and brighter as he looked. It was directly above the trap on the floor.

Making his way to the huge petals he saw many spirals of what looked like thin strands of blue smoke twisting in the centre, making lazy patterns in the air. Around and between them, sparks of light flashed randomly. It was too late, she was already coming through. Panicking he tried to move the device with his foot but it was too big and heavy. As he kicked it the glass rang clear as a bell in the tiny room. Wincing as the sound hurt his ears he tried twice more, each time succeeding only in making a deafening racket. The smoke became thicker and twisted in ever more complicated patterns. It reminded him of the patterns of DNA threads that they'd showed him in Biology at school. There were flashes of crystal light in the centre of the device and they flickered like shooting stars. He glanced up and saw the crystal protruding from the ceiling, glowing like a huge diamond, impossibly bright.

He glanced at the trap again and realised what it was. As she appeared it would close up and pin her within the petals. The smoke and sparks got more and more frequent and the crystal burned so bright. Desperately he stepped into the centre of the petals and his vision blurred, the scenery shifted and his stomach lurched. He was suddenly standing at the end of a long, ornately decorated corridor. Sophie Roberts was facing him at the other end, flowers in her hair and wearing a purple silk nightdress that moved slightly from a gentle breeze. She smiled serenely and was clearly unaware of what was going on. Behind her stood an open door and Jared glanced over her shoulder to see it led to a hospital room. Directly behind Sophie and down at an angle was Sophie again, lying in bed asleep with the green sheets pulled up to her chest. A woman sat by her bed crying and holding her hand and Jared could see what looked like a doctor with his back to him. Sophie floated towards Jared and her gaze was only on her destination, she did not see or register that he was there. Jared quickly glanced around and saw that the corridor's walls were pulsating, first pastel shades of peach and pink and blue and then fading to become transparent, revealing a black void of eternity beyond.

"SOPHIE!!" he yelled as loud as he could. She didn't respond and continued towards him. Jared knew that if she came into this world she would die.

"SOPHIE! STOP IT'S A TRAP!!" he yelled again, waving his arms frantically above his head to get her attention. Again she paid no heed. The sound of beating wings suddenly began to fill the air and Jared glanced around quickly to try and see what was making the noise. He saw nothing and his foot scraped on the floor as he positioned himself to stand in Sophie's way. She drifted on regardless and her smile was one of peaceful joy. Jared glanced down and saw that he was standing on nothing, the floor beneath pulsating to the same rhythm of pastel shades and then invisibility as the walls.

"SOPHIE ROBERTS!!" he screamed as loud as he could "MORDALAYN SAYS IT'S NOT SAFE!! PLEASE GO BACK, THIS IS A TRAP!!"

With a sudden jerk of her head Sophie's eyes snapped out of their glazed look and she stared directly at Jared. Her expression changed to one of confusion and alarm. She glanced over her shoulder at the open door to her hospital room and again back to Jared. The sound of beating wings became louder and louder. Jared screamed as loud as he could.

"KING JAMES BETRAYED YOU. THIS IS A TRAP! YOU HAVE TO GO BACK!!"

Sophie was now fully aware of what was going on and she frantically glanced around and down at her own body, the flowers in her hair tumbling to the floor and then passing through it and vanishing as the room pulsated into nothingness again. Jared looked at the walls and he could see red dots in the black infinity beyond them. As the corridor pulsed into colour and back into void again he saw they were dozens of eyes.

Sophie looked at Jared again and nodded in understanding, then turned and ran back down the corridor, her nightdress billowing and then she was gone, the door slamming behind her. Jared saw the corridor pulsate once more into colour and then it was gone. He was petrified, standing on an infinity of nothing, the sound of beating wings getting ever louder and the crimson eyes around him darting everywhere. Far in the distance, he saw corridors like this one. But these were gold, red, blue, silver. They faded as he stared at them.

Screaming in fear he suddenly fell and as his vision blurred again. He found himself sitting on the floor in the room, one of the open petals of the trap had tripped him. His heart racing he staggered to his feet and breathed slowly, trying to calm down. He glanced up and saw that the crystal was now dimmed, the brilliant light no longer glowing.

Chapter 34

Jared tried to calm down and forced himself to breathe normally. Slowly he staggered to his feet and lurched towards the windows. He looked out into the blue skies of Alegria. His heart gradually slowed down and he placed his hands on the cold stone. As he was about to turn he glanced up at the window and saw something move behind him. He ducked and whirled around as a piece of metal pipe missed his head by inches and smashed the window. He stared at the person in front of him, open mouthed.

"M, M, Madame Veer?!!" he stuttered, not believing what he was seeing.

The woman glared at him as she removed the pipe from the remnants of the window and turned to face him.

"Yes Jared. If you hadn't got involved you wouldn't have to die."

She raised the pipe and moved towards him, Jared moved back trying to get around to the door but she kept moving, keeping the trap and herself between him and his way out.

"Why?" Jared pleaded, perplexed and still not fully believing what was happening.

"Why?" she snapped. "WHY? Have you ever been in control of something and then had it taken away from you and then never, EVER been able to get it back?"

Jared's mind raced. He didn't know what she meant but ventured. "But you control the orphanage, everyone respects you there…."

"THE ORPHANAGE!!" she shrieked and then laughed bitterly. "The orphanage is nothing. Waifs and strays that think they have a right to be looked after."

"But what...no one wanted to hurt you. Why would you try and kill Sophie?" Jared asked, glancing past her and trying to see if he could make a run for it. She sensed his intentions and shifted her body again to block him.

"I WAS Sophie you little imbecile!" she shrieked and Jared still stared at her confused. "Do you think a little girl could rule this place forever? Time does not stand still here. Sophie is not the first ruler of this world nor will she be the last."

Jared finally realised what she was saying and realisation hit him like a hammer to the chest.

"But...but...YOU?!!"

"Yes me? Don't look so surprised I was young once too. I left this world behind when I grew up. Time moves three times faster here and when I wanted to come back no one remembered me.. Do you know what that feels like? Can you even begin to imagine how that feels?"

"But Sophie is...she must have known who you were."

Madame Veer snorted with disdain and the pipe wavered in her hands. She glared at Jared. "That girl knew but her sweet pretence and attempts to remind me that I was now nothing were worse than if she too had no knowledge of me." She paused and looked so sad and stared at the floor as she told her tale. "Head of an orphanage!!!" She sniffed and wiped a tear away on her sleeve, her normal fearsome facade was in tatters. "I ruled this world fairly and that was my reward? To become a headmistress for parentless brats?"

Jared tried to lunge past her but she raised the pipe and stood in his way again. She continued; "I'm dead in your world. I can't go back. I have to stay here now. If you hadn't interfered this would all have been put right. I could have ruled again, everything would have been perfect but YOU SPOILED IT." She shrieked the last words and then lunged at Jared. Frantically he ducked under the blow she aimed with the pipe at his head and pushed her backwards. "Nasty! Interfering! Little...!" She gasped as they tussled and then her boot snagged on one of the glass petals and with a shriek of fear she fell backwards into the trap.

Jared staggered back as her grip on him was released and as she attempted to sit up the petals suddenly all glowed a bright, buttercup yellow and silently began to rise.

Glancing around her in fear Madame Veer looked in horror as the trap closed in around her. "NO!!" she screamed and stood, trying to push her way through the gap between two petals but was forced back as they squeezed shut.

"HELP ME JARED!!" she shrieked in fear as the glass petals completely closed and with an almost inaudible "chunk" they met at the top and sealed the trap completely.

Madame Veer pounded on the glass and gazed imploringly at Jared. "Please, don't let this happen." Her voice was muffled through the glass and as Jared watched in horrified fascination, flashes of light began to appear from the bottom of the trap once again. The same thin blue tendrils of smoke rose, that he'd seen when Sophie had been coming through. They began to wind their way like plant shoots up and around Madame Veer.

Jared realised with shock that this trap would work equally well on Madame Veer as she had been a ruler of this world too.

She shrieked as the tendrils of smoke wrapped around her legs, torso and arms and strained to escape, futilely beating on the glass.

"Jared don't leave me like this, PLEASE!!" she pleaded. The petals began to glow brighter and Jared glanced up as they began to close in on themselves, shrinking in and becoming smaller.

The smoke inside now completely enveloped Madame Veer and she shrieked louder as the beads of light flashed rapidly. The trap continued to shrink and, pinned by the tendrils of smoke, Madame Veer managed to wrench her head and stare at Jared one last time. Her gaze became hard again and she snarled through gritted teeth. "To the nine hells with you Jared Miller and all who live in this filthy place."

Then the light inside became blindingly bright and Jared turned away. Shielding his eyes with his arm as the petals completely closed in on themselves and with a final flash of light the trap vanished. Madam Veer's final scream of frustration, fear and rage fading away.

Jared waited until the light ebbed away and, with spots dancing before his eyes, he looked at the place where the trap had been and there was nothing. Just a wooden floor and a ringing in his ears from the noise.

Chapter 35

The captain saw the crystal fade out and the lightning flashes over the tower die. The clouds parted and he lowered his spy glass. He turned to the king seated beside him who was looking up expectantly. Clearing his throat he spoke levelly. "Your majesty, the trap has been activated. Our mission was a success."

The king held out his hand for the telescope and the captain handed it over. King James squinted through the lens and trained the view over the battlements and towers of Alegria castle. The light in the highest spire was gone. The once brilliant and seemingly eternal brightness was no more. Only a dull grey crystal where the thousand year old beacon had once burned so brightly.

King James chuckled to himself and then handed back the telescope to his captain who bowed then stood to attention.

"Recall the Glavers, then send them back to Anghofio. We won't need them now," he said and the man moved to give the order.

The king sat on a throne of silver and gold. Encrusted with jewels, this was the chair his ancestors had used to oversee victories and battles for many centuries. The throne was now being used for the first time in aeons and King James wanted to savour this moment. Around him stood five of his most trusted guards, with a further ten men on perimeter duty further out. The field they were in was large, dotted with huge, ancient trees. Further back was the rest of his legion. One thousand men. More than enough to subdue the impotent and naked Alegrians now that their queen was gone.

Before him was a table, large and spread with fresh fruit, loaves of bread and a flagon of wine. Opposite him, holding a tankard in one hand sat Galfront Siavy who smiled as the king looked at him.

"You have done well Siavy," the king said taking a big bite from a succulent peach. Galfront bowed his head. "You will be richly rewarded for this. However, I need you for a short time longer." Galfront kept his face impassive at this but felt a twinge of worry. The king continued. "A man with skills such as yours is needed. I am sure a man such as yourself will not begrudge a grateful king such a request."

Galfront's smile did not fade but his blue eyes held the king's gaze. "Your majesty it would of course be an honour," he replied, running a hand across his closely cropped white hair. He knew he could not refuse the king but was uncomfortable of being right in the jaws of the Alegrians, regardless of whether the wolf was dying. An injured wolf is more dangerous he reminded himself and, like nearly everyone else, he was still shocked that their victory over Alegria had been so easy.

The captain returned and the king turned to him again and beckoned him forward. "Take four of my personal guard and ride to the castle. They are to be given one opportunity to surrender, unconditionally of course."

"Your majesty!" the man said, saluting, clicking his heels together and then turning. He pointed to four guards and barked at them. "You four, with me!" They marched after him as he made for the horses near an apple tree.

Chapter 36

The remaining men struggled, one soldier hauling down on the legs of his brother-in-arms as the man was pulled up by two cackling Glavers. They suddenly dropped him and with no warning sped away. The others did the same and as Mordalayn despatched the shrieking Glaver trapped under his boot with a downward swing, he looked to see them all shooting off into the distance over the bridge. Glancing up he saw the crystal had dimmed and the lightning display had stopped at the peak of the tower. Swallowing hard he hoped Jared had managed to do something.

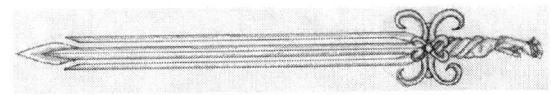

Checking around in case the enemy regrouped Mordalayn wiped his sword on the body of the Glaver beneath him. Where there had been a hundred or more men there were now only about forty. One man was weeping and clutching the lifeless body of his comrade. Others staggered around as if in a daze. The soldier who Mordalayn had rebuked for not having his sword was still alive, his face grimy. Mordalayn had seen the man fight bravely and he walked to him and placed his hand on the soldier's arm.

"You fought well," he said and the man muttered his thanks and tried to smile, his scared eyes darting around fearfully.

Some men were wounded and there were loud groans as their friends tried to move them. With a grinding noise the castle doors opened again and Degrezen appeared. He walked forward, the disbelief and shock evident on his face. Approaching Mordalayn he looked up at the blood spattered warrior. "Is hope lost Takoba?"

"That I do not know general," Mordalayn replied. The green fire burned in his eyes. They both glanced back as Jared emerged with Kloee.

Mordalayn moved quickly to him. "The crystal light has died," he said, the worry evident on his face. "Did you succeed or is Our Lady gone?"

Jared looked at him and said. "She's safe. I saw her. She looked at me and ran back."

Mordalayn breathed a sigh of relief but the look on Jared's face told him there was more. Jared saw it and before the Caracalic could speak Jared did. "Your traitor was Madame Veer. She ruled Alegria before Sophie."

The Caracalic's eyes widened in shock and the old man said "Veer!" in disbelief. "Is she..?"

"She fell into the trap meant for Sophie" Jared said and Mordalayn and the old man exchanged glances. "She's either dead or a long way from here. She vanished and the trap with her."

Mordalayn looked up at the dimmed crystal and then out towards the far fields where he knew King James'ss army was camped.

"What now?" Jared asked. Mordalayn was staring out at the woods beyond the main entrance, past the vast bridge. Jared was still shaken from the knowledge that the traitor had been Madame Veer. Her bitterness and rage as she'd pounded on the walls of the trap intended for queen Sophie was an image he would find hard to shake from his mind for a very long time.

"We wait," Mordalayn replied without looking back. "Sooner or later they will come to us. They saw the light fade when the trap activated. They believe the Emerald Queen is dead. Their treachery and cleverness will be their downfall."

Bue was helping soldiers to move the bodies of the Glavers to one side. One groaned and then was still. As Jared watched a small blue figure materialised out of thin air and waddled up to the corpse. He watched as the creature sat next to the body and started to talk.

"What's that?" Jared asked to Mordalayn who turned round and looked where Jared was pointing at the body.

Mordalayn looked at Jared quizzically. "It's dead. Does that matter now?"

Jared watched as the creature faded out again. "Not the Glaver the little blue thing." He pointed but the creature was gone.

Mordalayn looked concerned. "What did you just see?" he asked.

"Like a short…err, blue rat…kangaroo I suppose.."

Mordalayn looked around but no one else had heard Jared. "You could SEE that?" he asked quietly.

"Yes, why? Couldn't you?"

Mordalayn stared at him for moment then sheathed his sword. He looked Jared up and down and then gently placed his hands on his shoulders and said quietly. "Jared that was a Gryphoid. No one is meant to see them or know of their presence unless they have just died."

Jared swallowed hard. "Does, does that mean…?"

"No, you are not dead. It does prove however that you being in this world was something that was not meant to be."

"But you brought me here!" Jared snapped, exasperated.

"That was out of necessity. You are witness to knowledge and power that no one bar Our Lady is meant to know."

"Riders at the entrance!" a voice bellowed loudly and Mordalayn turned back to where a soldier was pointing.

Approaching the vast, curving, white entrance at the end of the huge bridge were five riders of King James's army. They galloped to the marble entrance and dismounted as one. One of the Alegrian guard went to them and after a few words of exchange the lead rider pointed towards Mordalayn. Mordalayn turned to Jared. "You come too," he said and Jared scurried to catch up as the warrior strode purposefully down the wide steps.

They reached the bottom and walked across the green grass of the gigantic, circular main courtyard. The soldiers could see them approaching and waited patiently. Mordalayn strode proudly forward, his jaw set in a hard, determined line. As they came to the waiting horsemen the leader bowed and spoke formally.

"Takoba Mordalayn. May I present myself. I am Captain Agostios Primmel of his royal majesty King James's army."

Mordalayn glared angrily at him and Jared looked nervously from the silent Caracalic to the captain. The man straightened up and adjusting his cloak continued.

"King James sends his regards to you. He respects your strength and your honour in defending your realm." The captain paused, feeling unnerved under Mordalayn's silent yet razor-like eyes. The Alegrian guards glared angrily at their counterparts who glared back just as hard.

"His majesty wishes you to know that he offers you terms of unconditional surrender."

Mordalayn said nothing. There were no others sounds in the vast courtyard. Jared didn't know what would happen next.

The captain was nervous and after a pause cleared his throat. "The alternative is that we take this castle and your kingdom by storm, which as I am sure you are aware, would not be a task now. Your queen is dead and your magic is extinct."

The two figures stared at each other and the captain spoke again. "Surely you can...."

"I agree," Mordalayn snapped.

The captain twitched slightly at the sudden response and then gestured his hand to Jared. "His majesty also insists that this boy is given to him."

Mordalayn glanced down at Jared and then to the captain. Jared's heart skipped a beat and he swallowed hard.

"Tell your king I will formally discuss surrender at the foot of the stairs to Our Lady's palace,"Mordalayn turned to the bottom step of the vast staircase. White marble statues of previous kings and queens and brave warriors of Alegria lined the high balustrades either side of it. "I'm sure your king will allow us that one piece of tradition in his flawless victory."

The captain smiled; relieved his task had been even easier than he had hoped. "But of course," he said curtly, bowing again and turned to signal to his men. They remounted their horses and as they wheeled them around. "We will return in two hours" the captain said loudly and then spurred his horse away, his men following at the gallop.

Mordalayn turned to Jared and placed his hand on his shoulder. He looked down. "Do not be scared Jared, this is far from over."

Jared stammered and then replied. "But you told him…."

"I know what I said Jared, but believe me this is not the end. We still have hope."

"Will you turn me over to him?" Jared said scared at the thought of being in King James's cruel clutches again.

Mordalayn stared at him. "Come, we have work to do," he said.

Chapter 37

The soldiers marched on Alegria. After centuries of living in the shadow of the accursed Alegrians and their ethereal monarchs, Anghofio would now be a proud and mighty kingdom once again. The soldiers marched happily, their feet stomping heavily on the road to the castle. Regularly the drummers leading them would beat four beats at double time and the soldiers would raise their rights fists high and shout at the top of their lungs "KING JAMES!

Every one of them was grateful to be there and everyone was hoping that the Alegrians would try to resist the conquest, so King James would give the order to sack the palace and city. He had ordered a peaceful march on the rival kingdom, solely to avoid the inevitable bitterness and resistance of a people who had not known oppression in over a thousand years. However, they also knew that their ruler would not hesitate to give the order if things did not go as he wanted.

The captain of the King's Shield had returned from his meeting at the castle and the excited buzz amongst the camp had been that it was none other than Takoba Mordalayn who had agreed the surrender. Many had seen his battle in the king's personal amphitheatre. While awed by his agility and skill, they were secretly pleased that the once mighty and legendary Queen's Sword had now been forced to humble himself.

"A pleasant day for an invasion don't you agree?" King James said to Galfront Siavy who rode next to him, near the front of the mighty column of men. Galfront smiled carefully, unsure if the king was speaking rhetorically.

King James smiled to himself. His Shield soldiers rode ahead, either side and behind him while the rest of the legion followed up. He could see the bridge ahead of them, maybe two hundred metres further and he braced himself, drawing in a breath as he savoured this moment. "*The final conquest of Alegria*," he thought. His forefathers had hated their impotent status in the face of Alegria's infuriating complacency and the tremendous power they wielded through their monarch. Anghofio's once legendary status as a mighty state of warriors had paled centuries ago, as soon as Alegria had found a way to bring a leader to their throne who wielded almost inestimable power. Their secrets were jealously guarded and it had taken the mysterious vanishing of Queen Sophie before anyone had been able to find out anything. The truth had been staggering and cost King James dearly in men and gold but the revelation of just where the Alegrian monarch came from had been shattering. With careful research they had found out exactly what was going on. The magic that had first created the devices to summon a child from another world continued. With appropriate bribery and subterfuge King James had found how to access the well protected portals that the Alegrians used to allow their queen free passage from her own world to this one. Now with her gone, there would be no more mythical rulers to infuriate stronger kingdoms with their sickening tolerance and desire to only use the magic to keep everything in balance. "*What was the point of power if you didn't use it?*"

As they approached the start of the bridge, as one huge voice the legion shouted "KING JAMES!!!", their fists again pumping the air.

The bridge was colossal. Pure white, solid marble. Around fifty metres wide and at least half a mile long. The walls either side were chest height to an average man and the view over the sides was heart stopping. Beneath the bridge was a drop of about half a mile, above a forest of trees and two snaking rivers. The kingdom's main city was four miles west. The castle could only be approached by this bridge but as Alegria had not had a standing army for centuries there was no longer any strategic advantage in the design of the defences. The huge main courtyard led up to the palace but the battlements either side again looked down via a sheer drop to the forest far below. It was a simple yet ingenious piece of engineering. Back in the days when Alegria had been a kingdom of warriors it had done the Alegrians proud in the many battles that history had recorded. Now the castle and all its power would belong to him and for that King James was determined to enjoy every second of this day. He needed someone to run the kingdom as his vassal and who better than a former Alegrian ruler unable to use her power and bereft of her magic. The king laughed out loud and the nearest members of his bodyguard twitched their heads in his direction. King James knew that Veer would rule as he told her, she was bitter and twisted after years spent having to pretend gratitude. That hatred of the kingdom she had once ruled would be the ideal tool to keep the confused Alegrians in line.

They crossed the middle point of the bridge. Ahead there were no guards. Alegria had no gate or portcullis to their entrance or their bridge. In hundreds of years they had needed no protection other than their magic and King James threw his head back and laughed once again as he thought of how such a mighty nation could be so oblivious to threat.

Further ahead and at the top of the huge steps they could see a few figures dotted along, outside the main doorway to the palace. The Caracalic and a smaller figure began to walk down the staircase to greet them and the King was pleased. The boy was the only remaining link to the waking world and would be a useful prisoner. He may also know much with the right persuasion and as they marched on the drummers again reached the beat and again the soldiers yelled out for their king.

Chapter 38

The legion was vast. Jared could see the huge numbers of men marching in time together, a moving wall of armour bristling with spears and swords. He and Mordalayn walked down the stairs to the bottom and stood on the last step, waiting.

He turned and looked at the tall figure who stared grimly at the approaching mass. "Let them come," Mordalayn said quietly and Jared didn't understand how he could be so calm in the face of such overwhelming numbers.

Some of the surviving soldiers were in the magisterial tower behind them, others formed a guard of honour. Their presence, although welcome was insignificant next to the mighty army sweeping across the land towards them.

The deafening "tramp, tramp" of booted feet resounded over the courtyard. Jared knew that while they had succeeded in saving Sophie's life they were far from safe and the kingdom may still fall without its leader.

A trumpet sounded as the troops neared the white marble palace courtyard, large enough to swallow four football fields. The orange and black cloaked men came steadily inside.

Jared watched open mouthed as hundreds of men marched into the building and stood in lines in the vast square.

Jared looked up at Mordalayn again and spoke above the steady pounding of feet. "I hope you know what you're doing." Mordalayn didn't look at him but moved back to one side. He looked to the soldiers around him. "Go back to the top of the staircase, do not come down it again no matter what happens," he said with finality. The soldiers looked at him and then moved away.

The approaching legion finally came to rest as the last of the troops stood in the circular plaza. With the sound of pealing trumpets they came with an almighty crash of feet to a shuddering stop.

There was a pause and then, as if by some unheard signal, the centre of the mass of men separated and a path appeared directly in the middle. Slowly two riders walked to the entrance and then dismounted. Handing the reins to a servant they slowly walked up the path cleared for them. "King James!" Jared said loudly and Mordalayn stared ahead, his face full of silent fury.

As the king approached he looked left and right and then up the huge steps to where Mordalayn and the others watched them.

He came to rest at the foot of the stairs and placed one foot upon the lowest one, saluting and then bowing with a flourish. Captain Primmel stood beside him.

"Gentlemen!" he shouted loudly, the sound echoing as there was absolutely no other noise in the huge courtyard.

"Gentlemen, I commend your loyalty to your departed queen." Mordalayn said nothing.

"Your loyalty knows no bounds. For that we are willing to spare your lives." King James paused for effect then looked round at the hundreds of men standing silent and armed behind him.

Mordalayn simply glared at him.

"Come, come" King James said laughing slightly. He turned to his gathered legion. "What do you think gentlemen?"

As one they responded with a deafening roar; "KING JAMES!!!"

He looked up again at the small group above him and smiled, the humour not fading from his eyes. "You are heroes now my friends, try not to become martyrs too. I offer this once only. Lay down your weapons and kneel to me and I will spare your lives."

Mordalayn replied in a rumbling voice. "James you are a traitor and a coward. My place is at the side of my queen. In this world, her world or the next world. I will never kneel to you."

James looked up and for the first time Jared saw disappointment on his harsh face.

"You agreed surrender Takoba," the king reminded him. "Are you willing to see your city and palace destroyed for your foolish pride?"

Mordalayn continued. "I agreed to discuss surrender. I never said whose. I now offer you one chance to turn around and return to Anghofio and never come back."

James stared at the Caracalic in disbelief. Then he threw back his head and laughed, a deep throaty roar. Agostios Primmel looked nervous, and glanced around quickly.

"My, my," the king said wiping his eyes with the back of his hand. He turned to the troops behind him and shouted. "What do you think men? Should we turn and leave with our tails between our legs?"

There was a mighty roar of laughter from the assembled troops and the king turned back to Mordalayn, still grinning. "Takoba Mordalayn, sword of the Alegrian queen. Your loyalty and courage are equalled only by your stupidity."

Mordalayn said nothing, his emerald eyes boring into the king. Then he spoke slowly and clearly. "Leave now and swear on what little honour you possess to leave Alegria in peace and I will spare your life and the lives of your men."

The king's face hardened and his amusement vanished.

"Very well," he replied and donned his helmet, the ornate gold and pearl armour shining in the bright sunlight. "You now leave me no choice. My men were hoping you would fight."

He turned to the gathered soldiers, drew his sword and raised it high above him. "Gentleman today we take Alegria."

His men roared louder than they had ever roared before.

Chapter 39

Jared was terrified. The king's obvious amusement at Mordalayn's arrogance had vanished once he realised the Caracalic was not simply making a gesture of defiance. As King James turned to face the thousand or so men assembled in the courtyard Jared's mind flashed to his family back home and wondered if they would ever find out what became of him. He looked up at Mordalayn to try to persuade him to accept the king's terms and to his astonishment he saw that he had his eyes closed and was silently mouthing words. The crystal on the pommel of his sword glowed brightly, green and clear as King James addressed his men. They roared as they prepared to follow his command to attack the castle. Jared then looked left and saw one of the huge, white marble statues on the staircase wall turn its head with a scraping noise and stare at Mordalayn. The statue was of a warrior, bare headed and designed with the armour of a knight. It frowned at Jared and then squatted down and jumped to the stair below it with a crunch.

Before he could say anything two more suddenly turned their heads and looked at King James. One looked like Kulkrain, with even the braided hair as part of the design and the tattoo chiselled on the upper left arm. The other was a woman, designed with a military uniform and holding a marble sword. A few of the front ranks of King James'ss men shouted in alarm and then the statues climbed down from their positions and jumped down onto the stairs with loud, crunching thuds. Mordalayn was still mouthing something almost silently. *"Whatever the spell was, it was clearly something that King James's research had overlooked,"* Jared thought.

The statues were elaborately carved and detailed. As King James turned in alarm, Captain Primmel leapt forward and stood in between the approaching statues and their leader. The nearest statue raised its arm to block the sword swing and then brought its other arm forward like a huge hammer into his chest. He flew back into the ranks.

The other statue reached King James, who was attempting to move back to the safety of his men, and took his arm. He yelled in fear and another soldier ran forward and tried to tackle the implacable stone figure. It brought its arm round and slapped the man who landed like a rag doll at the feet of his comrades.

The other soldiers began to shout in panic and the front ranks moved forward to assist their king. King James screamed. "Help me! Get them off me!" The first statue got a grip on his other arm and they began pulling him up the steps, roughly. As men spilled forward to tackle them the statues lashed out with arms and feet and marble swords. A total of six had stepped down from their positions on the walls and their vacant pedestals stood bare in the high noon sun. Two held James's arms and pulled him back while the other four stood in front forming a shield around the king. They completely blocked the stairwell, preventing anyone from getting past. Mordalayn grabbed Jared and picked him up once more, like he had at Heathrow airport. He ran in swift bounds to the top of the staircase. As they got to the top Jared turned to see the genius of what Mordalayn had done. Even though there were a thousand men in the vast courtyard none could make it past the statues that completely blocked their way.

It was so simple yet brilliant. None of King James's archers dared fire as they could not see their king due to the gigantic marble guards that stood in his way. More of his elite soldiers ran up to try and rescue their leader. Swords clashed on stone and the statues were relentless, simply shoving and swatting the men back as they methodically stepped backwards, their huge feet thudding on the stairs as they made their way to the top. A crush was forming as the once disciplined army tried to force its way through. After having been promised an easy victory they were not about to see it thrown away by a tactic such as this.

Mordalayn pulled Jared behind the right hand wall at the top of the stairs, looked at him once more and then drew his sword and dropped to one knee. He held the tri-blade out in front of him, both hands on the hilt with the green jewel facing the heavens and the blades pointing down. He closed his eyes and spoke slowly but loudly. "Our Lady, in this time of our darkest hour, of our greatest need, I invoke the most terrible of your protections to save Alegria."

With that he lunged down hard and with a clang the three blades penetrated the stone by about six inches. Sparks flew as the razor sharp metal ground into the smooth rock and Mordalayn shifted his grip on the hilt to touch the green jewel at the pommel tip.

King James was struggling violently against his two captors. One of them stood on his cloak and the king nearly fell, the fabric ripping as the marble foot tore a jagged shred from the silk.

More soldiers were running from the front ranks, their orange and black cloaks making them look like a swarm of ladybirds as they hurled themselves to protect their monarch. It was to no avail as the marble creatures contemptuously swatted each newcomer aside, their strength immense and with a clash of metal and stone the various soldiers who bravely tried to defend their king were thrown back.

Mordalayn placed his left hand on the top of the huge green jewel and said "watawashinda kebakaran" repeating the phrase again and again, his voice getting louder.

The statues had now managed to get King James half way up the stairs and he struggled and shouted for help. The front most ranks of his men were still trying valiantly to save him but despite their numbers they could gain no advantage on the narrow steps. One man tried a reckless move, darting directly at the king through a small gap between two of the stone figures and grabbing his hauberk, trying to pull him back. The left side statue grabbed him by the top of the head with one huge hand and threw him effortlessly against the vast stone wall. He hit it and fell hard, landing in the many multi-coloured flowers in the elaborate garden, his heavily armoured body crushing the delicate petals and stalks.

Mordalayn still chanted and Jared saw the green jewel glow brighter and brighter, like the one on his bracelet in the airport. He gazed, mesmerised, as swirls of green light appeared from the jewel and spun around it and upwards, lazily at first but then faster and faster. "Watawashinda kebakaran, WATAWASHINDA KEBAKARAN." The light wove in the air and a wind appeared, whipping Mordalayn's long hair and fur and Jared staggered in its billowing gasp. The Alegrian soldiers on the landing staggered back to the doorway and wall, squatting down and trying to shield themselves from the furious gale. A high keening noise rose and got higher and higher, like a scream of anger being slowly increased in volume.

Mordalayn stood now, his fingers still resting on the top of the sword hilt and he chanted louder and louder. He grasped the sword hilt with his other hand and tugged hard. The sword came free but the two outer blades remained locked in the marble floor, the lights weaving around them. He stepped back and one more time shouted as loud as he could, his voice carrying even over the din of the wind. "WATAWASHINDA KEBAKARAN...FOR ALEGRIA" and the whirling lights dove simultaneously into the embedded sword blades and made them glow an emerald green. Simultaneously the blades wrenched themselves free of the stone with a grinding noise and a shower of sparks and shot upwards. They hovered about five metres above and started to spin, clanging together faster and faster until they were a blur. Mordalayn grabbed Jared and pulled him back to the castle doorway, turning his face to the wooden door and pulling Jared's head into his chest as the sword blades merged and erupted into light.

The explosion shot forward, a streamlined blur of white and green brilliance. A wall of fire that swept past the statues, King James and those of his soldiers who were on the staircase. It halted for a moment at the base of the stairs and formed into a vast monolith of pulsing, dilating power and with a final scream of anger it erupted again into the vast courtyard.

The shock wave bowled all men before it over, their bodies ripped to dust by its immense and inescapable power. Only those on the steps survived its furious wrath. The wave rippled and moved back then forward again, purging all before it. The hundreds of men that had proudly and silently stood in the plaza were now rendered into ashes. A few screamed as they saw the devastation being wrought on the front ranks and a few at the rear tried to run. The whole thing lasted less than a minute. The pulsing, ebbing power of the spell Mordalayn had wrought left nothing in its wake but ashes and dust.

Suddenly and without warning the shock wave disappeared, the green and white light slowly calmed and faded, the motion slowing and then there was nothing. Only the blackened earth of the once beautiful plaza stood. After a pause a wind came and whipped up the dust and ashes, swirling them round and then blowing them out the main entrance and far out to the green lands and forests beyond.

Mordalayn released Jared and he staggered forward. He looked over the lip of the right hand balcony and saw the ruins of the once proud plaza. The scorched earth and blackened walls cast a depressing balance to the ruined gardens that had been destroyed and torn apart in the shock wave. He gazed open mouthed and then his gaze shifted to the struggling King James, now at the top of the stairs, his stone captors standing still. They held his arms firmly and looked silently through white marble eyes at Mordalayn. The other four escorting him also stood still, their heads turned to look at the Caracalic. The pursuing Anghofian soldiers who had survived were now uncertain of what to do. They stood a few steps down from their captured leader and looked around, confused, angry and frightened. They had been promised an easy victory without even a token show of resistance and now they had witnessed their legion decimated.

Mordalayn stepped forward and sheathed his sword, the remaining blade locking into place, the jewel now dimmed back to a milky shade of green.

He ignored the still wriggling King James and addressed his men.

"Survivors. You are loyal men. Willing to give your lives to defend your king. For that I offer you your lives. Lay down your swords and you will be spared."

The thirty or so men hesitated, unsure of what to do.

"Don't listen, SET ME FREE!!!" King James screamed at them.

Mordalayn glanced at the statues who pulled King James'ss arms until he squealed and then went quiet.

"You have nothing to bargain with. You are our prisoners. Throw down your swords."

The men still hesitated and then one, a helmetless man raised his sword. "You dogs think you can tell the King's Daggers what to do?" he snarled and hurled himself up the stairs. There was a twang and a crossbow bolt buried itself in him. With a gurgle he was hurled back, his body rolling down the steps with a crashing of armour until he finally lay still at the bottom.

"Ye-es!!" Bue exclaimed from his hidden spot in the main tower.

The other soldiers looked at Mordalayn and then slowly, one by one lay their swords gently on the steps and raised their hands in surrender.

Chapter 40

The Alegrian soldiers came forward with their swords brandished and rounded up the prisoners and took them to the main landing, against the palace wall.

Mordalayn turned to King James and motioned to the statues to release him. They did and then, bowing in respect to the Caracalic, moved off down the steps, making their way to their resting points on the walls. Their positions scarred black from the shock wave. Without hesitation they climbed back up and stood in their original positions. Still and motionless, no sign could be seen that they had ever moved.

King James was still wearing his sword and a soldier moved forward with his own weapon drawn and took it.

"Kill me you witch's lapdog," James snarled as Mordalayn stared at him, his gaze as cold as winter rain.

"I would love to," Mordalayn replied quietly. "But I serve the Emerald Queen and she set down rules that even I cannot break."

James snarled at him again and laughed, throwing his head back. "So put me in one of your jails oh mighty nanny to the queen. If you cannot kill me then you should know that no prison can hold me."

Mordalayn looked intently at him. "I cannot kill you without reason. You are too dangerous to be set free"

James then smiled and said slowly and loudly. "I invoke right of single combat."

There was a gasp from the people around, including the captured Daggers.

Mordalayn stared at James and replied. "That will not change your status as a prisoner, merely commute your execution to life in jail."

James sneered. "If I have to spend my life in one of your stinking cells I will smile every day knowing I put you in your grave."

Mordalayn looked at him solemnly. "This is an ancient law of our world. I will not break it. I accept your challenge."

James laughed again and cast his cloak to one side. "Very well, at least I will have the satisfaction of seeing you die."

Mordalayn drew his sword and glanced over to the soldiers. They understood and ten men created a circle around the two combatants. One threw a sword at James'ss feet. As Mordalayn walked up and stood facing him the final soldier took up position. Five others faced the captured men with their swords drawn and their eyes full of anger.

Mordalayn glanced over his shoulder to where he knew Bue was hidden. The boy saw the look on the Caracalic's face and lowered his bow.

James faced the Caracalic with wary eyes, his contempt never leaving his face. He began to edge around the inside of the circle of men, his blade held expertly before him.

"You know I am the best swordsman in Anghofio?" he taunted Mordalayn who stood stock still and simply turned his head to watch James as he tried to flank him.

"You talk too much," Mordalayn replied and with blinding speed he brought his sword in an arc over his head to where King James stood. The man parried the blow, the clash of steel loud in the otherwise silent theatre of combat. He jerked with the impact, adjusted his footing and then countered with a blinding side sweep. Mordalayn leapt back and snarled, avoiding the blow with ease and then lunged forward. James brought his own sword down and bent in the middle to avoid the lunge that would have disembowelled him. He then struck again and again, trying to drive Mordalayn back. The Caracalic simply stood there and countered the ferocious blows and then stepped to one side and brought his own sword round in an arc to James's head. He changed the angle at the last moment and James just managed to leap clear as the hilt caught him in the face, the hard metal gashing his forehead.

He stood back, panting and glared at Mordalayn, touching the small wound. Jared stared on awestruck and no one made a sound. The circle of Alegrian soldiers remained implacable, watching the fight emotionlessly.

James drew back his fingers and frowned. "It seems you have first blood," he said thinly. He then ran at the Caracalic and again tried to hammer his sword down in blinding, unpredictable arcs of blurring motion. Mordalayn simply dodged and weaved, both feet firmly on the ground and then parried the final swing, bringing his foot up and kicking James square in the stomach. With a whoosh of air he staggered back and folded slightly, then threw up his sword to parry Mordalayn's renewed attack.

The men broke apart again and circled each other. The wall of guards were now looking less than impassive. One or two were looking concerned.

Mordalayn launched himself at James again who span around as he came towards him, then ducked down and aimed his sword at Mordalayn's legs. The Caracalic saw the movement in time and jumped clear. James had anticipated his ruse being seen and simply brought his sword back in an abrupt reversal as Mordalayn leapt over the flashing blade. The Caracalic's reflexes were still so good that he managed to dodge that blow too, at least the full force of it. The blade nicked his chest, the droplets of blood spattering into the air.

The men broke again, James was panting slightly. One of the guards made to move forward but Mordalayn held up his hand again. "Hold! He's mine!"

The man stepped back, looking worried and stepped back into the protecting circle. James glared at Mordalayn who ignored the blood seeping down his shirt.

"You are good Caracalic, I give you that. Maybe your forsaken queen wanted you for more than your abilities as a wet nurse."

Mordalayn snarled and launched himself at James again who parried and the swords clashed. Both men struggled against each other, the blades locked. "You should have joined us," James hissed through gritted teeth into the Caracalic's face as they stared at each other over their blades. "What use is a dream warrior without a dreamer?"

"Loyalty is something you know nothing of," Mordalayn spat at him shoving James back hard. He fell into one of the guards who pushed him back into the centre.

"Clear the circle," Mordalayn shouted and the guards, after a moment's hesitation stepped clear. James smiled and wiped his forehead with his sleeve.

"Well, well" he said, spinning his sword over his hand and moving back into the larger space now given to him. He ran at Mordalayn again and their blades clashed, broke free and then rang out again. Steel upon steel the blades fell and rose again, a lethal blur of metal. The panting of James was now being joined by Mordalayn's. Jared was worried, he'd never seen the Caracalic look even remotely tired before now.

James jumped back and lunged again at Mordalayn who stepped clear and drove his elbow into James's face. There was a crunch and James screeched and broke clear.

Mordalayn paused and stared with expressionless eyes at the traitor. James recovered and spat out the blood that had run into his mouth.

"Did anyone ever tell you why you have no childhood?" he said and lunged at Mordalayn who parried the blow again. He didn't answer but continued to edge around where James stood, looking for an opening.

"Didn't you ever wonder?" James hissed at him gasping, his hair messy with sweat, sticking to his face.

Mordalayn again hurled up his sword, the blade catching James's blade. He still didn't answer but the flicker of anger and curiosity on his face was all James needed.

"Ever wondered why your life began when you were 14 summers old?" James said, lunging again and Mordalayn this time simply stepped away. The crowd watching were now spellbound, even the prisoners were unable to look away.

Mordalayn stopped circling and held his sword in front of him, the blade pointing at the sky.

James grinned and seeing that he had the Caracalic's attention he said with finality. "If you kill me you'll never know."

There was a long pause while everyone watched and then with a blood curdling snarl Mordalayn swung viciously at James, his blade curving again and again. James tried to parry but the fury of the blows was too much for him. He was beaten back and with a thud his back hit the chest-high wall overlooking the forests of Alegria.

He raised his arm to parry Mordalayn's blow, aimed for his head. With a cry of pain the sword was wrenched from James's hand. The blade span as it arced out and down to the trees far below.

James stared at Mordalayn not with a look of defeat but with triumph etched on his face. He rested his arms on the wall and stared at the victorious Caracalic through bloody, exhausted eyes.

Mordalayn stood in front of James. His rage was obvious to all watching as he slowly raised his sword and placed the tip at James's throat.

"Go ahead," James whispered. "Break your precious Queen's most sacred law."

Mordalayn continued to glare at the man, the sword tips not wavering in the slightest.

Jared stepped forward. "Mordalayn, don't. If you kill him like this he's won. Don't you see? That's what he wants!"

The cat face twitched as the emotions churned inside him.

"Don't let him make you worse than he is," Jared pleaded.

James grinned at Mordalayn as he drew back the sword. "Do it," he said.

Mordalayn's eyes flashed and, as if there were some titanic battle going on his soul, he quivered slightly and then slowly lowered his weapon.

James's face transformed once more from triumphant smirking to enraged frustration.

Mordalayn sheathed his sword and looked at two of the guards standing silently watching.

"Clap him in irons and take him to the dungeons," he snapped with finality and turned his back on James who looked frantically from left to right as the guards moved in towards him.

As the two men reached out to grab his arms he snarled in frustration and reached with incredible speed for the nearest man's sword, still in its sheath. He tugged the weapon free and lunged towards Mordalayn's unprotected back, a scream of rage bellowing from his mouth, his teeth bared.

Jared watched the scene as if in slow motion, powerless to do anything to stop it. As the two guards lunged futilely after James he brought the short sword down towards the Caracalic. Just when it seemed Mordalayn was doomed, he span impossibly fast, and grabbed James's sword arm by the wrist and twisted down and backwards. The blade sank to the hilt in James's chest and then Mordalayn released his grip and took James by the collar of his silk shirt, lifting him off the ground so that they were face to face. He stared into James'ss eyes as the man struggled weakly in his grip, his strength fading.

"Sometimes, you should be more scared of a man with his back to you," he hissed and then removing one hand he grabbed James by his leg, lifted him over his head and hurled him over the wall, out and down into the forests, far below.

Mordalayn moved to the edge of the wall and watched James fall until he was out of sight. Then he slowly turned to the astonished onlookers.

"He is gone," he said. "Let us try to rebuild our city," and moved past them all and towards the great doors of the palace.

Chapter 41

James's battered and broken body lay at the foot of a tree. The branches his fall had torn clear from it lay around him. He could feel no pain but knew he must be dead. Far above him he could see the castle of Alegria, the bridge where he had victoriously taken his men visible above him and the spire of the largest tower rising high above the wall.

He heard a rustling and tried to move his head but couldn't. A creature made its way out of the undergrowth and stood in front of him. It was baby blue in colour and looked like a large rat with a small kangaroo's face. It's tail was fat and long, tapering away to a fine point behind it. It's feet were too big for it and they had claws like a lizard. Its arms were stubby and appeared useless. It stared at James, it's big, brown eyes looked peaceful and serene. James managed to find his voice.

"Are you the Gryphoid?" he asked.

"I am," it replied shuffling forward.

"I always believed that you came when people died," James replied. "I suppose that counts for something."

The creature looked at him for a moment and then replied. "It does, but that's where your good news ends I'm afraid."

As James watched, helpless, the creature's baby blue skin changed to a slate grey and its eyes went from two pools of gentle peace to twin slits of black evil. It smiled at him and the grin was one of pure spite and malice.

James gasped as the creature stood in front of him and at the same time noticed that the birds had stopped singing in the trees and the breeze that had been blowing had ceased. Time had stopped.

"Now," the creature rasped, its voice like nails on a blackboard. "Where shall we begin?"

Chapter 42

Bue and Jared sat on the vast, ruined lawn in front of the palace steps. Mordalayn's spell had scorched the grass to a black and brown wasteland, flashes of desert-dry earth showing through in sporadic patches. Everyone was exhausted and knew that while they had won this battle the fight was far from over.

Kloee flitted around near Jared, concerned about the mess and upset to see the hurt and pain that had happened.

Bue leaned with back against the scorched marble wall, in the remains of what had once been a luscious bed of flowers. All the flowers were gone now, their stalks twisted ash and their petals merely a memory. The damage was immense and all the Alegrians knew that it would take many months or even years for the place to be brought back to its former splendour. The surviving soldiers were scattered in and around the courtyard along with the rest of the palace population who had come out of hiding once the battle was over. There was no fight left in the captured prisoners any more. They had all surrendered meekly and were now in the palace dungeons. Mordalayn had instructed that ALL prisoners were to be treated with respect and without suffering harm unless they initiated it. After so much loss and erosion of their beloved ruler's principles no one wanted to see any more of this wretched descent into brutality and anarchy.

Jared was tired. He was still shocked about Madame Veer. Wherever the trap had taken her she had gone out with vengeance in her eyes. Jared just hoped that she was somewhere far from any place she could hurt anyone else ever again. Her fury just before the trap disappeared was her true rage and the pleading and tears had melted in the face of her real anger.

Mordalayn walked over to Jared. His clothes were tattered and his jerkin was spattered from the fighting. Despite his ragged demeanour he still looked fresh and Jared was amazed at the Caracalic's stamina.

"Jared you need to rest now. There is no more we can do."

"But I...I, I saw Sophie. She was THERE."

Mordalayn shook his head and stared at Jared, his face showing no emotion. "Our Lady is still lost to us. Whatever brief break from her state you saw was not permanent."

"But...Mordalayn she SAW me, she was out of her coma. She must have been or she wouldn't have been able to run away." Jared was distraught. They had fought so hard to save everything and it seemed to have made no difference.

Mordalayn placed his huge hand on Jared's shoulder. "No Jared. This is not over. Whatever we have won here is just a small victory. We need to fight to keep what we have reclaimed. There may be other traitors who will rally their forces and try again. The Glavers will not come back now, but someone else may appear to lead them."

Jared's head drooped and he pulled away from Mordalayn's touch. He was tired, physically worn out and now THIS.

He moved to where Bue was resting, one hand protectively placed over his crossbow, his pack resting in the black ruins of a flower bed where he had placed his head.

Jared sat down heavily next to him and Bue immediately stirred. He opened one eye and squinted at Jared. "Alright?" he asked then grinned. "You look like leftover stew. Get some sleep."

"If only..." Jared said and stretched out next to Bue.

As Jared lay down, his mind full of the sound of clashing steel and Madame Veer's hateful glare as she was taken from this world he was suddenly startled by Bue yelping.

Sitting upright he shook his head to clear the descending syrup of sleep and shouted. "What? What's up?"

"Something's moving under me!" Bue shouted and jumped to his feet, grabbing his crossbow and attempting to crank it.

Jared stared at where Bue had been standing and saw nothing. Then the ruined earth rippled slightly as if there were worms moving underneath it. He stared again and heard other shrieks of surprise and shock from around the burned garden. The ripples became more fluid as he watched and with shock he saw a tiny green plant shoot emerge from the desiccated soil and wind its way upwards. Bue paused in the middle of fumbling for a quarrel. "What the....?" he gaped.

As Jared gazed fascinated the blackened ground began to slowly transform into a healthy, rich brown. All across the flower bed the earth changed and tiny plant shoots erupted from it. He and Bue gazed on as the shoots became longer and thicker and wound their way upwards. Then the tips began to form bulbs, one at a time like watching someone blowing molten glass. The stalks began to swell and then they suddenly blossomed into petals. The ones in front of him were white with splashes of pink and they were beautiful. The smell of the bouquet was intoxicating, like ten times more wonderful than the aroma of a flower shop back home. The other flowers burst into petals too, every conceivable colour available. Purple, yellow, pink, orange and red. He glanced quickly left and right and saw the most vivid display of colours he'd ever seen.

He turned and saw the other and people who had been sat or stood around were now on their feet, gazing uncomprehending at the transformation occurring in front of their eyes. The grass was returning too. First of all in small patches but then, like seeing a Mexican wave at a soccer game, the ripples spread and the desolate, blighted earth was flushed with lush, green grass two inches tall. The wave of green spread to the arched gateway and across the other side of the vast courtyard Jared could see the same effects as here.

He turned back to his side and the flowers were now fully grown, waving gently. Beautiful. The scorch marks on the marble walls faded like a thumb print on a computer screen and they shone in brilliance again. Jared stared and nudged the open mouthed Bue.

"What's happening Sharpeye?" he asked.

"No idea but at least it's not trying to kill us," Bue said, still looking shocked and glancing around rapidly. Kloee squeaked in fear and hovered behind Jared for protection.

They looked up to the palace steps and they too were now clean and glowing bright. Above them an emerald light shone from the huge windows in the throne room.

"Our Lady returns!" Mordalayn shouted and after a second's hesitation he leapt for the bottom of the steps and pounded up them to the main doorway.

Jared glanced around and saw that the whole area was now almost completely restored to its former glory.

The whole thing reminded Jared of watching the dents in a sheet of metal being pushed out on time lapse photography.

Mordalayn was at the top of the huge stairs now and he stopped in awed amazement as beams of emerald light sparkled from the front of the palace. The arched door was losing the nicks and scratches from the battle and was back to being solid, honey coloured oak again. The light radiated through the broken windows and one at a time the glass came back into place, snipping the light off as each pane was replaced one at a time. The stained glass patterns returned too, the exquisite artwork was rendered flawlessly. The myriad figures telling the history of the place, again acting out their eternal story through vivid pictures.

The light glowed brighter again. Jared, Bue and several others ran up the vast staircase to stand with the Caracalic who was as opened mouthed as they were.

"By the love of all that's pure," he half whispered as the building continued to restore itself, a pock mark from a Glaver board filled itself in and the wall was smooth again.

Finally the restoration was complete and the light gradually dimmed. The only emerald light now was above them, pulsing from the throne room windows and from the huge crystal in the main tower.

The vast entrance hall, although untouched in the battle looked as if a team of cleaners had spent a week on it. Everything shone and sparkled and looked clean and new. Flowers grew again and the vivid colours were just as beautiful as those in the courtyard. A huge silver vase of orange flowers was at the base of the vast staircase and the deep purple carpet that led up the centre and then forked off to the smaller staircases left and right practically glowed. The rich tapestry looking warm and inviting.

Mordalayn turned. "You five remain here, secure that door and check this area. No one is allowed in or out until I look upstairs."

Bue and four soldiers murmured their agreement.

Mordalayn turned to Jared and to five other soldiers. "With me," he said and then drawing his sword he quickly moved to the foot of the velvet stairs and began to cautiously go up them. At the junction he moved to the left and signalled the others to go right. They crept around and Mordalayn flinched as a parrot, layered in vivid colours flew squawking from the upper level. It settled on the big crystal chandelier hanging from the ceiling between the two winding stairwells. The crystals rattled slightly and it began preening itself, cocking its head and casting a quizzical eye over them.

Moving to the top they met again and Mordalayn saw the door to the throne room was half open. He signalled to Jared and the soldiers to move behind him and they approached the white and gold-inlayed doors. Mordalayn held his sword ready and taking a final look around he pushed the door open and Jared gasped.

Standing next to the crystal throne was Sophie. At least Jared thought it was Sophie but she looked different. Her body was shimmering like it was covered in sparkling dust and her elegant robes were vibrant green and silver. She appeared to be like some sort of spirit as her body was ever so slightly transparent. Her black hair was braided into a weaving pattern that tumbled down her back, tied with a purple ribbon where the braids met.

Sophie appeared not to notice them and was looking around the room as if she was seeing it for the first time in a long while.

As she looked at different things they would change or flowers would bloom from the formerly barren vases and pots. The throne room once again looked fit for the presence of a queen. She looked up and smiled, the dimples in her cheeks moving as she saw them staring at her.

"Mordalayn!" she exclaimed happily, "my sweet protector." She moved forward, her feet not touching the ground as she appeared to glide down the small flight of mottled marble steps. She raised her arms as she approached the Caracalic.

"Mordalayn!" she exclaimed again, "how I have missed you." She smiled and her eyes shone with joy as she approached him. Jared stared on, unsure of what to say or do now. The soldiers next to them were also at a loss.

As she stood in front of the towering figure, Mordalayn's impassive face softened and he silently lowered his sword and then slowly dropped to one knee. The other soldiers followed suit but Jared was too dumbstruck to copy them. No one seemed to notice.

Sophie looked at Mordalayn without saying anything, lowering her arms and standing expectantly as the Caracalic bowed his head.

"My Lady," he said softly, in his deep voice. "My Lady…I am moved beyond words that you have returned to us."

Sophie smiled again approvingly. "Come my friend, stand and hug me. I have missed you too."

Mordalayn remained on his knee with his head bowed and he spoke again after a pause. "My Lady I…I have strayed from the path."

Sophie looked puzzled but her smile remained as she stared lovingly at the kneeling warrior, her robes and a few stray locks of hair moving slightly as if in a breeze, although none was present.

"My most loyal and trusted friend," Sophie replied. "What could you have ever done that would earn my displeasure?"

Mordalayn raised his head and Jared saw to his astonishment that he was crying, a single tear on the huge furry cheek.

Mordalayn spoke again and his voice cracked with emotion. "My Lady I have let you down. I have killed men. I let my rage at your being taken from us hold sway on my emotions."

Jared looked on as Mordalayn gently turned the sword over so the hilt of the weapon was facing Sophie. "My queen," he croaked, his face incalculably sad. "I am unworthy to protect you. I failed in my duty."

He laid the sword at her feet and bowed his head again. There was a long silence Jared stared on at this most intimate and precious of encounters. The other men made no sound, even their breathing seemed quiet.

Sophie reached out and gently cupped Mordalayn's chin in her hand. Her jewelled fingers slowly raised his face to look at her.

She smiled again as butterflies flitted around her and then moved away to the open window nearest the throne. Jared glanced quickly at them as they flew to the outside world and then looked back to Sophie.

Sophie spoke softly. "Mordalayn, my most precious. You are my most loyal friend in this or any other world. I can forgive your indiscretions. I know how much you love me and I would have no other for my personal guardian."

Jared stared at Mordalayn whose face was a mask of sadness. His former steel tough demeanour was gone. The wall of his willpower had finally collapsed after so long.

He made a muffled sob and said in a choked voice. "I thought I'd never see you again."

Sophie took his face in both of her hands and leaning forward she kissed his forehead gently.

"You have nothing to be ashamed of and everything to be proud of. Now please, stand and embrace me my most beloved friend."

Mordalayn struggled to his feet and Sophie flung her arms around him, burying her face against his chest and hugging him tightly.

"Take your sword," she said and Mordalayn retrieved his weapon from the floor and silently sheathed it. Turning to the others she smiled. "Please rise, loyal subjects of Alegria."

The soldiers rose as one and bowed their heads to their queen.

The room was adorned with flowers and the musk of blossom. Sophie turned her head to Jared.

"You must be the one who saved me from entrapment," she said holding out her hand. "Come," and Jared moved to her.

"You have my eternal gratitude," Sophie said to him. "Now, before my people meet their queen again I think you all need to tell me what has been happening since I left."

Chapter 43

The people came from the city and from every village and hamlet in the kingdom.

The green beacon signalling the queen was in Alegria had been dulled for over a year now. As news spread of Queen Sophie's return and the vanquishing of the tyrant James, they came in their hundreds to see their beloved ruler once again.

The emerald light in the castle glowed for miles, as far as the untouched lands in the north and the kingdoms of Estorlan and Flintor. Within half a day the palace plaza, signs of the destruction that had taken place upon it long gone, had filled with eager and excited citizens, buzzing with conversation. Gossip flying thick and fast as to how the queen had finally come back. Some said she had been kidnapped by King James and had escaped just this morning. Others said she had been held prisoner and had cunningly let King James think he had his victory before destroying his army and letting her champion Mordalayn best him in fair single combat. Others still said that the queen had abandoned her kingdom but returned because she could not bear to leave her beloved people behind to face the horrors of rule under Anghofio.

Whatever they said, it was nearly always inaccurate and only a handful of people knew what had really happened.

Above all, no one hated the queen any more. No one despised her for leaving and no one was resentful that she had been gone for such a long time. The fact she had returned was enough for them to love her once more.

Thousands of people filled the huge plaza and the feeling was almost something you could touch. A buzz of excitement was everywhere.

Jared looked up at Mordalayn from near the windows of the throne room. Sophie was talking with the members of her inner council who stood in respectful audience in front of her. Below the window Jared could see the multitudes thronging to welcome their ruler home. "So many people," he murmured in awe and Mordalayn turned to him and smiled. The first time Jared had seen him smile since they'd met.

"Our queen is loved by her people Jared," he said, his eyes sparkling. "They are grateful she is here once more." He placed one giant hand on Jared's shoulder. "You have been a true friend to Alegria Jared Miller. For that you have earned my friendship." Jared was slightly uncomfortable under the Caracalic's steel gaze but he realised that the fire and anger had gone. Mordalayn's eyes were still intense but his face shone with something other than the fury that Jared had seen over the last few days.

"Thank you," he said quietly and extended his hand. Mordalayn shook it firmly and clapped Jared on the back.

"Soon you can return home, I promise."

Jared bowed his head. Wanting to go back but also wanting to stay. He had seen so much here and he knew there was so much more he could see.

"I've been here for days. I probably have Interpol and God knows who looking for me now," he said shaking his head. "All that stuff at Heathrow will be on the News you know."

Mordalayn smiled again. "Your world's people have a habit of trying to explain everything. Even things they cannot explain. I believe what happened will be given a rational, yet wholly untrue explanation by those who think they know best."

Jared looked outside, the echoing noise from the crowd still loud. Kloee flew up next to him, smiling and perched on his shoulder.

They turned as Sophie rose from her throne and the councillors parted to let her through, bowing as she glided between them.

It was dark outside now, the daylight having faded and Sophie smiled at Mordalayn and linked her arm through his. "Come my friends," she said, looking at Jared. "It is time for me to meet my people once more."

Mordalayn moved to the large glass doors near the window. Checking, by habit, over both shoulders and also that the balcony was clear he pulled the doors open and as Sophie stepped out into the cool night air, there was a roar from the thousands gathered in the plaza. Sophie walked forward to the carved ornamental wall at the front of the balcony, Mordalayn striding purposefully one step behind. She turned and looked back at Jared, then beckoned him forward. "Come, you should be here too," she said and Jared nervously stepped up next to her.

The crowd were going crazy. Cheering and waving madly. The sight of their beloved queen whipping them into a frenzy of joy. Sophie smiled and waved at her people and they cheered and cheered.

Jared stood transfixed by the sight below him. He looked around and saw the moonlight casting cool velvet shadows on the balcony around him and down to his left onto the main landing and the staircase and its elegant carvings and statues.

Overhead the crescent moon was bright in the cloudless sky. Like a sickle it hung in the starry void, casting its protecting light over the crowd below it.

The people below rippled gently as if made of water and Jared could see them surging as one, their arms raised in greeting to their queen, finally returned after so long. Their hearts soared as they gazed upon her once more, the terrible threat from Anghofio and King James now gone.

Jared looked up, beyond the vast entrance to the circular plaza and saw the huge bridge vanishing behind it in the distance. The dark woods black as ebony. Still more people were coming across to join the multitude at the foot of the palace. He looked up at Mordalayn who leaned forward and whispered quietly. "Now watch."

At that moment Sophie stepped forward and raised her arms. Again the crowd roared. She sang loudly in a sweet, lilting voice that carried loudly across the plaza above all other noise, the word long and drawn out:

"ALEGRIA!!!"

The crowd roared back. "ALEGRIA!!!"

Sophie smiled and again sang in her high voice:

"ALEGRIA!"

Once again the crowd answered her. Then to Jared's astonishment she floated up, her glittering green gown sparkling in the moonlight and sailed up over the balcony.

The crowd cheered even louder and yelled again. "ALEGRIA!!!"

Jared looked at Mordalayn, alarmed but the Caracalic simply smiled again.

Sophie paused and looked around and then sang:

"Alegria, for joy we are here.

In Alegria there's no hate or fear"

The crowd paused and then as one sang the lines back, their voices deafening but sweet in the night air.

Sophie floated out in mid air above the plaza and turned around, glittering whirls sparking around her, like Jared had seen with the fairies in Maximo's house. Then she looked down and a random member of the huge crowd floated up from the floor to join her high above the others. The man's legs kicked the air as if treading water and then he laughed as he came face to face with Queen Sophie. She embraced him and then sang.

"When the demons of night reappear.

You are safe if you are in Alegria"

The man laughed as he span gently around and with the thousands below him he repeated the line.

Two other people floated at random from the crowd, this time a little boy and an old woman. Again Sophie embraced them as they came level to her, thirty metres above the ground and they laughed with joy as they gently span in the air like leaves on a calm river.

Around them more and more people slowly began to rise out of the crowd. With much laughing and murmurs of approval from their fellows below they joined their queen. Singing their wonderful song of gratitude for all that she and this kingdom had given to them.

Kloee tapped Jared on the shoulder with a tiny hand. "Come on, let's join in."

Jared glanced at Mordalayn who smiled. "Go Jared, this is as much for you as anyone."

"You coming?" Jared said as Kloee began to glow again and he felt himself rising off the balcony like in the Phase game.

"No, I will remain to watch you."

His stomach flipping Jared gulped as he looked down and saw the sea of heads below him. He looked ahead as Kloee's little wings beat fast as they moved to the other people treading the air. They turned to them and the nearest one smiled warmly and as Jared approached him he reached out and hugged him. Sophie turned as about a dozen more people rose from the crowd. All different. All the same. United by their love of this moment and for their child queen. She smiled at Jared and then at Kloee and Jared saw that there were now about fifty or so people floating above the crowd. Sophie raised her arms again and from her a bright green light slowly rose to encompass the whole square. The crowd gasped and within a few seconds the square was as bright as daylight. Jared glanced back and saw Mordalayn standing impassively on the regal balcony. As steady as a rock and as reliable as steel. The Queen's Sword standing firm in his duty to his monarch and her people.

As the murmuring of the crowd finally died down, Sophie sang again but this time the entire crowd sang at the same time.

"Alegria. Alegria for joy we are here.

In Alegria there's no hate or fear.

When the demons of night reappear.

You are safe if you are in Alegria.

The wrath of angels will not touch you, nor suffer you harm.

The crown will protect you, enclosed in the palm.

Peace is our journey and light is our path.

Serene is our temper but fearsome our wrath."

Jared laughed as the people either side of him linked hands with him and Kloee stood on tiptoes on his shoulder. Her little red shoes shining in the bright light. All the people in the air linked hands and formed a huge circle around the queen. She span gently in a complete circle and then the circle of people began to ever so gently rotate. The crowd below were shouting and raising their hands in the air. Sophie paused and then she and the crowd began again:

"For the lost we will find you, for the sad there is joy.

No one need be lonely, no girl and no boy.

We welcome you brother, sister and friend.

Leave all woe behind you, your troubles we'll mend.

Alegria the joy, Alegria the light.

Alegria the torch through the darkness of night."

The crowd sang in harmony the sound carrying for miles and miles and Jared hoped the singing would last forever.

Chapter 44

Siavy was tired and filthy.

He'd fled as soon as he had seen the statues brought to life by Mordalayn's magic. As he galloped away, he had turned to see the destructive force rip through the legion. No one else had made it out alive.

He knew he had to get as far from Alegria as he could and after an exhausting day's riding he finally reigned in his horse, the beast lathered in sweat and panting roughly.

He lit a small fire in the woods and sat near his tethered stallion as the daylight faded. Cursing his luck he knew his life was in danger now. He owed money to so many people for this grand venture. Money he could no longer pay. With no victory there would be no reward and with no reward Galfront Siavy was now a wanted man.

He heard a squeak and a thrashing noise and stood up. The snare he had rigged had caught a squirrel. Grinning he took his dagger and quickly killed the animal.

As he freed the twine and lifted the creature up a furious voice behind him hissed angrily,"and just WHAT do you think you're doing?"

Chapter 45

Eventually the singing stopped and Sophie returned to the palace. Her people continued to sing her name and it was well into the late hours before the plaza was clear again.

Next morning the business of running a kingdom took over and the matters of most pressing importance were dealt with. The council was convened and Maximo was brought before the queen. The orphans that had been left with him had never known of his betrayal and were astonished when they had been taken from his home by guards in the early hours. His tears and obvious guilt over what had happened were listened to by Sophie and a quiet yet murderous-looking Mordalayn, in front of the council. He told them about Madame Veer and that his whole house and family had been threatened. He added that just to ensure his silence and continued co-operation, Veer had killed his beautiful sunflowers after he had sent Jared and the others to Anghofio. Sophie listened and as the man knelt in front of her, tears on his fat cheeks, she rose and astonished everyone by ordering him to rise and then embracing him. She then said words Jared would never forget.

"Maximo I know you are a good man. There are very few of us that can be the people we hope to be at all times. You were placed in a position that gives no one except me the right to judge you. I forgive you and I bid you to return to your home with my blessings."

Maximo wept with shame, overcome with emotion and was then allowed to leave to continue with his life with his beautiful house and family.

Kulkrain was still too ill to be moved but a physician had been despatched to remain with him until such a time as he could visit the palace and be duly rewarded for his loyalty.

Bue was personally thanked by Sophie for his efforts and Mordalayn himself spoke up for the boy, citing his bravery and loyalty to both his friends and Alegria. However everyone could see the pain in his eyes at the loss of his beloved bow master Leppard. They knew it would take a long time for that scar to heal. Sophie offered him the chance to remain in the palace and to learn skills from Mordalayn and the boy had accepted.

Challandra returned to the orphanage to be its new Headmistress. At 16 everyone knew she had more common sense than most people and clearly cared deeply about the boys. Sophie's shock at the betrayal of her predecessor who had become jealous and vindictive at her fall from power was not something she tried to hide from her council. She left Challandra with a promise that her loyalty meant she could personally call on her queen at any time.

The survivors of the King's Daggers were brought up in chains to be judged. They had been stripped of their armour and were clothed in only their shirts, trousers and boots. Sophie's anger finally made itself clear and Jared was shocked to see her usually peaceful demeanour melt as she showed her true feelings to those that had not only attacked her people but had been willing to kill them just to make a point. As they knelt in front of her she stood and moved towards them.

"Do you believe you deserve mercy after what you have done?"

None answered. Their previous arrogance replaced by the knowledge that they now faced a person with unimaginable power and there was nothing they could say to change whatever fate decided to hand them.

"My kingdom is peaceful and your king tried not only to kill me when I was helpless but also to hurt my people. Innocents have died and all through your wicked greed."

The soldiers remained on their knees with their heads bowed. Mordalayn glared at them, his fists clenched tightly as he stood to one side.

"You were not merely soldiers following orders. You were the elite of King James's army and even if you were to say you were sorry I would know you did not mean it. You made a free choice to follow your dead king's vile plans and for that you have earned my utter contempt."

She looked at them. "What do you think would be justice?" she asked angrily

She stared at the men before her for a long moment. "You are men who have lived your lives relishing in the power of your strength and physical abilities. My judgment is this. I take from you your youth. You will no longer be a threat to those you sought to make suffer just because they were weaker than you."

With that she raised her left arm out straight and spoke a few words in a strange tongue. Purple light shone at the tips of her fingers and the kneeling men yelled out in pain and grasped the sides of their heads with their hands. Yellow light shone from their faces and shone so brightly no one could look on them. They collapsed on the floor and screeched in pain and then, suddenly the light faded and Sophie stood in front of them.

Slowly they rose from the floor and Jared saw to his shock that they were all elderly. Sophie had kept her promise.

The men groaned and one or two reached up to touch their faces, their hands exploring the lines and wrinkles. Horror creased the looks of many as they realised what she had done. Once virile and young, not one of them over 35 years old, they were now in their 70s and 80s. Old men whose ability to fight was gone.

"Go back to Anghofio and tell what remains of your royal family what happens to those who prey on the vulnerable and the weak," Sophie said, anger edging her voice.

The men staggered to their feet and faced her, the shock and misery evident on their faces.

Sophie looked at them. "However I offer you one chance to redeem yourselves." They stood in silence waiting to see what she had to say. "Make one selfless gesture that you fundamentally believe will change the life of an innocent and your youth will be restored to you. If you can prove that your brutality is extinguished then I will give you back what I have taken from you."

She looked to her guards who ushered the men out of the throne room.

Once the important issues had been dealt with the council left the throne room leaving just Mordalayn, Bue, Jared and Kloee. Sophie turned to Jared. "Time to go home now."

Jared was sad. He had seen so much here.

Sophie smiled at him, her eyes sparkling. "You are always welcome in Alegria Jared. Come and see me in our world. I would like to be friends there too."

Jared smiled back. "I'd like that. Which hospital are you in?"

Sophie laughed, her voice musical and high. "I do not know," she replied and Jared looked puzzled. She continued. "I am powerful here but in our world I am just like you."

Chapter 46

They moved through the throne room to a small door on the left. Mordalayn opened it and they walked through, the guards in the throne room taking up positions either side. Jared saw the long path ahead of him and the golden gate at the end. They walked slowly along together, the orange petals soft beneath their feet. Soon they reached the gate and Sophie took a small key from a necklace at her throat and inserted it into the large golden padlock. Mordalayn reached forward and slid the huge bolt and the gate swung forward. There was nothing beyond, just blackness. An infinity of black. As Jared turned startled to them, Sophie placed a hand gently on his arm. "It's ok, don't be frightened. Just step through and imagine where you want to be. You will find yourself there."

As Jared looked at them both, something caught his eye. Turning back he saw standing midway along the path, in front of one of the trees a tall man but with huge wings like an angel. He stood staring at them, his wings folded behind his back. No one else seemed to notice him. The man had blood red eyes, piercing and deep. Sophie saw Jared's expression and looked back. The man's eyes shone brighter, then he faded away.

"Who was that?" Jared said, confused that this world could still show him things that were able to surprise him.

"The Claviger," Sophie replied. "They watch over this world and others. Now order has been restored they are happy. Even I answer to somebody"

Kloee was crying as she hovered next to Jared and he smiled sadly at her. "Don't cry. I'll come back one day, I promise," he said. She gently kissed his cheek before flying over next to Mordalayn.

"Take care mate," Bue said winking, then shook Jared's hand.

"Goodbye Jared," Mordalayn said in his deep voice. "Remember I am always your friend."

"Thank you," Jared said and extended his hand which once again Mordalayn took in his huge grip.

Sophie stepped forward to hug him one final time and then stepped back. "Just think where you want to end up and you will be there."

Jared looked at his new friends for the final time then took a deep breath and walked through the gateway, the darkness enveloping him as he stepped forward. Everything went dark and as he turned he saw Sophie, Bue, Mordalayn and Kloee standing on the threshold and then suddenly they sped away from him as if he had been pulled backwards by a hugely powerful hand. He gasped as they faded into nothingness in the distance and was frightened at the absolute blackness that covered him. He felt he was both falling and moving in every direction at the same time. Just as he started to flounder and waved his hands around, light suddenly flooded around him and with a jerk he found himself standing on solid ground. He staggered and almost fell but managed to retain his footing. Feeling dizzy he looked around and saw that he was on the doorstep of his own house. It was night time and the light was on over the front door. No one was around and as he finally regained his footing he saw the curtains were drawn on the living room window. He looked up and down the street. It was empty. Turning to face the doorway he reached up and pressed the doorbell which gave its reassuring two chime tone. After a few moments the bolt slid on the door and it opened to reveal his astonished looking father.

"Hello dad," he said smiling. "I'm home."

The end....for now.

Acknowledgments

To Dad, Paul Rose, Mitchell Small, Robert Maltby & Mich Altschuler for their superb artwork.

To Fox (8), Cameron (9) and Chloe (15) for scrutinising the manuscript.

To Charlotte Elizabeth Thompson for her proofreading skills (first edition had some quite horrid errors) and her inexplicable crush on Mordalayn.

To the guys at Hip-Lok.

To my English teacher Mr Hardy, the only decent teacher in a very bad school.

To Kevin & Lisa Murphy, Simon JB Davy, Richard Wilson, Graham the Grinning Demon, Ian Miller MBE and Gary M...who all have Alegrian counterparts.

To Inspector Gadget for the First game diversions while writing this.

To the tremendous Alexandra Harrington and the mighty Sister Joseph Clare for inspiring Madame Veer.

To every bully I ever met for shaping the walking nightmare that is Mordalayn.

To Marco Zanitzer at Krav Maga Rome, for showing me that fighting "fair" will only get you killed.

And most of all to the English Police. For cringeworthy security flaws that led to the *complacency in power* themes of this book.

~COTEQ

Excerpt from the sequel The Sunder of the Octagon.
Coming soon!!!

Josie's feet thudded across the wet grass as the rain poured down.
Her breath was raw in her throat. The yells followed behind her.
The gang had stopped her at the Jephson Gardens park entrance.
She'd seen them before but stayed away. Tonight they were
drunk and they had wanted to chat. She'd tried to be nice, her
heat hammering in her chest and at first they'd been polite. She'd
even given them a couple of cigarettes. Then as she walked away
she heard one of them say, "Let's get the freak!" Josie had run
then, knowing that this would happen and praying she could
make it to the main road through the park in time.

It was around 3am and no one was around to help her. There
were seven or eight of them. She didn't stand a chance. As she
ran past the closed café she saw the lights in the distance, outside
the old pump rooms. The rain was heavy but she ran faster, her
old leather boots limiting movement and her long braided hair
soaking wet.

Suddenly she skidded and tumbled forward on the wet
tarmac. Josie fell hard, the wind rushing from her lungs and then
they were around her, snarling.

"Well, well! Looks like we caught the freak!"

"Shouldn't go out looking like that, you're a disgrace."

Josie looked up, tears burning her eyes as they stood around
her. "Please, just leave me alone," she said weakly, holding out
one hand, the black nail varnish chipped on the first two fingers
where she'd fallen. They laughed at her.

She looked up to their ugly, hateful faces. The circle around her got smaller. She could smell the beer on their breath.

"Shouldn't be here," one said raising his fist.

"Not in our park," said another.

"Weirdo!"

"Mosher!"

"FREAK!"

She put her hands over her face and tried to curl up away from their hate and their beer and their violence, wishing she was anywhere but here. "Please!" she said again in a whisper.

As they moved in, laughing nastily and one drew back his foot to kick her he was suddenly yanked backwards, vanishing into the darkness of the bushes. The others looked around in shock. "What the hell...?" The circle broke, the teenage thugs looked around wildly. The lad emerged again, trying to get free from something that was holding him.

"Help me!" he screamed as he was yanked back briefly and then he seemed to fly from the bushes and sail over their heads, screaming in fear before landing with a splash in the ornamental lake in the middle of the park.

As the lads looked around, Josie took her hands from her face and looked to where a huge figure emerged dripping wet, his face hidden in the shadows of a hooded robe. Next to him was a smaller person, also hooded.

The leaves on the trees rustled in the wind but then there was silence except for the steady rain.

The taller figure then spoke slowly. A deep voice that was edged with menace. "You would attack a woman? What manner of animals are you?"

The boys simply stared, dumbstruck at this change in fortune. They glanced to their friend in the lake, splashing and yelling for help, then back to the newcomers.

The nearest lad overcame his fear and sneered back at them. "Think you're hard do you? No one messes with the Bury Boys!" He clicked a knife open, the blade shining wetly in the artificial lights.

His friends regained their bravado for a moment and sniggered. One said "go on Steve, show them!"

Steve moved in smiling and the hooded figures separated. The other lads came at them, fists flying in wild, erratic curves. As Steve swung his flick knife the tall man blurred into motion, trapping his arm and throwing Steve over his shoulder and onto the ground with a crunch. Steve yelled and dropped the blade. He staggered to his feet but with a shove he was thrown sprawling onto the tarmac again. Two others tried to jump the man from behind but his hand darted out, faster than a snake and caught one by the throat. The lad's eyes bulged as he was pulled off the ground, his legs spinning. As the other attempted to punch the hooded attacker, he kicked out without even looking over his shoulder. His foot caught the lad in the chest, who flew back gasping, hitting the metal fence. He span backwards over it and landed with a sopping thud in the wet earth.

Josie sat up, watching spellbound at the fight before her. Even though there were so many of the thugs, they were posing no threat to her saviours. She saw it as if in slow motion, time blurring as the two strangers punched, blocked and kicked out at the gang, effortlessly beating them back.

The smaller figure was facing three at once. He struck out at the nearest, catching him in the head, then kicking him hard in the guts and the lad fell. The other two came to their senses and turned and ran, their trainers splashing on the wet ground. The hooded figure extended his right arm and with a click, a block of what appeared to be smooth wood and bright metal suddenly appeared from his sleeve into his open palm. As Josie watched mesmerised, the block changed shape. Warping, twisting and clicking into alignment. A tiny crossbow, merged with his gloved hand. He reached to his belt and slid a bolt into the firing groove of the weapon. Dropping to one knee he whispered a strange few words and the bolt glowed.

"No way," he said quietly as he glared at the retreating figures. The arrow's wicked point dripped as he paused to aim.

His partner whirled. "BUE! NO!!!"

The arm wavered; the figure cursed then lowered his aim a fraction. He triggered the weapon and the bolt sang out. As it flew it separated, with a flash of golden light, into two arrows and with an almost simultaneous thud, landed in the backsides of the two runners. They sprawled forward, screaming in pain as they rolled around.

Steve had managed to crawl towards his knife but as he turned holding it and tried to stand, the tall man simply kicked him in the hand. The knife span into the dark shadows and Steve shrieked, clutching his ruined fingers.

Josie looked around, the rain was heavy and it blurred her vision as the huge figure turned. He stood over her, green eyes glowing like fires in the depths of his hood. Gently he reached down and after a pause she took his hand. Helping her to her feet he asked, "Are you hurt Miss?"

She looked at him, then at Steve and then to the screaming lads on the ground 30 metres away, still trying to pull the arrows out. She looked further across to the lake and the lad who had been thrown there was splashing to the shore, yelling in fright and clearly having trouble.

For the first time she saw the huge sword, sheathed on the figure's back, the hilt shaped like a kneeling woman with her hands clasped in prayer. His friend returned to them, his crossbow hidden once more.

She looked from one to the other and then slowly said, "No, I'm fine. Thank you."

The taller figure nodded. "Come. Let us escort you to the gates."

As they walked either side of her in silence, the rain dripping off their clothes she felt she was dreaming. She wanted to ask them who they were but couldn't. Her voice was stuck in her throat. They were slowly scanning the area ahead and around as they walked. They passed the ornamental flower beds and she saw the fountain to her right. When they reached the gates the shorter figure spoke. "There you are young Miss, you'll be safe now. Don't worry about them; they won't bother you or anyone else like that again."

She looked at them, silhouetted in the light from the main road opposite the library and finally asked, "Who are you?"

The same one chuckled and said, "Friends. Now, please go Miss. You'll catch a fever in this rain."

She walked over the road to the libray. As she turned they were gone, just the entrance to Jephson Gardens standing open in the pouring rain.

As she walked away up the road the taller figure turned to the other and said, "We need to find Our Lady."

The other chuckled and replied. "Couldn't she have put the portal nearer to where she lives?"

~COTEQ

~COTEQ

~COTEQ

~COTEQ

~COTEQ

~COTEQ

Made in the USA
Charleston, SC
07 March 2016